DARKEST
ECSTASY

Books by Tawny Taylor

"Stark Pleasure" in *Yes, Master*

Darkest Desire

Dangerous Master

Darkest Fire

Decadent Master

Wicked Beast

Dark Master

Real Vamps Don't Drink O-Neg

Sex and the Single Ghost

DARKEST ECSTASY

TAWNY TAYLOR

APHRODISIA

KENSINGTON PUBLISHING CORP.

www.kensingtonbooks.com

APHRODISIA BOOKS are published by

Kensington Publishing Corp.
119 West 40th Street
New York, NY 10018

All Kensington titles, imprints, and distributed lines are available at special quantity discounts for bulk purchases for sales promotion, premiums, fund-raising, educational, or institutional use.

Special book excerpts or customized printings can also be created to fit specific needs. For details, write or phone the office of the Kensington Special Sales Manager: Kensington Publishing Corp., 119 West 40th Street, New York, NY 10018. Attn. Special Sales Department. Phone: 1-800-221-2647.

Aphrodisia and the A logo Reg. U.S. Pat. & TM Off.

eISBN-13: 978-0-7582-9033-5
eISBN-10: 0-7582-9033-0
First Kensington Electronic Edition: September 2014

ISBN-13: 978-0-7582-9032-8
ISBN-10: 0-7582-9032-2
First Kensington Trade Paperback Printing: September 2014

10 9 8 7 6 5 4 3 2 1

Printed in the United States of America

For David

Acknowledgments

To my editor, Martin Biro, thank you for being awesome.

opped. There they were, her new partners. Her ticket to a ew, wonderful life.

Smiling, she entered the car.

"Bro, time to man up. You know what you've gotta do."

Talen Gryffon grunted a response. If he'd actually enunciated the words, his oldest brother, Drako—who'd lately become a hell of a nag—might have tried to kick his ass. Of course, Drako would have failed. As long as he kept the fire thing out of it.

"Yeah. I hear you." Lying on his back, on the weight bench, a loaded three-hundred-pound barbell in his hands, Talen completed his sixth rep. *Four more to go.*

Drako, the nag, stood at his head, ready to spot him if he needed it. He wouldn't. "Any ideas yet?"

Talen lowered the bar to his chest. "No."

"Want some advice?"

"No." Chest and arm muscles working, Talen completed rep number seven.

"Fair enough." Drako watched him finish up the last three repetitions, then helped him place the bar on the stand before stepping to the side. "Look, I know where you're at. I've been there. I promise it's not as bad as you think. Rin and I had our rough times, but I'm happy. Really happy." He tossed a towel at Talen.

Talen snatched the white terry cloth out of the air and patted his face with it. What Drako, the leader of the Black Gryffons, had said was true. It was obvious he was happy. Now. In the beginning, when Drako had first married Rin...not so much. Drako hadn't been any more ready for marriage than he was. Why they had to marry at such a young age, he simply didn't get. There was plenty of time to have kids. Years. Decades. He and his brothers had only recently stepped into their positions as the Black Gryffons. Three brothers. Three guardians of The

1
_____

In general, people complicated things too much. Life
ple. Human beings were simple. They were creatures. In
animals. And like every other beast in nature, they wer
by a handful of common motivators. The most powerl
preservation.

After decades of searching, living in fear, she had fou
way to end the struggle. And she would do somethin
for all of humanity in the process. Talk about a win-wi
ation.

Her heart pounding with excitement, she signed the le
her new apartment. She had a new lease on a home and
lease on life. At last she was free from fear and frustration
life would never be the same.

After shaking the leasing agent's hand, she stepped out
the warm, sunny day. For the first time ever she felt alive, e
gized, ready to start her new life.

This was just the first step.

A black Mercedes-Benz prowled around the corner

Secret. They didn't need to think about the next generation so soon. "Yeah, sure. But there's no saying I'll find the same thing you did."

"Malek's done okay, too."

"Sure. Okay. Right."

He didn't want to talk about this. Marriage. Ugh. He didn't want to think about it, either. Drako didn't know, didn't understand. He wasn't ready yet. He needed more time.

What the hell was the hurry, anyway? Both of his brothers' wives were pregnant already. If they were carrying boys, two out of three future Black Gryffons were already on the way. He could wait awhile, at least until they found out what they were having.

"I'm not trying to be an asshole," Drako said. "You know the deadline is getting close. Father told us we all needed to marry this year. Not to mention, the enemy has almost wiped us out. Twice. They've been on our asses lately." That part was true. They'd been forced to pack up and leave, take new identities, and start over. It was a hazard of the job.

But there were the powers they'd somehow developed. Drako's fire. Malek's strength. Those would help them, keep them safe. So far, they had.

"Any sign of the Chimera again?" he asked, deciding a change of subject was a great idea. Finished with his workout, he headed for the door.

"No, not yet. But last time was close. I don't think it'll take them long to find us again."

"Yeah, I know." Some of the most powerful men in the country belonged to the Chimera. Scientists, politicians. Men with means. And the occasional nut job who was crazy enough to use those means in dangerous ways. The Chimera's one and only goal was to get its hands on The Secret. Talen's job, and the job of his brothers, the Black Gryffons, was to keep them from succeeding.

That job had almost cost them their lives. More than once already. And it would become the duty of their sons someday, when they were too old, too fragile, to continue.

That was why they all needed to marry. To have sons. As many as they could. But finding a wife, the right wife, was going to be hell. Plain and simple. She would not only have to share his life, and the dangers associated with it, but also somehow either satisfy his darkest erotic hungers, or be willing to allow him to satisfy them elsewhere. While both of his brothers had enjoyed some of the same things as he did before they were married—erotic bondage, discipline, among them—they had both made some compromises in the name of love.

He didn't compromise. He wouldn't compromise.

His mood sour, he waved his brother off and stomped into the bathroom to shower. Where the hell would he find the perfect wife? A woman who was strong, and sexy, and brave, but also trusting and submissive. He doubted she existed.

As he rounded the corner, he heard voices in the private dungeon he and his brothers shared. Malek was in there, enjoying a little downtime with Lei, his wife. Malek was happy, too. Well, fucking great for him. They were expecting their first child, as well. Lei's delicate petite form was already softening from the effects of her pregnancy.

A little twinge of jealousy raced through him, but he shoved it aside, just like he had for the last few months.

Lei. Beautiful, delicate Lei.

When Malek had started pursuing Lei, he hadn't realized how strong Talen's feelings for her were. But Talen, on the other hand, quickly saw how strong Malek's were becoming. And so, being the brother he was, Talen stepped out of the way the minute he realized what Malek was thinking.

He'd lost her. To his brother.

For months he'd kept his disappointment to himself. Malek didn't need to know about it. Nobody did.

He pushed on, moving quickly to put the sounds of Lei's moans and whimpers of pleasure out of earshot. It had been hell, living like this, watching Lei and Malek together, witnessing the connection between them strengthen each day. Not so long ago, he'd expected to be the one to help Lei heal from the wounds of her past. He'd expected his to be the strong arms holding her when she was afraid.

Oh hell, he needed to stop fucking thinking about what might have been. Lei was Malek's wife now. End of story. It was time to move on.

It was his duty to move on.

And move on he would.

First step: a shower. Then, a trip to the new club he'd just joined.

Since he couldn't have the woman he wanted, he'd find someone else, someone very different from her. Someone who would make him forget how great she smelled, or how sexy she looked first thing in the morning, when her glossy blue-black hair was mussed, or how creamy and smooth the skin on her back was.

Maybe a blonde. With long legs, big tits. Curvy and soft and tall, instead of lean and petite and delicate. A woman who craved the kinds of things he did, who loved to live on the edge. A woman who was adventurous and fearless.

As he showered, he made a mental checklist of his future wife's traits. They were, in any and every way, exactly opposite to Lei. After he dried off he wrapped the towel around his hips and pulled open the door.

A pair of almond-shaped eyes met his. A small, perfectly shaped mouth formed an O of surprise. Then porcelain skin stained pink as a blush tinted her cheeks. "Hello, Talen. Excuse me," Lei muttered as she scurried down the hallway to the bedroom she shared with Malek.

Talen gritted his teeth as his cock thickened, hardened. His body tightened. His blood simmered.

Would she ever stop affecting him that way? Would he ever be able to look at her and not wish he could throw her onto the nearest horizontal surface and make her his?

His mood even darker than before, he locked himself in his room to dress. Maybe Drako knew more than he thought. Maybe he could sense the growing tension between him and Lei. And maybe that was why he was pressuring him to find his own wife.

Maybe it wasn't too soon after all.

With one purpose in mind, Talen dressed. Black button-down shirt. Black pants. Black socks and shoes.

After making sure he was satisfied with what he saw in the mirror, he headed out to find himself a wife.

Tonight, she would celebrate.

She'd done it. The contract was all but signed. Not only had she saved her own ass, but she'd saved the company's, too.

Thank you, God.

Half-walking, half-dancing, Michelle Linsey pranced through the parking structure toward her car. In the distance she heard voices echoing off the concrete walls. The screech of tires and *thump* of car doors slamming. A little chill buzzed up her spine.

Normally, she wouldn't be walking through the structure this late alone. She always tried to time it so she'd be heading out with someone from the office. But tonight she'd had to stay a little late to tie up some loose ends. It was a good problem to have. A great one.

But when she spied a pair of young men walking toward her, her heart jerked against her rib cage. She didn't like the way they were staring at her. She didn't like the way their hoods were shading their faces.

This is Mason, Ohio, not Detroit. When was the last time someone had been jumped in a parking garage here?

They were getting closer. And they were still staring at her.

Feeling like she was a mouse about to be pounced on by a pack of alley cats, she hugged her purse to her side and fisted her keys tightly. She stared right back at them, letting them know she'd seen them and wasn't afraid.

What a lie that was.

She felt herself shifting her path to the right to put as much space as possible between herself and the men. She stopped glaring at them as they passed her, dragging in a small sigh of relief.

She was being paranoid.

Of course.

She was swallowing a nervous chuckle as someone behind her grabbed her arm. Her scream of terror trapped in her throat, she whirled around.

"Excuse me," the man holding her arm said. "But—" He released it, lifting his hand, palm out. "Sorry, miss. Didn't mean to scare you. Are you okay?" At her nod, he smiled and asked, "I feel like such a fool for asking, but have you seen a red pickup truck? We forgot where we parked."

He felt foolish. So did she. She really needed to stop watching those Lifetime movies. Seriously.

After tonight. She couldn't miss *My Husband Is a Serial Killer.* She'd been waiting almost a month for it to air.

But then she would give them up. Yes. Absolutely. Positively.

Maybe.

A girl had to have at least one guilty pleasure in life.

2

He had his quarry.

There. That one. The lush blonde in the black dress. She was perfect. Just the right combination of sweet temptation and seductive siren. Long legs. Full tits that made his mouth water. A hundred carnal promises glittering in her eyes.

Another man stepped up to her and set a hand on her shoulder. Her gaze flicked to the man, then back to Talen. Her lips curled in a sultry half smile.

His cock hardened. *Let the games begin.* Energized by the challenge, he waved the waitress over.

"A bottle of champagne. To that woman. In the black dress." Then he leaned back in his seat and waited, watching her every move as the bottle was delivered and as the waitress told her who had purchased it.

The woman smiled in his direction, then excused herself from the man who had thought he'd be fucking her tonight. Her glass in one hand, the bottle in the other, she crossed the crowded bar, collecting stares from admiring men and glares from women along the way. She moved with the smooth fluidity of a dancer. Her hips swayed seductively. Her shoulders were back, her full breasts pushed out.

Stunning.

"Hello," she said, smiling down at him as she approached his table. "Thank you for the champagne." She set the bottle on his table. "I couldn't possibly drink this whole thing by myself, so I thought I'd come over and share some with you."

"Thanks. Please, sit." Pushing his full glass aside, he motioned to the waitress. "May I have an empty champagne glass please?" he asked her.

"Sure. Can I get you anything else?"

Talen looked at his new companion. She shook her head. "No, thank you."

"I'll be right back."

He turned his attention back to Blondie.

"I'm Angela."

"Angela." He extended a hand, and she placed hers in it. Her grip was neither too tight nor too loose. "Tage Garner."

"It's good to meet you, Tage Garner. Thank you again for the champagne. It's delicious."

"I'm glad you're enjoying it." Lips. She had very nice lips. He could imagine them circling his cock while he fucked her mouth.

Peering over the rim of her glass, she sipped. "Have you been to this club before?"

"No. I just joined."

"You'll love it. I've been a member for about a year. I'm here at least twice a week."

"Dom or submissive?" he asked.

"Oh, submissive. Most definitely."

He felt himself smiling. "I was hoping you would say that."

"Were you?" She tipped her head. "You know, I haven't had very much of this champagne yet, only a few sips. We could take this party somewhere private if you like."

That sounded like a great idea.

When the waitress stepped up, he accepted the glass and the bill. After signing for it, he escorted his quarry to his newly leased private suite upstairs. As they climbed the steps, he admired her fine ass as it swayed back and forth in front of him. He couldn't wait to get his hands on it. On the rest of her, too.

Upstairs, she allowed him to steer her toward his suite with a hand on the small of her back. Beneath his fingertips, he felt her muscles flex as she responded to his touch.

This was going to be fun.

Inside, she walked straight to the center of the room, turned so her back was to him, reached around, and dragged the zipper of her dress down, exposing a deep *V* of smooth skin.

"Are you sure you haven't had anything else to drink?" he asked. He hadn't noticed any signs of intoxication, but he wasn't so lost in need yet that he'd be willing to ignore the first rule of D/s. Safe. Sane. Consensual.

"Nothing else. Just a few sips of champagne." She pulled the garment down to her waist. She wasn't wearing a bra.

"Limits?"

"None." The dress slid to the floor. She wasn't wearing panties, either.

His cock twitched at the sight of her beautiful body. "None?"

Slowly, she turned to face him. Her lips were curved into a semi-smile once again. Her eyes were downcast, as a submissive's eyes should be. "I have been a submissive for a long time, trained by some of the most demanding, sadistic doms around. I can handle *anything.*"

His balls tightened.

He had found his dream sub. But was she wife material?

To hell with that. I just want to fuck her.

Smiling to himself, he decided he would put her to the test.

He knew exactly how he wanted to test her first. He unzipped his pants.

Her little pink tongue darted out, swiped across her lower lip. Yes, that was exactly what he was thinking. He stepped up to her, close enough to reach, grabbed a handful of silky blond hair and said, "Suck my cock. Hard."

"Yes, Master," she murmured, then eagerly opened her mouth for him.

"Oh damn," he growled as he rammed his cock deep into her mouth, then withdrew, only to thrust deep again. Over and over. She took him easily, greedily. Her little tongue cushioned the bottom of his rod as he glided in and out. The head of his cock hit the back of her throat, but she didn't gag, she didn't pull away. No, she opened to him, taking him to the hilt, slurping and sucking until he was seeing stars and on the verge of coming.

Mere seconds before losing control, he jerked out of her mouth. There was so much more to do yet, pleasures to explore, limits to test. He couldn't let it end so soon.

"You've been well trained," he said as he tucked his still-erect cock back inside his pants and zipped up.

She placed her hands at her sides and kept her eyes downturned. "Thank you, Master. It's my pleasure to serve you."

"Hmmm." His body thrummed as possibilities whirled around in his head. A submissive with no limits could be rather useful to him. His gaze meandered around the room. Having just leased the room, he hadn't set up some of the bigger pieces yet. The St. Andrew's Cross was waiting to be assembled. Same with the large table he liked to keep in the center of the room. For now, he would have to make do with the bench. There was plenty of fun to be had with that.

He positioned her as he wanted, kneeling, legs spread, chest and stomach resting on the upper support. Ah, perfect. Now he had full access to that ass he'd admired earlier. "Safe word?" he asked as he cuffed her wrists and ankles in place.

"Red is fine."

"Red, it is." He stepped back to admire the view. How he wanted to bury his rod deep inside her. She was clean shaven everywhere. Her folds glistened with her juices. She was wet. Wet and ready. He went to his storage cabinet and gathered a few things, dildo, condoms, lube. He wasn't in the mood for discipline. Just fucking. Lots of fucking. His eye went to her puckered anus.

There. He would take her there.

"Anal?" he asked.

"Love it."

His whole body tightened. Could this woman be more perfect for him?

He unwrapped a condom and rolled it onto the dildo. Then, without warning, he shoved it into her cunt.

She shuddered with pleasure. "Thank you, Master," she whispered, hips rocking forward to take the toy deeper. It plunged to the entry of her womb. He left it there and switched it on. "Ohhhhhh," she mumbled. "Thank you."

Damn, that was a pretty sight. Once again he stepped back to admire her. Her legs were long and lean, her stomach flat, breasts full and natural, ass round and firm. Her smooth skin was starting to shimmer with sweat as the toy buried in her pussy made her insides burn for him.

He was burning for her, too.

Working quickly, he rolled on a rubber. Then he squirted out some lube onto his fingers to test her anus.

Two fingers in. Oh, she was tight but willing, giving just enough resistance. As he plunged his fingers deeper, the ring of muscles tightened around them. Damn.

He couldn't wait.

At his withdrawal, she whimpered. The sound sent a wave

of heat blazing through him. It was sweetly seductive. He had to hear it again.

He smoothed some more lube around her anus. Slowly. He entered her slowly, inch by inch. Oh, it was hell. And heaven. Both. As he drove deeper, his body tensed more. By the time his stomach was resting against the pillow of her ass cheeks, he was sure his hair was singed, he was so hot. "Damn."

Her muscles tightened, and a pulse of carnal heat blasted through his center. Just as slowly, he withdrew, letting her body caress him as he pulled out. She was perfect. Completely and utterly perfect. This once wouldn't be enough. He had to have her again. In the ass. In the pussy. In the mouth. Anywhere and everywhere.

"Meet me again," he said. To his own ears, he sounded breathless.

"When?"

"Soon." The tip of his cock still remained inside. This time, he thrust quickly inside, driving deep.

She cried out. "Yes!"

"Yes," he echoed as he jerked back to thrust deep. "Yes," he repeated as he buried himself in her ass. "Damn. Damn."

"Master," she said. She whimpered. The sound nearly sent him over the edge. "Please. May I come? Please."

"Not yet." He pounded into her with no mercy, and she took him, rocking back to meet his forward thrusts. His fingers dug into her hips. The soft flesh of her ass rippled with each impact. The sound of skin striking skin and husky, fast breathing was like a symphony. This was fucking at its finest. This was what he couldn't live without, would not live without. Faster, he fucked her. Harder. Each stroke amped up his temperature higher, raised his heart rate. He was spiking a fever, hot and tight everywhere, balls ready to explode.

Her cry as she lost control echoed through the room and sent him careening over the edge. His orgasm blasted through his body like a nuclear explosion. His voice joined hers as he shouted in ecstasy, pounded away the last pulse of carnal pleasure. When he was spent, he withdrew, removed the condom and the toy from her pussy.

"Thank you, Master." Her whole body trembled, he noticed, as he unbuckled her wrist and ankle cuffs. Once he had her completely free of the bindings, he helped her turn around and sit. For the first time since they'd entered the room, she lifted her eyes to his and smiled. "I look forward to serving you again soon?" she asked.

"Yes, very soon." And often, he hoped.

3

Six feet something.

A face that inspired wet dreams.

Hair that begged to be touched.

There he was. Tall, Dark, and Mysterious. God, was he something to look at.

He was way out of her league. Miles and miles.

With her heart pounding so hard she wondered if he might hear it, she stepped aside to let him into the elevator. Like she did every morning, she moved to the right just enough to let him in. God, she loved the way he smelled. And standing so near made her knees get a little soft. She wanted to speak to him. She wanted to do more than that.

But...but...he was so good-looking. Would he even notice someone like her?

Just go for it.

Trying to hide how nervous and excited she was, she watched the numbers light up on the display above the doors. Two, three. *Just say hello, you chicken.* Four, five. Darn, her floor was next.

Do it! Now!

She sucked in a deep breath and blurted, "Are you new?"

Tall, Dark, and Mysterious turned his head. His eyes met hers, and something flashed in their dark depths. It seemed as if the world dropped out from under her feet. A zing of electricity buzzed through her. Her heart did two flips inside her chest.

He reached toward her, his hand roughly waist high. Was he going to touch her? To take her hand in his? Her entire being seemed to become energized as her senses heightened.

Just as his hand was about to make contact with her, he bent forward and poked a button on the panel.

"I think this is your floor." His lips curled into a smile that made her heart do a third flip.

"Oh." She jerked her eyes up and saw that the six above the door was illuminated. Her cheeks burned. *You're such an idiot.* "Yes, yes, it is. Thanks. I guess I should get going, huh? Wouldn't want to set off any alarms."

"I don't think that'll happen." Still holding the button, he tipped his head. "To answer your question, yes. I am new."

"Well...welcome to the building."

"Thank you." His smile amped up another thousand watts.

"Well..." Her skin sizzled as she stepped through the opening. "See you tomorrow."

"Sure. Tomorrow." His eyes tracked her as she moved away from the door so it would close. She felt the heat of his gaze. Literally. It was the oddest sensation, like nothing she'd ever experienced before. It was as if his eyes produced heat. She took a couple of steps down the hall, but at the sound of the doors rumbling behind her, she glanced over her shoulder.

Once again their gazes tangled, and it felt as if arcs of static charged the air between them. Frozen in place, she sucked in a little gasp of surprise. When the door shut, she shook herself out of her daze.

That was intense. And weird. Weirdly intense. At least she

had finally spoken to him, and he had responded. That was a major victory for her. She had always been so painfully shy around men. It took Herculean effort for her to talk to a man. As a result, she could literally count the number of dates she'd been on this year on one hand. Every one of them had been blind dates. And none of them had led to second dates.

When she'd first seen Tall, Dark, and Mysterious a week or so ago, she had felt this strange attraction, as if he were a magnet, pulling her toward him. She'd told herself he was far too good-looking for her, but still that odd energy kept buzzing and zapping through her every time he was near. She had to know if he felt it, too. If he did...oh God, what if he did?

Standing at her work's suite door, she ran her sweaty palms down the sides of her legs. It was time to focus on work. Focusing on work was easy. She loved her job, a junior account rep with a small advertising company. It allowed her to be creative.

She waved at Lauren, the receptionist, on her way back to her desk. Lauren beamed a greeting in return, just like she did every morning. Tom, her boss, was in his office. The door was shut. Through the window, she could see he was talking to her newest client, the one she'd just signed yesterday. She wondered if she should join them, hesitated at the shut door, and waited until Tom looked her way. It took a while, but he finally made eye contact. He didn't motion her in, which was a little strange. Confused, she headed for her desk and dropped her stuff.

"I heard there's a problem with the Quadtex account," Jessica, the other junior account manager, whispered. She was leaning out of her cubicle, to peer into Michelle's. Today, like every day, her dishpan-blond hair was scraped back into a bun, and she wore big J.Lo-style hoop earrings that nearly hit her shoulders. Her lips were the shade of ripe cherries.

Michelle scooted her chair toward Jessica and whispered, "What did you hear?"

"No specifics. Just that they were pulling out."

"What? Why?"

Jessica shrugged. "No idea." She jerked around. "Oh, I have a call. I'll let you know if I hear anything else."

"Thanks. God, I hope it's just a rumor." Uneasy, Michelle powered up her computer and checked her e-mail, skimming for anything that was time-sensitive. Just as she was wrapping up an e-mail to another prospective client, Tom approached her desk. He was alone.

"Michelle, I need to speak with you." His tone was clipped, his expression serious.

"Sure." Not certain what to expect, she followed him into his office.

"Please, close the door," he said as he rounded his desk to have a seat.

Michelle shut the door, then sat in the chair facing him, the one that had been occupied by her new client not so long ago.

He smoothed his tie. His features were taut, mouth drawn into a line. "The Quadtex contract has been cancelled."

Oh God, it was true. This wasn't just a big problem for her. It was a catastrophe. An epic one. "What happened?"

"It seems you made a commitment that you couldn't keep. Did you tell Robb Lara that you could guarantee a five-star review from *IndigoTech* magazine?"

Her heart jumped. Tom thought it was her fault? "No, of course not."

"That's what he's claiming."

"I'm sure he misunderstood—"

"What did you say that led him to believe you could?"

"Nothing that I recall. I swear."

Tom opened a folder and pulled out a sheet of paper. He slid it across the desktop, toward her. "Did you send this e-mail?"

Her hands trembled slightly as she picked up the paper to read it. First thing she checked was the header, to make sure it had her name on it. It did. And the correct e-mail address. Then she read the message.

Oh God, did she really write that?

"Yes. I did," she confessed. Had the oxygen been sucked out of the room? She couldn't breathe. "What I meant—"

"It doesn't matter what you meant. What matters is what you said." He poked an index finger at the paper. "This is a problem."

Her heart started pounding so hard it hurt. Her hands. They were trembling. "I wasn't intentionally trying to deceive him."

"Perhaps not, but it was taken that way."

"I don't know what to say. I was just trying to show him how hungry I was for his business, and how hard I would work for him."

Tom smoothed his hands over his thinning gray hair. "There's nothing wrong with being enthusiastic. But you went too far."

"I'm sorry." That was an understatement. But what else could she say?

"Yes, well, so am I." He cleared his throat. "We've lost the account. They're going to the Mattex Agency."

She felt like absolute crap. Just a few words had cost her an account worth over a million dollars. There was nothing she could do, other than to say, "It won't happen again. I promise."

"It *can't* happen again."

No mistaking the tone of that statement. She nodded.

"That's all for now."

She hurried out of her boss's office. What a freaking mess! All because of one little sentence in one little e-mail. Who would've ever guessed something so insignificant would lead to such a huge blowup?

At her desk, she flopped into her chair and let her head fall into her hands. How would she fix this? How?

She couldn't. Shit. Shit, shit, shit.

Tears burned her eyes, and she sniffled. Someone tapped on her shoulder.

"Are you okay?" that someone asked.

She knew that voice. Jessica.

"I screwed up," she said into her hands. "Big-time. I put something in an e-mail I shouldn't have." At the sound of a door slamming, she jerked her head up and checked Tom's office. He was standing in front of his door, staring at her. "Oh crap. Tom is looking this way. I'd better get to work," she muttered.

"Okay. You can tell me at lunch. What do you think? Antonio's? I'm in the mood for Italian."

"Italian sounds great, but I should probably work through lunch today. And tomorrow. And all week. Maybe all month." After giving Jessica a little wave, she dug into her work, letting her angry boss see there was good reason not to show her the door.

Because Michelle had stayed busy all day, time passed quickly. By seven-thirty, she was so hungry her stomach was trying to digest itself and her feet were hating her for wearing her most expensive, but most painful, pointy-toed pumps. She'd been at work for over eleven hours. Nobody, other than Tom, was still in the office.

She shut down her computer, stood, and stretched muscles that were sore and tight. Neck. Legs, Back. After loosening up, she grabbed her purse and headed out of the suite. As she was waiting in the hallway for the elevator, her phone rang.

Mom.

Glad to hear a friendly voice, she answered. "Hi, Mom."

"Hello, honey," her mother said. "Thank you for the nice gift."

Gift? She hadn't sent a gift. "Mom, I have no idea what you're talking about," she said as she pushed the elevator button again. Why was the stupid thing taking so long?

"The box was delivered a little while ago. It's my favorite chocolates. It had to be you."

"No, Mom. It wasn't me. Are you sure you didn't order them for yourself and forget?"

"No. I wouldn't do that. Let me see if there's a card or a receipt." The sound of rustling paper echoed through the phone. "No, nothing."

"That's odd."

"Yes, it is. If it wasn't you, who would send me these?"

"I have no idea. Why don't I come over to check it out? It's a little strange that you've received a gift out of the blue and you have no idea who sent it. You can never be too careful. Maybe you should set the box aside until I get there?"

"Well, that's just silly. Who would send a gift to hurt me?"

"Good question. I'm sure it's fine. But just in case, you should probably either figure out where they came from or toss them." Finally, the bell chimed.

"Throwing away Epiphany Chocolates would be a crime. I won't throw them away."

The elevator door rumbled open, and she scurried inside. It was empty, except for her. She poked the button for the first floor. "Okay, then I'll help you figure out who sent them. I'll be there as soon as I can."

"Good. I'll make your favorite for dinner."

"Wonderful. See you soon."

"Bye, dear."

She clicked off, dropped her phone into her purse, and took a few deep breaths.

What a crazy day. First she'd almost gotten fired for losing a huge account and now this. The car lurched to a stop. The bell chimed. And approximately a zillion seconds later the door opened.

Feeling extra creeped out in the dark parking structure, she didn't walk, or even race-walk, to her car; she ran like a scaredy-cat. When she reached it, she remoted the locks, tossed her purse onto the passenger seat, flung herself into the driver's seat, and rammed the key into the ignition. The second she grabbed hold of the gearshift, a knock pounded on her window.

Her heart slammed against her breastbone.

Her head snapped to the left.

It was Tall, Dark, and Mysterious.

Where the hell had he come from?

Her hand trembled a tiny bit as she powered down the window.

He smiled. It was so bright and friendly she couldn't help smiling back, despite the fact that her heart was still racing so fast she felt light-headed. "Hi," he said through the open window. "I just found a phone over by the door." He tipped his head toward the building. "It looks like you're the only one out here, so I thought I would check to see if it's yours." He lifted the phone so she could see it. "If it isn't, I'll turn it in to security tomorrow."

Black. Touch screen. With a hot pink cover. "I think...it looks like my phone. It might be mine. It was in my purse." After flicking a glance at her open purse, still sitting on the seat beside her, she extended a hand out the window. As he placed the phone in it, his fingers lightly brushed against her skin, and a little zing of electricity buzzed through her. After she recovered from the mini-electrical shock she'd received, she swiped the screen. There could be no doubt. It was hers. "Gosh, I hope I didn't lose anything else." She grabbed her bag's handle and pulled it closer so she could check if anything else was missing. Because she'd been so freaking paranoid, she'd run through the garage with the stupid thing hanging open. Brilliant.

Her wallet was in there, thank God. That was the only thing that mattered, really. Except her phone, of course.

Lifting an arm to rest it on the car's roof, he angled over the window, peering down at her. "I didn't find anything else on the ground. Just the phone."

"My wallet's here. That's all I really care about." Setting her ransacked purse back on the passenger seat, she turned to Tall, Dark, and Mysterious. "Thank you again. I would have been lost without my phone. Absolutely lost."

He flashed a smile that was bright enough to illuminate the entire city of New York. "No problem. I'm just glad I caught you before you'd left."

"Me too."

Their gazes tangled, and Michelle became a little breathless and warm. There *was* something there. It couldn't be her imagination. There was a chemistry that zinged and sizzled through her body. It almost made her forget where she'd been in such a hurry to go. Almost.

"Um, I'm sorry, but I have to go," she mumbled a hundred heartbeats later.

"Oh, sure." He stepped back and gave her another smile, this one not quite as bright. "See you tomorrow."

"Yes. Tomorrow." She made sure he had moved out of her way, then backed out of her parking space.

She couldn't help peering at his reflection as she drove toward the road.

That was twice now. Twice, she'd spoken to him. She was on a roll.

Talen didn't move.

What the hell was that? What the hell?

His cock was so hard it could bust concrete. And his heart was thumping against his rib cage as if he'd run a marathon.

That little brunette was so strange and quirky, an odd mixture of awkward and sexy. Never had a woman like that made him feel this way.

He thought back to all those times he'd ridden the elevator with her. She hadn't spoken for the first, oh, ten or so days. And he hadn't really noticed her much. But this morning... this morning his body had been tense all over by the time he'd reached his office. He'd thought it was because of last night, with Angela. Angela, his perfect submissive. Sexy as hell. Eager to please. *Able* to please—so fucking good at sucking cock.

But now, after running into the little stuttering brunette again, he wasn't so sure it was the memory of last night with Angela that made him hot and tight all over.

Still standing exactly where he'd been since she'd roared away in her little compact car, he glanced down at his hands. He could swear he'd felt an electric current zap him when he'd touched her.

Static, he told himself. He was grounded. She was in a running car. It had to be static.

Shaking his head at his own foolishness, he strolled toward his car. He had a sexy, hot submissive waiting for him at the club. There was no time to stand around, imagining things that weren't there.

4

For some silly reason Michelle held her breath the whole drive to her mom's house. She hoped she was being paranoid. She hoped this whole thing was a silly mistake, and Mom would remember she'd either ordered the chocolates for herself or mentioned them to a friend. It was just so weird if it wasn't.

But her heart rate hadn't slowed down by the time she'd parked in her mom's driveway. And, in fact, it sped up as she *click-clacked* in her painful shoes to the front door. It amped up another notch when there was no answer.

Michelle rang the bell a second time. At least a dozen gruesome images flashed through her head.

"That's it. I am never watching another Lifetime movie again."

She scurried over to the window and peered in. Her mother was on her way down the hall, heading toward the foyer. "Oh, thank God." She teetered back over to the door and waited to be let in.

A gust of delicious cooking smells wafted out the doorway as Mom opened it. "Honey, this is such a nice surprise."

Surprise.

"Dinner smells scrumptious," she said as she stepped inside. She kicked off her shoes at the door. Her feet thanked her. "Where's the box?"

Mom motioned toward the kitchen. "On the counter. I didn't touch it after I called you. But I think you're being silly about all of this."

"I probably am. But that's okay." She padded into the kitchen, bare feet on linoleum, following behind her mother.

Mom smiled over her shoulder. "I hope I get more mysterious packages. At least I'm getting a visit from you."

Guilt knocked Michelle in the belly, the impact as painful as a punch. "I'm sorry it's been so long. I've been busy. But that's no excuse," she said as she approached the box. "I promise I'll come over more often. At least once a week."

"I know you're busy," Mom said as she headed for the pots boiling and steaming on the old gold-enameled stove. "It's okay. Once a week is too much for a busy young woman like you. I understand."

"No, it isn't too much. And I mean it." Michelle checked the outer shipping box first. There was a clear plastic pocket glued to one side. Inside the pocket was a receipt. The buyer's name and an address were clearly marked on it. "Mom, do you know someone named Robert Kepley?"

"Robert? Oh gosh. Yes, I do. He's a friend I met on the Internet."

Michelle handed her the receipt. "He was the one who sent you this package."

"Well, isn't that sweet! Now that I think about it, I did tell him how much I loved Epiphany Chocolates, but I didn't expect him to buy me some." She looked down at the paper in her hands. "Where did you find this?"

"Inside an envelope glued to the side of the box."

"Ah. I didn't see it."

"Now you know, if you get any more mystery packages, check for an envelope with a shipping order on the outside, okay?"

"I will. Thank you, dear." Grinning a little guiltily, her mom set the paper on the counter and went back to the stove. "Now, how about something to eat? Are you hungry?"

Did her mom...? Had she intentionally overlooked the shipping order?

She wouldn't.

Yes, she would.

"You knew all along who sent you those chocolates, didn't you?"

Her mom shrugged and batted her fake eyelashes. "Maybe."

"Please don't do that again. You had me terrified."

Her mother's coy smile wilted. "Okay. I promise I won't."

Michelle went to her sneaky little mother and gave her a hug. "I'll make sure you don't have any reason to trick me into coming over again. I promise."

"Good. Now let's eat. I've been smelling the food cooking all day. I'm starving."

She had learned from the best. She'd learned to outwit the enemy, to find a weakness and use it to her advantage.

And all men, including the Lion, the Dragon, and the Eagle, the Black Gryffons, had one common weakness.

After weeks of waiting, planning, preparing, she was ready.

The first step: to set the trap.

Twice in recent months the Chimera had tracked down the Black Gryffons. The Secret had been within their grasp. But then they'd fucked up.

They'd sent the wrong *man*.

Not this time. She knew exactly what to do. The brothers

would be subdued, separated, manipulated into revealing the location of The Secret. This time they would not fail.

She would not fail.

Already, her plan had been set into motion.

He was watching her. Oh God.

Michelle's skin sizzled. Her heart pitter-pattered.

Trying not to notice Tall, Dark, and Mysterious standing in the corner of the room, tracking her movements with dark eyes, she cut through a thick crowd of dancers. As she passed between the writhing, gyrating bodies, hands caught her by the waist, spun her around.

She looked up.

It was him. How had he caught her so quickly?

He pulled her flush against him. His heat made her blood burn. The heavy, throbbing beat of the music pounded through her system. His lustful stare made her heartbeat erratic. "Are you running from me?"

"Running? No. Are you... are you following me?"

His hand skimmed down her side, stopping at her hip. Every nerve in her system electrified. His gaze darkened. "You should run."

"Why?"

Without warning, he spun her around and slammed her against the wall.

Trapped. She was pinned against a cool wall and a hot man. Both were hard. Both were immobile. The sensation thrilled her.

He tipped his head slightly, eyes fixed on hers. "I'm dangerous," *he whispered.*

Dangerous.

He looked like a god.

He was strong and sexy.

He made her feel things she had never felt before.

Oh yes. He was most definitely dangerous.

She opened her mouth to respond, but he slammed his mouth over hers.

The kiss was darkly erotic. A feral possession. His tongue pushed into her mouth and caressed and tasted and claimed. His hands explored her body, making her writhe and shudder and whimper.

When one hand cupped her ass, his fingers slipping lower, to her hot center, she gasped.

Was he going to take her right here? In a crowded club? With people all around them?

His fingers slid beneath the crotch of her satin panties.

He groaned. "Wet."

That she was. Wet. Ready. So warm. Her tissues clenched.

Empty.

He hooked his fingers in the sodden material and yanked. It tore away, leaving cool air to caress her simmering, sodden tissues. "Unzip me."

Ohmygod, he was going to take her.

She said, "Shouldn't we—"

"Unzip me."

She could not resist his demand. Reaching between their bodies with shaking hands, she unbuckled his belt, then unfastened his pants.

No underwear.

She pushed the sides of the zipper apart to expose his erection. It sprang free. Thick. Hard. He would fill her. Perfectly. Completely.

He grasped one of her legs by the knee and lifted it, opening her center to him. The head of that gloriously big cock prodded at her opening.

"You're mine," he said, cupping her face with his free hand.

"Mine." His hips slammed forward, driving his cock deep inside her.

The pleasure was almost unbearable. Her body went instantly tight. Everywhere. Stomach. Chest. Legs. Her inner walls clamped around his cock as it glided out, then slammed back in, filling her over and over. Erotic heat rippled through her body in waves, each one building bigger, hotter. And all she could do was cling to him and ride through the bliss as it threatened to overtake her.

She could feel the heat blasting from his body. His hips slammed forward and back, forward and back. Fast. Faster. Hard. Harder.

This was fucking. Reckless. Wild. Feral. She had never been fucked before. She'd never thought she was the type of girl to fuck.

Oh, she was.

She felt herself losing control. A scream of ecstasy was gathering in her chest, whirling around and around. Enormous waves of pleasure were crashing through her system, sweeping her toward a swift, hard, tooth-gritting climax.

Almost there.

He rammed into her hard and demanded, "Now. Come for me now."

His words sent her tumbling over the precipice. Her body spasmed. Her pussy rippled around his cock. That scream that had been trapped in her chest surged up her throat and out.

Breathless, Michelle jerked upright.

What a dream.

Her pussy was still spasming. She was sweaty, trembling, breathless. She'd had an orgasm in her sleep. That was a first.

She'd had an orgasm dreaming about him.

Mr. Tall, Dark, and Mysterious.

Mr. Tall, Dark, and Dangerous.

She settled back down and, smiling, closed her eyes. Maybe if she fell asleep quickly she would have another dream about him throwing her against the wall and fucking her brain-dead.

Maybe, if she were really lucky, someday he would fuck her brain-dead for real.

5

Today things were going to be different; better. The sun was shining. The birds were tweeting. Her belly was full of her mom's wonderful home cooking—she'd indulged in leftovers for breakfast this morning. And Tall, Dark, and Dangerous had just stepped into the elevator.

Oh, the dreams she'd had about that man last night. If only they could come true.

He gave her one of those stunning, traffic-stopping smiles as he stepped in. "Good morning."

Her heart did a triple flip. "Good morning." Today she didn't move over. She stayed right where she was. Instead of standing there like a goon and staring at the glowing numbers above the door, she pivoted to face him. Oh, was he big. Tall. Strong-looking. His shoulders were very broad. His chest, too. His clothes fit him perfectly, as if they'd been made for him. And they emphasized his perfect proportions.

Life had to be good for him, looking so freaking perfect.

She said, "Thank you again for finding my phone."

He slid one hand into his pants pocket and leaned against the wall. "It was no problem. Really."

"My phone's my lifeline."

"Yes, mine, too. Now that I've had it for a couple of years, I can't imagine life without it."

"Me, either."

There was a brief silence as the car slowly climbed higher. As time ticked slowly by, the tension between them amplified.

Say something, you twit. Now's your chance. You were doing so well.

"My name's Michelle," she said, extending a hand.

He took her hand in his. It was big and warm and strong. "Tage."

"It's good to meet you, Tage."

Once again, a heavy silence fell over them. He was still holding her hand, and her skin was warming. Her face, her chest. Her stomach. It was such a strange and unexpected reaction. Yes, he was insanely handsome, with his penetrating eyes and chiseled features. He held himself tall and proud, and he emanated a strength and command that she couldn't seem to ignore.

His concentrated gaze remained tangled with hers as his tongue darted out and swept across his lower lip. She felt herself mirroring him, moistening her lips, holding her breath. The air between them was so charged with energy it practically crackled, and her heart was pounding so hard she could count the heavy beats. *Thump, thump, thump.*

The elevator stopped, and the bell chimed. Her gaze hopped to the illuminated numbers above the door. The sixth floor. Her floor.

"I...this is my floor," she whispered.

"Yes. Okay." He released her hand, and a little buzz of disappointment swept through her. His touch. She missed his touch. The touch of a stranger?

Slightly shaken, she took a step toward the door. Before she crossed the threshold, the doors started rumbling closed, trapping her inside. A strong, thick arm shot past her shoulder, so close. His bulky frame leaned toward her as he caught the door. Instantly, her right side, the one closest to him, simmered, her skin tingling, nerves sizzling, pulses of awareness blasting through her. The intensity of the sensations took her breath away. She stood transfixed. Her eyes found his again, and she murmured, "Thank you."

"Have dinner with me," he blurted. Then he blinked. His brows scrunched ever so slightly, as if he was confused by his words.

He shifted back and the doors shut, closing them inside again. The elevator started climbing up to the next floor.

Had he just... had he just asked her on a date?

"When?" she somehow managed to utter.

"Tonight."

"Tonight?" Her mind raced. Did she have plans for dinner? What day of the week was it? Was it Friday? Yes, Friday. Did she have plans? She never had plans. What was she thinking? "I—I think it'll be okay. What time?"

"You were working late last night. Should I make the reservations for... seven? Seven-thirty?"

"Seven-thirty sounds good."

"Okay, then." The elevator stopped again, this time at the top floor. When the doors rolled apart, he stepped out, then turned to look at her. "I'll come down and pick you up at seven."

"I'm in suite six-ten."

The doors shut, and she took her first breath in at least ten minutes. Down she rode, to her floor. The door opened, and

Angela, the company's lead account rep, grabbed her hand and dragged her out of the elevator. This was not a common occurrence. No. In fact, since Michelle had started working for the Bauer Agency, Angela had spoken to her maybe three times, total.

"Who was that?" Angela asked, jerking her head toward the elevator doors.

"Who?" Michelle echoed, feeling her face warming with embarrassment.

"That guy," Angela said, tugging her around and escorting her toward suite six-ten. "The one with the eyes. And the body. And the hair." She sighed.

"He's ... his name is Tage. He works upstairs. On the tenth floor."

"Ah, I thought I recognized him. He is to die for, isn't he?" Angela opened the door for her. "Are you seeing him?"

Angela knew Tage? "Not ... technically."

"What do you know about him?" Angela asked as she dragged Michelle past Lauren.

"Not much." On the way by the reception desk, Michelle gave Lauren a quick confused look and a wave. "We've only spoken a couple of times."

"Did you see a ring?" Angela asked as she steered Michelle toward her cubicle.

"I didn't look for one," Michelle admitted, feeling a little stupid for not having thought of it. Here she was, all this time, trying to talk herself into speaking with him, and he could be married. But if he was married, why would he ask her to dinner? And if Angela knew him, why didn't she know if he was married or not? Clearly she didn't know him well.

"That's okay." She flapped a hand. "I'll do my own detective work."

Michelle merely nodded, not bothering to tell her new

friend about her dinner date. For one thing, it was only dinner. It could lead to something. Or it could not—especially if he was married. She was not interested in being the other woman.

She fished her phone out of her purse, then she put it away in the cabinet above her desk.

Angela shouldered the half-wall and crossed her arms over her ample chest. "I didn't realize he worked in this building. You said he works on the tenth floor, right?"

"Yes," Michelle answered as she powered up her computer.

"Did he tell you his suite number?" she pressed.

"No. Um, how do you know Tage?"

"I . . . just recently met him." Thrusting out a hip, she tossed her glossy blond waves over her shoulder. There was no missing the determined look in her eye. "I'm sure it won't be hard tracking him down." She sauntered off, a girl on a mission.

A little wave of defeat washed through Michelle. Angela White wasn't just any girl. She was beautiful. She was intelligent. And she was damn good at everything she did. No doubt she'd be just as accomplished at seducing a man as she was at everything else.

Unlike her.

At least she would have tonight. She hoped.

Shoving aside thoughts about what might happen later, she forced herself to concentrate on work. After that terrible screwup with Quadtex, she needed to stay focused. Her job was her first priority.

Her family was second.

Her love life was, and had always been, last.

At ten to seven, Michelle had a mini panic attack.

Her hair was a wreck. Her makeup wasn't much better. Her clothes were wrinkled (why, oh why, had she worn linen to work today?). And she was so freaking nervous, she felt sick to her stomach.

In the bathroom, she did her best to sexy herself up a bit. There was no getting her mouse-brown waves back into the neat French twist she'd had it in, so she pulled out the pins, tossed her head back and forth a few times, and opted for the disheveled look, hoping she would pass for sexy instead of just plain messy. A quick dig through the depths of her purse scored her an eyeliner pencil and a lipstick she hadn't worn in ages. She darkened her eyes and smoothed on the lipstick.

The result was acceptable.

Now, what to do about the clothes?

Her linen skirt was what it was. A wrinkled, creased mess. There wasn't much she could do about that. So she focused her efforts on the garments from her waist up. For work, she'd worn a crisp white blouse. And over that she'd buttoned on a cardigan sweater. Then she'd buckled a narrow leather belt around her waist. The belt was the first to go. Then the sweater. Finally, she unfastened a couple of buttons to give her date just a little peek at her cleavage.

She took a step back, sighed, then turned to head out of the bathroom. She was practically slammed off her feet by a blur of blue as she pushed open the door.

"Ohmygod!" the blue blur said. "He's here." Angela stopped in front of the mirror, dropped her purse on the counter, and started digging through its contents with one hand while popping open buttons on her blouse with the other.

Michelle had to give it to her, Angela was quite the multi-tasker.

Hurrying out, so she could get him out of the office before Angela made her appearance, Michelle sucked in a deep breath.

It left her lungs in a huff the minute her eyes met his.

He smiled.

She practically melted.

"Hello," Angela said as she sauntered past her, hips swaying, hair bouncing, smile beaming. "Do you have an appointment with someone?"

"Yes, I do." He motioned toward Michelle. "With her."

Angela's perfectly plucked brows scrunched. "You do?" She swung around to look at Michelle. "She didn't mention it."

"I was a little busy at the time," Michelle explained.

Angela's scrunched brows pulled in closer. "Is that so?" Her expression changed in a blink, from confused to happy. "Well, that's okay." She thrust her hand out, offering it to him. "I'm... Angela. Michelle's supervisor. We can all sit down and discuss your needs together."

Supervisor? Since when?

Tage's puzzled look bounced from Angela to Michelle and back again. His lips twisted. "Um...this is a private meeting."

Angela's lips formed a perfect *O* as she jerked her head around to look at Michelle. A little muscle in her jaw clenched as she measured up her competition. "I see." She stepped back. "Sorry for the misunderstanding."

"It's okay." Tage motioned to Michelle and, feeling as though she had won some kind of contest, she stepped up to him, then preceded him out the door. The skin on her back burned as she walked out. She wasn't sure if it was the awareness that he was behind her that made it sizzle, or the heat of Angela's furious stare. Either way, she did her best to ignore it and stepped inside the elevator. For the first time, she rode it down with him.

Down, to the parking structure. And out she went, walking beside him.

At this time of year the sun hung low in the western sky by 7 P.M., the angle creating long, cool shadows in the structure. Michelle hugged herself as she followed Tage's lead through a long row of parked cars. He stopped in front of a Range Rover, circled around to the passenger side, and opened the door.

Her arm brushed against him as she moved between his bulk

and the car. A bolt of heat blazed through her at the brief (much too brief) contact. Her face warmed. "Thank you," she said softly. Her gaze lifted to his face. A powerful face. A stunningly masculine face.

"You're welcome." With long, land-eating strides, he wound back around to the driver's side. Within a second or two he was seated beside her, his hands on the steering wheel, his gaze once again locked on her face. He opened his mouth, as if to say something, but then closed it. The car's engine roared to life, and in a blink, they were zooming down the road. "Your coworker thought I was meeting with you for business."

Coworker? He wasn't going to admit he knew Angela? "Yes. My personal life is none of her concern." She tried to smooth her skirt over her thighs.

"Then she's not a friend of yours."

"No," she responded flatly.

He chuckled, and she immediately decided she liked the way it sounded. A deep, vibrating rumble that echoed through her body. "Is she an enemy, then?" he asked.

"I wouldn't go that far, no. I don't have many enemies."

"That's a good thing."

"What about you? The way you said that...?"

"I have my share, I suppose." His gaze flicked to the rearview mirror as he steered the car onto the freeway. "But it comes with the job."

"Which is...?" she asked as she studied his (stunning, drool-worthy, extremely attractive) profile. His features were so classically beautiful. They reminded her of the world's most treasured sculptures, Michelangelo's *David*, Cellini's *Perseus*, and the *Antinous Mondragone*.

"Computer programmer."

"Computer programmer? Enemies? Really?"

"You'd be surprised," he said.

"I'll take your word for it."

"I see you work for an advertising agency," he said as he eased the car toward the exit ramp.

"Yes. I'm a junior account representative. I haven't been with the agency for very long. So far, I like it, though I was hoping I would be more involved with the creative side of things. That's where my true strengths lie. I hold two bachelor degrees. One in commercial art and one in creative writing."

"Interesting. My strengths lie in my creativity, too."

The car rolled to a stop at a red light, and he turned to look her way. Again, their gazes tangled and a zap of electricity buzzed between them. It felt like the charge was zinging across her skin, energizing her nerves. She'd never felt that way with a man before. It was strange. And thrilling. Both. She decided Angela was a non-concern. Clearly Angela was interested in him, but he wasn't in her. Too bad. So sad.

"Yes, I suppose it would be, considering what you do," she said, her voice barely above a whisper.

A honk jerked her out of her haze.

Tage's head snapped to the front and he hit the gas. The car surged forward like a jet.

She inhaled deeply, exhaled. This was the oddest date she'd ever been on already. And it had hardly started. The chemistry was insane. Staring straight ahead, she tried to decide if she should break the silence that had fallen between them with more small talk or not.

"I was thinking," he said, doing it for her. "I have been wanting to look into some advertising for my company, maybe some color brochures."

"Sure. That would be great."

"I would insist on working with you. And I would also request you do the layout."

She couldn't help giggling. "You say that without even seeing any of my work."

"Something tells me you're not the boastful type. That you are truly talented."

"I'd like to think I am," she said, face burning with embarrassment. She really did hate talking about herself, and she truly wasn't the type to brag about her gifts. "I tell you what, you can come over anytime you like and determine that for yourself. I'll show you my portfolio."

"I'd like to see it."

"Just say the word. Anytime."

"Okay." He pulled into a grocery store parking lot and shifted the vehicle into park. There was no restaurant in sight. Not one.

She gave him a questioning look.

"You'll have to tell me where you live," he said.

Did he mean...now? "Oh. We're going to my place first? I thought we were going out to dinner."

"You said anytime."

"Yes, I did."

"We can order in. Unless you had your heart set on sitting in a restaurant."

Slightly shaken at the sudden change of plans, she took a moment to think. She determined, rather quickly, that things were going very well. "No, of course carryout is perfectly fine. I live on Third Street in Maineville. Are you familiar with the area?"

"No. I just moved into town a few months ago. You'll have to give me some directions."

"We'll need to head back north."

"Okay." He steered the car around and turned onto the road, heading in the opposite direction from which they'd been driving. "What kind of food do you like?"

"Anything."

"Anything?"

"I'm a total foodie."

"I like you already." The light turned red, and once again they were waiting, gazes tangled. Her breath lodged in her throat, and her heart pounded hard against her breastbone as she stared into the darkest eyes she'd ever seen. The longer she looked, the more lost she felt in the shadows she saw there. And she couldn't help wondering what his story was, where he'd come from, what kind of life he'd led up to this point, and what he dreamed about.

"I like you, too," she said. The light changed, and she pointed. "Someone is going to honk."

"Let them." He reached for her head, slid his hand across the back to cup it, and pulled while leaning toward her. His gaze, which had been fixed on her eyes, slid lower, to her mouth.

He was about to kiss her.

Kiss her!

A flurry of butterflies launched in her belly.

6

What the fuck was he doing? What. The. Fuck?

This woman wasn't his type. The one he'd left behind, Angela, she was his kind of woman, the type he'd told himself he would marry. What the hell was this he felt with the little meek Michelle? It was as if he were being drawn in, ensnared.

Was she Chimera?

Think with your brain, dickhead, not your cock.

He closed his eyes and dug deep, searching for the strength to pull away.

Then she sighed. The sound was so enthralling, so enticing, he leaned closer. He inhaled, drawing in the sweet scent of her skin. She smelled so good. His heavy eyelids lifted. She had closed her eyes, those mesmerizing eyes. Her full lips were waiting for him, pursed ever so slightly for his kiss.

One taste. Only one. That wouldn't kill him. He'd always been able to maintain control, even while white-hot need was thrumming through his veins. It would be no different with this woman.

Using the hand he'd cupped around the back of her head, he

pulled her toward him and lightly brushed his lips over hers. A tiny gasp filled the silence. Her gasp.

Her reaction pleased him. It made him hard, ready. Hot. He wanted her. Wanted to possess her. Now. Right there. In the car.

A horn blared behind him.

Fuck them.

It honked again.

Oh hell.

He couldn't get to her house fast enough. Yanking himself back to reality, he stomped on the accelerator. Until he was parked somewhere, he was going to have to keep his hands off her. And his lips, too. His tongue darted out, swept across his lower lip. Her sweet flavor still lingered there. It was delicious. He couldn't wait to taste her again. He couldn't wait to hear another sigh, too.

That was one sound he doubted he would ever tire of.

Had she died? Was she in heaven? In hell? The way she felt at the moment, it could be either...or both. Her body was burning, from her scalp to the soles of her feet. Agonizing blazes of need were rushing through her system, and she couldn't quite catch her breath. Between her legs her tissues were moist, warm, pulsing.

How was it that one tiny kiss could do all of that to her?

Staring out the window, she concentrated on breathing. Innnn. Outttt. Innnn. Outttt. Her head was a little less swimmy after a few deep breaths. But her body was still as hot and tight as ever.

And she was about to spend the next...who only knew how much time...alone with this man. Alone. In her apartment. And he wanted her. She could see it in his eyes.

I'm going to sleep with him.

A bolt of energy charged through her, knocking the air from

her lungs again. Her face and neck heated. Yes, she was going to sleep with this gorgeous, sexy man.

Her voice was very quiet and small as she delivered directions to him. She could hear the nervousness in it. She wondered if he could, too. If he did, he said nothing, just quietly followed her directions. He drove skillfully, following the speed limit. Even though there was little to no small talk during the rest of the drive, she found herself gradually relaxing. They stopped at her favorite Italian restaurant on the way to her place. She ordered her usual, a pasta dish that she'd never had anywhere else. It was rich and decadent and delicious. He followed her advice and ordered the same. While they waited for their dinners to be cooked, he suggested they sit at the bar and have a drink.

His gaze was locked on hers when he asked, "What would you like?"

Another one of those kisses would be great. Her heart *pitter-pattered*. "A glass of wine would be nice."

He ordered two and while the bartender filled their order he swiveled his stool to face her. "Are you nervous?"

Oh God, her face was going to ignite. "Is it that obvious?"

"No. I'm just...I notice those kinds of things."

The bartender set the glasses on napkins in front of them. Michelle appreciated the bartender's timing. It kept her from having to explain her jittery nerves to a man who had probably never felt nervous on a date.

Tage pulled out his wallet, fished out a couple of bills, and handed them to the bartender, telling her to keep the change. She responded with a wide smile and a "Thank you" and moved to the man on the other side of Tage.

His attention focused, Tage waited for Michelle to pick up her glass. "Shall we?" He tipped his glass.

"Sure." She raised hers and gave him a go-ahead nod.

"To...fortunate coincidences."

"I'll drink to that." She tapped her glass against his, then sipped. Delicious. Smooth. As she swallowed, she could feel her nerves untangling a little, the tightness in her neck and shoulders easing. She took a few more swallows.

"Why are you nervous?" he asked as he set his glass on the bar.

Shit. "Oh. Um." She took another big gulp. She couldn't tell him everything. Some of it was just plain embarrassing. "I haven't been on a date in...a while."

"Really? That's hard to believe." He set his left hand on the bar's polished top.

No ring. Definitely no ring. Or tan mark. That didn't guarantee he wasn't married, but it made it more likely.

"It's the truth." So much for her pride. "Lately I've been so focused on work, I haven't had much time for anything else," she explained, deciding that rational excuse would make her less pathetic than the truth.

"Hmmm. I understand that. I've been there before, too. But I've learned more recently that it's one thing to work to live; it's another thing to live to work. I love what I do, but I don't let my work be everything anymore."

His confession intrigued her. If what he said was true, it explained why she didn't see a ring on his left hand. "I would like to get there, myself. I will. But I have some things to prove to my boss right now. So, it's mostly work and very little play for this girl."

"I see." He scooted a little in his seat, sliding his arm along the bar top and leaning closer to her.

Her nerves sizzled at his nearness. She explained, "I kind of screwed things up with a huge client, and the client cancelled the contract and went with another company."

"Hmm. I'm sorry." He lifted his glass and took a couple of swallows.

"I'm just glad I wasn't fired." Feeling as if the conversation had veered off into dangerous territory, specifically her messed-up career, she waved a hand. "Enough about my problems. Tell me about your work. You said you're a computer programmer."

"It's not very exciting, I'm afraid. My brothers' careers are both more interesting."

"You have brothers?"

"Two. I'm the youngest."

"The baby."

"Not anymore." He smiled. It wasn't a sweet smile. It was the kind that said, *I'm-very-much-not-a-baby.* "I definitely outgrew the baby thing a long time ago."

"Oh, I didn't mean to imply—"

"You didn't offend me." He winked. "I just thought I'd clear that up."

"Ah, got it." Like he needed to point out the fact that he was physically as far from an infant as a man could be. He was big and hard and masculine. He carried himself like a man who knew what he was doing, what he wanted, and how to get it. The latent power that she sensed lay below the surface intrigued her. No, it excited her.

She took one last swallow of her wine, emptying the glass, just as the bartender came scurrying toward them with a bag in her hand. She set the bag on the bar. "Sorry for the wait."

"No problem." Tage stood, grabbed the bag's handles, and, turning his attention back to Michelle, motioned toward the door. "Shall we?" Turning back to the bartender, he waved.

Michelle couldn't help noticing the bartender's sparkly-eyed stare as she returned his wave and called out, "Have a great night."

A little jolt of something charged through her at the sight of those sparkles. She immediately shoved that something aside and produced some sparkles of her own as she stepped through the restaurant's door, brushing past Tage as he held the door for her.

Outside, she took a few deep breaths. The wine had helped

settle her jangly nerves somewhat, but she still tensed up whenever she got close to him. The tension was strange. It wasn't entirely bad.

Outside of telling him when and where to turn, she didn't say much as they drove the rest of the way to her apartment. Her heart started pounding really hard when he pulled into the visitor parking space next to her building a few minutes later.

He motioned for her to stay in the car, then opened his door and unfolded his bulky frame. Within seconds he was standing next to her open door, offering her a hand out. She accepted, which put her almost chest to stomach with him as she straightened up. Her head tipped back, and she looked up into his dark eyes.

"Thank you," she murmured.

Something flashed in his eyes, and she froze in place. His fingers moved, tickling her hand. The touch sent blades of wanting piercing through her body.

"You're welcome." He moved, blocking her in, and her heartbeat raced even faster. There was something very dangerous and exciting about this man. At times he emanated this strange energy, almost predatory. But rather than being scared by it, she was drawn to him, mesmerized.

Most men she'd gotten that vibe from made her nervous in a bad way.

Feeling sexy, alive, she let her lips curl into a flirtatious smile. "Did you change your mind?"

"About what?" he asked as he shifted his weight, moving closer.

"About going inside?"

This pretty little thing had no idea she was playing with fire. None. He could tell she was inexperienced. Much to his surprise, her awkwardness and shyness made his blood burn. He'd never reacted to a woman like that before. Evidently he'd been wrong all these years, thinking he needed women with experience, submissives who knew what their limits were and understood the rules of the game.

He hadn't touched a fresh one like Michelle ever. He couldn't wait to see her on her knees, begging for release. He couldn't wait to taste her kiss, to hear her whimpers and sighs. To smell the sweet scent of her desire.

He cupped her chin and stepped closer, and a wave of need pulsed through his body. Oh yes, this was intense. He could tell by her wide eyes, dilated pupils, and deep, quick breaths that she felt the chemistry, too. Maybe it frightened her a little. He imagined it did. That was good. The little edge of fear would make her pleasure so much greater.

His thumb ran across her lower lip, and her sweet breath warmed his hand. "I haven't changed my mind. Have you?" Her lips were lush, plump, pink temptation. Not waiting for her to respond, he dipped his head down and tasted them. Delicious. He needed another taste. Decadent. And another. Intoxicating.

She shifted forward, pressing her soft, curvy body against him, and he hardened. His cock strained against his pants. How he wanted to spin her around, bend her over, and take her. Hard. Right there. Right then. His thick rod would make her shiver with pleasure.

"Ohmygod," she whispered into their joined mouths. Her little hands curled into fists, his jacket caught in them. He pushed a thigh between her legs, and she trembled. The heat of her desire burned his leg through his pants. She was so incredibly responsive. This was going to be fun. This was going to be hell. Both.

Taking advantage of her lips parting as she drew in a breath, he slipped his tongue inside to deepen the kiss. As he'd expected, she was sweet. Sweeter than any nectar, any fruit or berry. His body tightened even more. He tipped his hips, pressing his throbbing hardness against her, and wrapped his arms around her, pulling her flush to him. She fit against him perfectly, her soft femininity a perfect contrast to his hard, lean masculinity, her inexperience a perfect contrast to his wide and varied experience, her innocence a perfect contrast to his corruption.

Would he taint her by taking her? Would he ruin what was most beautiful?

"Please," she whispered.

He broke the kiss and forced himself to step away. Studying her in the dim semi-light of the weak, yellow parking lot lights, he pulled in a deep breath. A second one.

What was he doing? What the hell was he doing? This wasn't the kind of woman he should be playing with. It wasn't fair to her. Unlike the women he met at the club, like Angela, she didn't realize what kind of depraved man he was. All she knew was that he made her tremble with need. Made her wet and hot and ready. He licked his lip. Damn, her kisses were intoxicating. Addicting. He wanted another one. And another.

Leave her. Now. Before things get out of hand and you ruin her.

"Actually..." His voice wavered ever so slightly as he spoke. He lifted a hand to stroke her soft cheek, but before his fingertips touched her satiny skin, he pulled it back. "I should be going. I have to work early tomorrow."

The lips that were still swollen from his kiss puffed out in a semi-pout. "I—I understand." Her hand shook slightly as she lifted one to finger her mouth. "I'll see you Monday. Normal time. Normal place."

"Yes, Monday." Placing one hand on the small of her back, he escorted her to her building's entrance, handed her the bag of food, and waited until she was safe inside before he climbed back in his truck. He cranked on the engine, hit the gas, and steered his vehicle back to the road. As if it were on autopilot, it took him to the club, which was a good thing. There was no way he'd sleep tonight without burning off some of the heat blazing through his body first.

With tension wound through every inch of his body, he strode inside. Hoping to find a new submissive—someone athletic, maybe a little brunette with a high tolerance for pain and a flexible little body—he made his way into the open dungeon space.

Hmmm. That one. The brunette playing with a dom who clearly didn't know what the hell he was doing. She had some potential. Yes. That was the one he'd invite back to his room.

That is the kind of woman you should be marrying. Someone you can't taint, can't break, can't ruin.

Waiting for her scene to end, his gaze scanned the crowd. Tonight the club was a little busier than usual. Not only was just about every piece of equipment being used, but there were small clusters of people gathered around the participants, watching, waiting.

In the back corner, he caught the shimmer of dark hair. Was that Lei? A man had stepped in the way, blocking his view. As he moved toward the woman, someone tapped his back.

He swiveled around.

Instantly, he recognized her.

7

"Well, hello there," Angela said, giving him the up and down. She'd traded her sleek business skirt and blouse for a clingy black dress that fit her curves to perfection. "Looks like we have more in common than just where we play." Her eyes narrowed slightly. "How long have you been working in our building? I've never seen you there before today."

"Hello," Talen said as he continued to scan the crowd.

She stepped to the right, directly blocking his view. "Looking for someone?"

Slightly put off by her aggression, he moved to the left. "Yes, I am."

"Maybe I can help. I've been here for a while. Are you searching for a female or a male?"

His gaze meandered back to the woman in front of him. He gave her a thorough up and down. She was attractive. There was no denying that. And she definitely knew how to dress to make the most of her assets. And she had a few assets that were definitely worth highlighting.

But, gauging by the way she stood today, the way she held herself now, he suddenly didn't see her being a submissive. And after what happened earlier, when he'd run into her with Michelle, he wasn't sure whether he wanted to play with her again. "Female. Tall with dark brown hair. She told me she's a regular. Name is Jodie."

"I know Jodie. She's a close friend of mine." Angela pulled her lips into a semi-pout that reminded him somewhat of a certain other woman's pouty, lush lips. "Sorry, I think she's busy tonight. But maybe I can help you find another play partner?" She batted long eyelashes at him. That expression was one hell of an invitation, one he would have accepted without thinking before today.

One that he should be able to accept without feeling like he was doing anything wrong. So why did he feel slightly uneasy now? Was it because he didn't like Angela's attitude? Or was it because of someone else. A little brunette?

Couldn't be the latter. He owed Michelle absolutely nothing. They'd shared a couple of kisses, and then he'd left, before things got carried away. He hadn't even stayed for dinner.

"Are you looking for a girl with experience?" Angela asked.

Was he?

Yes. Of course. Experience was good.

Experience was essential.

And a certain level of independence and inner strength.

Remember, you're looking for someone who won't have any unrealistic expectations. Someone who won't be torn apart if you don't fall in love with her.

He gave Angela yet another up and down. While she was a little overly tenacious, she also seemed independent and self-assured. And, as he'd hoped, she was physically as different from Lei as he could get. She was tall and willowy, with long golden waves and blue-gray eyes. Her breasts were full, her hips wide, waist tiny. Classically beautiful.

He jerked his head toward the hallway. "Let's go."

Her lips curled into a broad smile, then straightened out as she adopted the serious, obedient expression she'd had last time he'd taken her to his room. "Yes, sir. Or...do you prefer Master?"

"Sir is fine." He steered her down the hall.

Monday morning Michelle's heart rate was galloping at an insane level as she boarded the elevator. Her hands were literally trembling. As she turned around, she clenched her purse, hoping holding her bag would help them stop. It probably didn't.

The car didn't move for several drawn-out moments. She waited, watched, her heart in her throat. He would step around the corner any second now.

Any...

Second...

Any time now...

He's going to miss it.

He had said he would see her today, same time, same place. Where was he?

The doors started closing. Her view of the lobby narrowed until it was completely cut off.

No Tage. He hadn't come.

Was it an intentional brush-off? Why? What had she done on Friday? Things had seemed to be going very well, at least that was what she'd thought. He had kissed her. Oh God, that kiss. She would never forget it. In fact, she'd dreamed about it last night...and the night before that.

But then he'd abruptly left. He hadn't even taken his dinner. He'd thrust the bag into her hands and left her on the front stoop of her building. He hadn't asked for her phone number. Nothing.

Once again, she'd screwed it up.

When the elevator stopped on her floor, she shuffled down to suite 610. Once inside she gave Lauren a wave, like always. Then she plopped down in her chair and started up her computer.

"You will never guess who I saw on Friday night!" Angela exclaimed as she bounced around the corner.

Michelle was so not in the mood for a bouncy Angela. "Who?" she grumbled.

Angela shouldered the wall and crossed her legs at the ankles. She pinched a blond curl between her fingers and twisted it. "Tage."

Michelle's insides felt as if Angela were twisting them. "Tage."

"Yes. Around eight-ish. I'm a member of a private social club. That's where I met him before. He showed up Friday night just as I was about to head home." A wicked gleam sparkled in her eyes. Michelle didn't care for that gleam at all. No, it made her feel a little sick inside. "We spent some *quality* time together at the club."

"That's...nice," Michelle said as she swallowed her breakfast for the second time. That bitch had to know what she was doing by telling her this. She wasn't going to give her the satisfaction of reacting.

And Tage...that jerk. He'd run out on their date just to go out to the club and meet up with someone else? What the hell? He'd sure acted like he was interested in her at first. So why did he leave so abruptly? Had Angela texted him an invitation he couldn't resist?

More importantly, why, oh why, did he have to pick Angela for his little sordid one-nighter? Of all the women in town, why her?

Angela's waxed and tweezed brows scrunched. "Michelle, are you okay? You look a little run down."

"Yes, I'm fine. Just tired. I had a late couple of nights this weekend."

Angela's overly lined eyes widened. "Oooh! I'm intrigued. Tell me."

"Maybe later." Michelle motioned to her computer, which had finished starting up. "I have a lot of work to do."

"Sure, sure. Later. Say, why don't we go to lunch? I can tell you about Tage. He's coming by this afternoon, by the way. He said he wants to talk about some advertising campaigns for his company."

Dammit, Angela got him in bed, and now she was getting the account, too. The bitch!

But what could she do about it? Nothing, that was what. Absolutely nothing. If he wanted to follow his dick, and go to Angela for help at work, that was his choice. There was no law against it. But it did suck.

Michelle pulled her mouth into what she hoped would pass for a smile. "That's great." She started poking at her keyboard, hoping Angela would get the message and leave.

She didn't. Ignoring Michelle's hint, Angela stayed put. Her expression turned all girly and wistful. "Yeah. It'll be really hard sitting there, talking business. He's so incredibly handsome, don't you think?"

"Yes, he's handsome." *And a complete ass.*

"You know," Angela said, twirling that stupid lock of hair, "when I saw you leaving with him on Friday, I thought you two were dating or something."

Me too.

"Well, if you were seeing him, I would want you to tell me. You can say a lot about me, but I wouldn't steal another woman's man. Never."

Great, now she had to either keep her mouth shut and listen to Angela spout on and on about Tage's prowess in the bedroom, or admit that she'd misunderstood his invitation to dinner, thinking he was interested in starting some kind of relationship with her. Either way, it was a shitty situation.

She opted for preserving her pride, smiling, and saying, "Oh no. We're just friends. He's not my type."

Angela's brows rose so high they practically blended into her hairline. "Not your type? Tall, handsome, and rich isn't your type?"

"No, I prefer short, fat, poor, and pasty white." Michelle forced a grin.

Angela's laugh was nauseating. "You are so funny. Why am I just realizing that now?"

Because Angela hadn't bothered to talk to her much before last week, perhaps? "Oh, I think I hide it pretty well when I'm at work."

"Well, you shouldn't. People around here like someone who can make them laugh. It doesn't always have to be serious business. So don't be afraid to let that inner comedienne out every now and then."

"I'll try to remember that, thanks."

"You're welcome." Angela tossed her hair. "See you at lunchtime." And off she flounced, to her office with the door and the window.

Some people got everything in life. The looks, the promotions, the men. Michelle hated those people.

Michelle knew he was nearby before she saw him. The air around her felt warmer. And little crackles of energy were skipping over her skin. She looked up from her computer screen, swiveled to glance over her shoulder.

He was watching her.

She felt her cheeks heating as their gazes met. His lips curled into a semi-smile that made her heart stutter and her mouth dry out. "Hello," she said, trying not to let him know how much he unnerved her or how hurt and disappointed she'd been after hearing about his little thing with Angela.

"I'm here to talk about advertising plans."

"Yes. Angela told me you were coming in today."

Some odd expression flashed across his features for a fraction of a second. It was almost too fast to be sure she'd seen it. It was most definitely too brief to read it. "Did I tell her that?"

"She's waiting for you." Michelle motioned toward Angela's office.

He strolled across the room, stopping just outside her cubicle. His brows pulled together. "She is?" His gaze jumped back and forth from Michelle's face to Angela's door. "I thought I would be meeting with you."

A little flare of heat blazed through her. "Me? Oh. I thought... well, never mind what I thought. I guess I made an assumption I shouldn't have." She stood, which put her in very close proximity to him. Another blast of awareness surged through her.

Her skin tingling, she pointed in the general direction of the conference room. "We can go talk in there."

"Sure." He didn't move. His gaze remained fixed on hers. His tongue darted out, flicked across his lower lip, and a little quiver buzzed up her spine.

Was it her imagination or was he acting a little strangely?

She motioned again, and he shook his head, as if to wake himself from a trance. As she brushed past him, her arm skimmed across the front of his body. With that miniscule, innocent contact a reaction fired inside her, like an atomic detonation. It took everything in her power not to stagger as she walked toward the conference room. Leaving the door open, she stood at the entry and motioned for him to sit. He stood next to a chair but didn't sit until she'd taken a seat herself.

"Before we begin," he said, leaning toward her, his voice barely above a whisper, "I feel I need to say something about Friday—"

"That isn't necessary."

"Angela. What did she tell you?"

"She met up with you Friday at some kind of private club she belongs to."

His gaze intensified as he listened, until it almost felt probing. "I see." A tiny muscle on his jaw twitched, which made her think he might be upset or angry with Angela for spilling the beans about seeing him. That almost made her feel better about the whole situation. Almost. Another part of her wondered if he was trying to do something underhanded and sneaky, like sleep with both Angela and her. She was so *not* into players.

She cleared her throat. "Anyway, your personal business is not something we need to discuss here and now. Agreed?"

He nodded, but that twitchy muscle still hadn't stopped clenching.

It was time to get things rolling. Her work was top priority, especially after what had happened last week. She needed to bring a new client on board. She hoped that client would be Tage. "So, tell me, what kind of advertising were you thinking about? What are you trying to accomplish?"

"I was thinking about doing some color brochures," he said, sounding as if advertising was the last thing he wanted to talk about. He glanced over his shoulder then jerked his head around again. "Can we close the door?"

"I suppose." She stood up to get it, but he literally lurched in front of her, beating her to it. He had it about halfway shut before a familiar face appeared in the gap between the frame and the edge of the door.

The door, which hadn't been completely shut, swung back in, and Angela sauntered into the room. "Tage?" Her contact-enhanced gaze ping-ponged back and forth between him and Michelle. "Am I interrupting something?" She checked her watch. "Michelle, why didn't you tell me he was here already? I wasn't expecting him until this afternoon."

Tage said, somewhat gruffly, "I didn't... My plans changed."

"Well, it's a good thing, then, that I'm available this morning."

Michelle glared at Tage, giving him a what-the-hell look. "We were just chatting for a few minutes. I was going to get you in a second."

"Actually, it's my fault," Tage said, standing. "I needed to talk to Michelle in private. And we're not through yet."

Angela's cute little lipsticked mouth formed an O. A handful of seconds later, her jaw snapped shut, and she jerked a nod. "Fine. Come and get me when you're done talking, Michelle." Her hips swung like a movie starlet's as she *click-clacked* in her expensive shoes toward the exit.

Tage closed the door behind Angela, then returned to his seat. "I've really fucked things up for you, haven't I?"

Oh buddy, you have no idea. "Did you tell Angela that you would work with her on the brochures?"

"No."

"She sure thinks you did."

"Yes, I see that." He shoved his fingers through his hair, messing it a bit. It looked better messy, which irritated Michelle even more. "But I'm telling the truth, we didn't discuss work on Friday."

Either he was lying or he was telling the truth and Angela had found out about his promise to come down somehow. Which meant they'd spent their time together discussing... other stuff. Personal stuff. Or maybe they didn't talk at all.

Maybe he kissed Angela like he'd kissed her. And maybe he didn't stop there.

Michelle's insides knotted. She swallowed hard, trying to force down the big lump congealing in her throat. It didn't work.

His expression darkened as he shifted closer. "Are you all right?"

She opened her mouth to speak, but nothing came out.

Swiftly, and with no warning, he jumped up, caught her by both arms, and pulled her against him. His gaze wandered over her face as his brows pinched together. "What's wrong?"

This time she took a deep breath in, and with more force, she pushed it out, blurting the word, "Nothing," as she exhaled.

"Are you sure?"

"I'm fine." Becoming increasingly aware of how close his big, hard body was to hers, she raised her shoulders, trying to pull her arms free. If he knew what she was trying to do, he didn't cooperate.

"Are you sure? You're breathing very fast."

His proximity sure wasn't helping that.

"I'm sure," she said, tugging on her arms again. "Please, just let me go."

At last he released her. And she was sad he did it. Sad but also relieved. She hated how mixed up and confused she became around this man. Absolutely despised it. "Now, let's get back to business." She tried to put a little force behind that sentence. She failed.

"What's wrong?" he asked, still standing much too close.

She sat, which at least put a little more space between her body and his. "Can we just get back to our discussion? I have other appointments."

His gaze sharpened. "I really screwed things up with you and your friend—"

"I told you, I don't give a damn about your personal life. It's your business, not mine. Now please"—she motioned to his chair—"sit down so we can discuss your brochure."

Instead of sitting, he placed a flattened hand on the table next to her and angled himself over her. "Why does that pretty face of yours get so tight every time I mention her name?" Grabbing her arms yet again, he jerked her to her feet. "And why do you pout those lips for me when I pull you near? Why?"

"I don't pout anything for you. Wow," she said as she flattened her hands against his chest and gave him a hard shove. "Are you so egotistical that you think every woman is dying to be your next conquest?"

"I don't think that. But I do believe you want to sleep with me."

She snorted. "That's ridiculous."

"Is it?"

She glared at him, and he slanted challenging eyes back at her. She stood frozen in place, her gaze locked to his, and fought to breathe. She was angry. Confused. And...alive. So alive. More alive than she'd ever felt before. Electric currents zoomed through her body at the speed of light. Zaps and tingles and buzzing heat pulsed up and down along her spine, down her limbs. When she saw his gaze flick to her mouth, her heart started thumping against her breastbone.

He wouldn't kiss her here. Not in the office. Not now.

He yanked her against him and slanted his mouth over hers, and a tsunami of erotic heat slammed through her. She trembled as his lips claimed hers, and for a tiny fraction of a moment she forgot where she was. But when a distant phone's ring reached her ears, her common sense kicked in. And once that happened, desire turned to anger. White-hot and fiery. Her entire body stiffened as that rage charged through her. She was able to break the kiss. Her right arm arched up, her target set. But before her hand made contact with his cheek, a steel-like fist clamped around it and jerked it behind her back.

She was so furious tears burned her eyes. She blinked. "You bastard, what are you trying to do? Get me fired?"

"No, of course not."

"Then what the hell?"

"I'm..." As he stared into her eyes, his expression shifted from one unreadable emotion to another. At last he released her and stepped back. "I don't know what my problem is today."

"Yes, well, all I can say is, you need to keep your hands to yourself if you don't want to be arrested. This isn't your 'private club'." She made air quotes.

"What did Angela say about my private club?"

"Nothing. But I figure if there is such a club, it would be the same as any nightclub I've been to, where that kind of thing isn't going to get you arrested."

He didn't respond immediately. "Yes. To some extent, I suppose that's true."

"Anyway," she said, moving farther away from him so that she could focus more on getting to business and less on how hot he made her when he kissed her, or how incredibly thrilling it had been when he'd pinned her hand behind her back. "I have work to do. Since you can't seem to focus on business with me, I guess I'll turn your project over to Angela. I'll tell her you're ready for her." Taking the long way to the door, circling the large conference table, to avoid getting within reaching distance of Tage, she made her way toward the exit.

Tage blocked her. "Would it be a problem if I insisted on working with you?"

"Yes," she stated as she shoved past him. "It would." Extremely aware of his gaze on her back, she yanked open the door and scurried out of the conference room.

She'd just walked away from a potential contract. Not because she was afraid of Angela, but because she was afraid of working with Tage.

That man was trouble. The more she distanced herself from him, the better.

Praying Angela couldn't tell how shaken she was, she waved her toward the conference room. Then she made a beeline for the bathroom to get herself collected.

8

What the hell was that? Seriously, what the hell?

As confused as fuck about his behavior earlier, with Michelle, Talen stuffed his cell phone into his pocket and fisted his keys. It was almost seven. During his brief meeting with Angela, she had confirmed Michelle usually went home at about seven. He was hoping she'd told him the truth.

Somewhat anxious, he locked up his office and headed down the hall to the elevator. He checked his phone for messages while waiting for the elevator to make the slow climb from the ground floor.

One message. From his brother Malek.

The bell chimed, and the door rumbled open. The car was empty. He stepped inside, hit the button for the ground floor, and clicked through his text messages while he waited for the elevator to make its descent.

The bars on his phone grayed out. Damn elevator. He couldn't get decent reception in there. The car lurched, bounced. It was rough, slow, and jerky. Someone needed to call maintenance.

It stopped on the sixth floor.

That was her floor.

There was no possible way he'd get so lucky as to have caught Michelle at the precise moment she was leaving. Could he? The doors rolled open, and Angela stood there, smiling, as if she had planned everything.

Wrong girl.

No, right.

"Hi," she said, full lips curled into a wide smile.

"Hello." He motioned to the panel of buttons in front of him. "Going down to the parking garage?"

"Yes. I'm done for the day." She flattened a hand over her stomach. "I was thinking about trying that new place down the street, Durmark's. I heard it was good. Would you like to join me?"

He really wasn't in the mood for company tonight, although he wouldn't have minded receiving an invitation from someone else. A very specific someone else. "Thank you for the invitation, but I have plans."

"Spoken like a true diplomat." She sighed and stepped closer. Now she was near enough for him to smell her cologne, to feel the heat of her skin. "Tell me, have I said or done something wrong? Or is it Michelle that has you so tight?"

"You've done nothing wrong."

"Then it's Michelle?" She shuffled a tiny bit closer yet, and he felt himself leaning away. "What's the matter? Maybe I can talk to her. We're not the closest of friends, but I've been going out of my way to help her at work. She's still pretty new to the company."

"That's very nice of you to offer, but no thanks. Has she left the office yet?"

"Oh yes. She left earlier than usual tonight." She checked her watch. "At least a half hour ago."

"Ah."

Her smile faded slightly. "How about a rain check? I'll take you out to dinner tomorrow, and we can discuss your campaign."

"A rain check sounds good."

"Good." Her grin was back up to full wattage as the car bounced to a stop on the parking level. "Well, I guess we'll talk later. I'll pull together some numbers and get them to you ASAP."

"Thanks," he said as he watched the doors open. He motioned her to precede him out into the lower level lobby.

She turned to look over her shoulder as she sauntered toward the exit. "You won't regret going with me. I promise."

"I'm sure I won't."

Angela stopped directly in front of the door and turned to face him, eyes lifted to his. Talen could tell she was waiting for him to do something, kiss her perhaps. But he couldn't do it. He didn't want to. He just gave her a nod and pulled open the door, standing aside to let her pass through first.

She tossed a stunning smile over her shoulder at him as she stepped through the open doorway. "Talk to you soon."

"Yes, soon." He had taken several steps toward his car when he heard her clear her throat behind him.

Swiveling, he turned. This one was far too aggressive. He didn't like aggressive women.

"A couple of times a week, Michelle grabs dinner over at her favorite restaurant. I think someone she knows owns it. The place is called Noodles. It's just down the street."

"I've heard of it. Thanks," he lied as he took longer, swifter strides toward his car.

"Have a nice night," she called out.

"You, too." He ducked into his car, poked the ignition button, and while the engine kicked to life, he looked up the restaurant on his phone.

It was less than a quarter of a mile away.

He pulled into the parking lot within minutes, despite the heavy rush-hour traffic. Hoping he would catch her before she left, he headed inside the modest family restaurant.

The interior was slightly tired. It wasn't the kind of place he would normally go for a meal. But the smells were mouth-watering.

Standing just inside the door, he scanned the open dining space, looking for her.

There. The back table. She was sitting with someone. A man.

She glanced his way, and suddenly he felt out of place. What the hell was he doing here?

Their gazes met, and his mouth went dry. Her eyes widened, as if she was shocked to see him. He couldn't blame her for being surprised. Now that he was standing here, staring at her as she was having dinner with another man, he couldn't believe he'd chased after her like this, either.

She lifted a hand, a small, polite wave, and after he returned it, she turned her attention back to the guy sitting across from her.

"How many?" a girl wearing a ponytail and a black uniform shirt asked as she bounced up to him.

"One," he said. He might as well eat. It was the only way to not look like a fucking stalker, he reasoned.

"Follow me." The girl led him to the table directly behind Michelle's. "Is this table okay?" she asked as she set a menu on the table.

"It's fine. Thank you." He sat in the bench facing Michelle and tried to pretend he wasn't watching her. As he was giving his drink order to the waiting hostess, he noticed the man who had been sitting with her stood up. He was wearing a black uniform shirt, too. As the guy stood, he glanced over his shoulder—at him.

"I'll be back in a few with your drink." The hostess scurried off.

Trying hard not to stare at Michelle, Talen checked out the

rest of the restaurant, the long counter with a couple of patrons chatting quietly, the young couple at the table on the other side of the room, the family sitting by the entry, their baby propped in a wooden highchair, arms flailing.

He tried not to stare. He really did. But somehow his gaze ended up back on Michelle anyway.

She was watching him.

She thinks I followed her. Which I did. I'm not fooling anyone.

Ready to confess the truth, he went up to her table and jerked his head toward the now empty seat. "Do you mind if I join you?"

Her brows scrunched together. "I guess it's okay." It wasn't an enthusiastic invitation, but it wasn't a get-lost-asshole, either.

He lifted an index finger, returned to his table, grabbed his menu, and finally took his seat across from her.

Now, this was better.

Her eyes hardened. "How did you find me here? Did you… follow me?"

"Not exactly. Your friend Angela told me you come here on Monday nights for dinner."

"So, you did come here looking for me. Why?" she snapped.

"I owe you an apology."

Her lips thinned slightly.

He continued, "What I did earlier today was unprofessional."

"I appreciate the apology." Her voice was a little short, her tone slightly clipped. The sound, and the way she was looking at him, made something tug inside him. It was the strangest feeling. Not a whole lot different from how he felt with Lei sometimes. He didn't like it.

"And I appreciate your ability to forgive me," he said.

Their gazes locked for a moment, and he felt another surge of emotion buzz through him. What was that feeling? Why did he feel it with this woman? What was it about her that made him think about her, dream about her?

She jerked her gaze down to stare at her plate, which still remained mostly full. "The food here is really good. I recommend the fried chicken."

"Thanks, I'll try it." Needing a little break from the tension between them, he searched the restaurant for a waitress. The only waitress he saw was standing next to the counter, talking to the man who had been sitting with Michelle. "Is he a friend of yours?" He indicated the guy with a tip of his head.

"Yes. A friend."

"Then I'm not interrupting anything?"

"No, it's nothing like that. We're friends. Only friends." She flicked her gaze toward the subject of their conversation. "Carter used to be engaged to my sister."

"I see." He saw no reason to ask why she'd said that in past tense. "You have a sister?"

"I..." She bit her lip. "Kathleen died last year."

Damn. "I'm sorry."

"It's okay. You couldn't know."

Another wave of emotion washed through him, and suddenly he felt the urge to pull the sweet, strong, sexy little woman sitting across from him into his arms and hold her. Thankfully, the waitress chose that moment to approach the table. She looked at Michelle first, then him.

"Will you be joining Michelle for dinner?" she asked him.

He looked askance at Michelle.

"Sure," Michelle said, sounding a little tense.

"Michelle told me your fried chicken is very good. I'll take that, please."

"Okay. Salad?" the waitress asked.

"Sure. Blue cheese dressing."

"I'll put a rush on your order." She hurried off.

Michelle poked at the food on her plate. She definitely

looked stressed. Talen figured it was probably because of him. Clearly the apology wasn't enough. Or perhaps it was something else.

"If you'd rather I go back to my own table, I will," he offered.

"No, it's okay. Really." She lifted her eyes to his, and he couldn't help staring into them. They were a dark, cool blue, the shade of deep ocean water. "I don't like being rude, but..." She sighed. "I'd sure like to understand what you are doing."

"Doing?"

"You're playing this weird game with me, and I don't like it."

Ah, the truth was finally coming out. "I'm sorry. If it seems I'm playing a game, it's not intentional."

"Then why are you so hot and cold? One minute you're kissing me"—her gaze flicked to the side, and he followed the direction of her glance—"and the next..."

The waitress was heading their way, a bowl in her hands. She set the salad in front of him and asked if there was anything else.

"No, this is fine. Thank you," he said. Then, when she was out of earshot again, he leaned forward and said softly, "I won't offer any excuses for my behavior. I've been an asshole." Looking into those gorgeous eyes, he felt something happening inside, unspoken words pushing to get out. He tried to swallow them down, but they kept surging to the surface again. *I don't know what I'm doing, what I'm thinking or feeling. When I'm around you, something inside clicks, and these urges surge through me. To touch you. To kiss you.*

As if she'd heard his thoughts, her lips parted, forming a small *O*. But she didn't speak. She simply sat there and stared at him. The longer she stared, the harder it became for him to inhale.

"I swear I've never been such an asshole before," he whispered.

That confession earned him a tiny semi-smile, and instantly, he was breathing easier.

"Maybe I'm being a little bit of a bitch, too."

"No, you aren't."

One of her brows lifted. "I shouldn't argue with you on that point, I suppose. Okay. I've been a saint, and you've been an absolute bastard."

His heart suddenly felt a hundred times lighter. "Good. Now that we've settled that, I hope you'll be able to eat." He plunged his fork into his salad, lifted it, and filled his mouth with lettuce and blue cheese dressing.

This guy was either a total nutcase or... what? *He's gotta be a nutcase.*

Just her luck, she had a soft spot for crazy guys. Case in point, the one man she had ever had a serious relationship with. The man who had broken her heart less than a month before her sister had died.

There were some similarities between Greg and Tage. She didn't know Tage well at all, but already she could see a few traits they shared in common. But one thing Greg had never been able to do was deliver what appeared to be a genuine, heartfelt apology. Nor had he ever been able to confess to any of his (many) faults. Not even when they were glaring in broad daylight. There were always excuses, explanations.

Maybe that was why she felt this little tug in her heart now, as she sat there watching Tage eat salad like he hadn't eaten a meal in weeks. He barely seemed to be chewing. He was able to admit his faults. And he could apologize.

But she was terrified.

Not only did he confuse her with his on-and-off, hot-and-cold game he was playing. But he was also way out of her league in the looks department. And he was miles ahead of her in the experience department, she guessed from his confidence.

Would he turn around and dump her the minute she let her guard down?

Would he find someone else, someone prettier, someone who wasn't so freaking awkward around him? Like Angela.

Would he change into an egotistical asshole once he thought he had her? Given some time, would Tage fall into the same trap, of rambling off excuses for his mistakes?

Why me? she asked herself.

As she poked at her salad, her thoughts wandered. When they'd been alone in his car, things had been going so well. The way he touched her, kissed her. She could melt right there and then, just thinking about it. But then he'd abruptly cut things off, rattled out an excuse, and practically run away...only to go to a club and hook up with someone else. Why?

She wanted to know why, but it wasn't really her place to ask. What explanation did he owe her? They weren't dating. They were virtual strangers. He could sleep with anyone he wanted, even Angela, and so could she.

But still, she wanted to know why.

"Angela told me she met you at some kind of private club," she said, thinking that might be a way to skirt around the issue while still getting to know him a little better. "Is it the yacht club? Angela is always talking about the parties she has with her friends at the yacht club."

"No. I'm not much of a water person. I don't care for boats."

Something they had in common. "Me, neither." She encouraged him to elaborate with a tip of the head.

He set his fork down and placed his empty salad bowl at the end of the table for the waitress. "It's more of a...social club."

"Like the Elks?" she offered.

"The Elks? I doubt it." His lips curled up at the corners, as if he was trying not to laugh at an inside joke.

"I'm intrigued."

That ghost of a smile faded. He studied her for a few minutes. "Maybe you should ask your friend about the club."

"Now you have me really curious. What is it, some kind of secret cult or something?"

"No." His gaze flicked to the side.

The waitress came tromping up with a plate in her hand. After asking if he needed anything else, she took away Tage's empty salad dish, and in a blink she was hurrying off to take care of someone else.

Michelle's gaze meandered over his handsome face. "I apologize if I'm being nosy. We don't have to talk about the club anymore. I was just curious how the two of you met."

"Why?"

She didn't want to say what she was thinking, but she felt she'd backed herself into a corner. "I'm assuming the two of you are seeing each other. Dating. Which is why...earlier... um, she told me...you..."

"I figured as much. We did have sex. But it's nothing serious. There's no commitment. It was just...a casual thing."

"I see." In truth, she didn't see anything. Sex wasn't casual to her. She didn't sleep with strangers just for kicks. She slept with men she cared about, men who meant something to her. Which was why she'd had exactly two partners in her whole life. This guy clearly had very different thoughts about sex.

It was probably a good thing he'd run out on her that night, now that she thought about it. No, it was *definitely* a good thing. If she had slept with him and then he'd gone off and slept with Angela immediately afterward, she would have been hurt, confused, and thoroughly disgusted with herself.

That was it, she couldn't eat another bite. She felt a little uneasy now. Uncomfortable.

His expression changed, intensified. "You don't have casual sex, do you?"

She shook her head. "No."

"I respect that."

"Is that why you left?" she blurted, before she realized what she'd said.

"Yes. It is. In a way. I could tell you are...different. I could have stayed. But if I had, I would have slept with you that night. And eventually, you would have regretted it." He pushed his plate aside and leveled a very serious look at her. "I'm going to be brutally honest with you. As much as I would love to strip off your clothes and take you, right here, right now, I won't. I'm not the kind of man you need. No, correction, I'm not the kind of man you *deserve*."

Her head spun at the dark hunger she saw in his eyes. A blaze of heat rocketed through her. Slowly, as the warmth faded, his words sunk in. When they did, a chill spread through her, snuffing out the fire his erotically charged gaze had ignited.

He wanted her. He. Wanted. Her.

But he didn't want to want her.

9

This wasn't happening. Her plan couldn't be failing. Not after all the work she'd done to make sure everything would go perfectly.

It was time to make some changes, to look at other options. She could not fail. Everything that mattered hinged upon this.

Somehow she would turn things around.

As Kim Jong-il once said, "A man who dreads trials and difficulties cannot become a revolutionary. If he is to become a revolutionary with an indomitable fighting spirit, he must be tempered in the arduous struggle from his youth."

She was a revolutionary.

A half hour later, the remainder of Michelle's dinner (most of it) was in a foam box on the table. The bill was paid. By Tage. And his empty plates were stacked up, ready to be taken away. While she had gotten an answer to the one question that had been nagging her, she felt more conflicted and confused than ever.

Tage was interested in her. There was no denying that. But

he was convinced she was wrong for him, or rather, he was wrong for her. And, from what she could tell, it had a lot to do with their different attitudes toward sex. He had sex with whomever he wanted, whenever he wanted, wherever he wanted. She did, too, but (and this was a big but) only if she was in some kind of committed relationship. She didn't do one-night stands or friends-with-benefits. To her, sex was an expression of caring and trust and commitment. If she needed to burn off a little excess energy, she had a vibrator. It always had fresh batteries in it.

As she stood and picked up her foam carton and purse, her skin tingled. It was as if he somehow electrified her nerves when he came near. He didn't even have to touch her. The air between them was always warm, too.

"Thank you for paying for my dinner," she said.

"It was my pleasure." He waved his hand toward the door, indicating she should precede him.

The skin of her back burned a little as she walked through the restaurant.

"See you next week," Carter called from the counter.

She angled her body to give him a wave and a smile. "You bet."

Tage stopped abruptly, a split second after she had, and placed a hand on her waist. The touch sent a current of energy buzzing through her body. The shock took her breath away, and a crazy, insane, completely out-of-character thought flashed through her head.

Sleep with him.

Feeling a little unsteady, she took a step toward the door. He reached around her and opened it. Outside, she pulled in a deep breath.

"Thanks again," she said, sounding breathless, despite the huge gasp.

"Thank you. If it hadn't been for you, I would've never known about this place. The food is excellent."

"Glad you liked it."

"I did." His gaze scanned the parking lot. "Where are you parked? I'll walk you to your car?"

"Actually, I walked here from work." She motioned in the general direction of the building in which they both worked.

"Then I'll drive you back. You shouldn't be walking alone. It's dark."

She pulled the strap of her purse higher on her shoulder and tucked it back between her body and arm. "I do this every week. This is a safe part of town."

"Even so, I would feel better if you let me drive you."

She could tell by the set of his jaw and the tone of his voice that she wasn't going to win this debate. And so she acquiesced with a nod. "Okay. Thank you. I accept your offer."

Once again he placed his hand on her. This time it rested on the small of her back. She fought a shiver of sensual heat at his soft touch and let him gently steer her toward the sleek black car parked under a light. He opened the door for her, and she sank into the leather seat. While she waited for him to circle around to the driver's side, she inhaled deeply. The car smelled good. Like leather and him.

He folded his large frame into his seat and started the car. The engine roared like a jungle cat. And it prowled, low and smooth, like one, too, as he steered it toward the road.

"This is a very nice car."

"Thank you. I have a weakness when it comes to cars."

"I have a weakness when it comes to handbags," she confessed, lifting her latest purchase, a Louis Vuitton she'd bought secondhand from an online boutique.

"I guess everyone has a fault," he said, laughter lifting his voice.

Relieved to have the tension eased somewhat, she slid a glance his way as they rolled up to a red light. Mistake. Their gazes locked, and it felt like all the air had been instantly sucked out of the vehicle. She parted her lips to try to pull in some air, and his gaze flicked to her mouth. A wave of sensual heat pulsed through her.

The chemistry she had with this man was insane.

He jerked his head, returning his eyes to the road. "We'll be there in a minute," he said. Whether he was telling that to her or himself, she wasn't sure.

"Thanks again for driving me."

"You're welcome." He focused on the road for the rest of the drive. At least, that was what she assumed. To be safe, she didn't check. She stared out the passenger side window, silent, her hands gripping the foam box with her leftover dinner so tightly the top collapsed a little. When he finally pulled into their building's parking structure, she was finally able to pull in a complete lung full of air. The oxygen to the brain was most definitely needed.

As he turned the car down a row, she pointed. "I'm parked down at the end."

"Okay." He pulled up behind her car and shifted his vehicle into park. Twisting, he turned toward her. She did the same, and opened her mouth to thank him. But before a single word came out, he had his hand cupped around the back of her head and was pulling her toward him.

Her heart rate kicked up to the stratosphere the instant their mouths touched. A little whimper slipped up her throat. She swallowed it back down, closed her eyes, and surrendered to the pleasure his kiss was building inside her.

Warm. She was getting so warm. Everywhere. Her chest. Her face. Down there, between her legs. A second little whimper slipped up her throat. Her breathing rasped. The soft slough of fabric added another layer of sensual sound as he moved closer. Getting hotter, her body tensing, she caught the fabric of his sleeves in her fists and held on.

While he held her head in place, his tongue traced the seam of her mouth. Eagerly, she opened to him, welcoming his intimate invasion.

He tasted sweet, decadent. His kiss was intoxicating. It did things to her she didn't think were possible. It scrambled her brains and ignited blazing fires through her whole body.

Just when she thought she couldn't take another second of torment, he placed his hand over her breast. It felt like a lightning bolt blasted through her. With that blaze, what little resistance she had left burned up. Her brain shut down, and she was overcome with need. Desperate, overwhelming need.

Her spine arched, pushing her breast into his hand. Her hips started tipping forward and back as the throbbing heat between her legs intensified. She needed a touch, a stroke, down there, where the heat was the worst. She needed a big, hard cock pounding away this horrible need.

Somehow she found the strength to release his sleeves. While his mouth vanquished hers, her hands wandered down his body until they found the waistband of his pants. She tugged on his tucked-in shirt, pulling it out, and slid her hands beneath the crisp fabric.

Smooth skin. Soft like satin. With deep furrows between thick, bulging muscles. In her mind's eye, she saw him shirtless, defined abs flexing, thick chest muscles clenching, arms bulging. Oh, he was glorious. The most beautiful man she'd ever seen. And he wanted her.

Blindly, she forced the material out of her way and explored higher, higher. One fingertip found a hard, pointed nipple. He growled. The sound vibrated through every cell in her body.

Take me. Please, take me now.

The hand that had been resting on her breast slid down her body to her stomach. Over her mound. Along one thigh. Under her skirt.

Oh yes, under her skirt.

A shudder swept up her, starting at the base of her spine and racing up her back. She groaned as the kiss became more urgent, as his tongue plunged deep inside her mouth, stroking hers. No longer a seduction, it was now a possession, a claiming. And she was so willing to surrender to it, to him.

She had waited so long for this. At last she would feel what it was like to be taken by this strong, powerful man. "Please," she said when he broke the kiss to nip the side of her neck. Her voice was raspy, breathy. "Please, I hurt. Everywhere."

"Dammit," he growled. "Dammit."

He kissed her again. He didn't wait for her to open to him, no. He pushed his tongue inside her mouth. He tasted, he took. The hand that had been inching up her bare leg made a swift leap to the apex of her thighs. A deep rumble vibrated in his chest.

Fisting her hair with his other hand, he jerked her head back and kissed the tender, sensitive skin of her neck. Goose bumps burned the entire front of her body.

"Please," she whispered as she pulled at the waist of his pants. Her fingers found the button of his fly, and she tried to pull it open, but her fingers were clumsy, the trembling sweeping through her body making her movements uncoordinated. Frustrated, she cupped the warm bulge lying beneath the zipper and rubbed.

She was rewarded with a tender stroke between her legs. Her cotton panties felt like a thick shield between his fingertips and her burning tissues. They had to go. Had to. The pulsing heat shooting through her body was becoming unbearable. It had to stop. Soon. Now. "Yes," she whispered.

He stopped kissing her. He stopped caressing her. "Open your eyes," he commanded. "Open them now."

She did as he asked. She couldn't resist his command, as much as she wanted to. She was afraid what he might say. "You have no idea what you're getting into."

"I don't care."

"You will."

"I get it. You have sex for the sake of having sex. I don't. At least, normally I don't. Tonight, I want to. And I won't become a crazy stalker afterward." She had made up her mind. She would have this man. He would have her. There wasn't going to be any more talking.

"That's not what—"

She pulled her shirt up over her head and flung it away. That shut him up. His gaze snapped to her breasts, covered with scraps of lace, then climbed to her face.

He took a quick glance around, shrugged out of his jacket, and handed it to her. "No."

No?

It was a terrible blow, being rejected by this man. Who would do such a thing? Who would turn down a sure thing? Why? This was the second time he'd done this to her. Twice. Now would he run off, find someone like Angela again, and pound away all that male need with her?

Eyes burning, she pushed one arm through a sleeve, then the other. She held the front closed to hide herself, her shame.

Anxious to find her discarded top and escape to the safety of her own car, she turned to search for her shirt. "Okay. Well—"

"Come with me." He opened his door, and while she squirmed around, searching for her top, he circled the car and opened the passenger side for her.

She said, "I can't find my shirt."

"We'll get it later. Come." He extended a hand.

Later?

Completely confused, she placed her hand in his and stood. Her knees were a little wobbly as she stepped aside to wait for him to close the door. She held her purse and the foam carton of food in her hands.

When he had the door shut, he placed a hand on the small of her back and motioned toward the building. "Let's go inside."

So he wasn't shoving her into her car and racing off? He wasn't dumping her like he did last time?

A silly, giddy feeling rushed through her. Then came the nerves. Dozens of skittery butterflies fluttering through her insides.

Ohmygod, something was going to happen.

She hoped.

Then again, maybe he was going to take her inside and let her down easy.

Unsure what to expect, she followed his direction. They boarded the elevator. She moved to the back, resting against the rear wall. When the door closed, he turned around and looked at her. "You look sexy as hell in my coat."

The deep timbre of his voice made her shiver.

"Are you cold?" he asked.

"No."

His lips curled into a bone-melting smile. Moving swiftly, he trapped her between his bulk and the elevator's wall, arms outstretched. His suddenly aggressive move sent a wave of thrill pulsing through her. Her breathing quickened as she stared into his dark eyes, waiting for what he would do next.

Bending his arms, he angled his upper body closer, and she tipped her head back, maintaining eye contact. It was no wonder this man made her melt. He was different from anyone she'd ever met. Not only was he absolutely glorious to look at, but he emanated a certain feral energy. It was that vibe, of barely restrained power, of danger, that made her heart pound so hard in her chest. Yes, that was it.

She never would have guessed she would respond to a guy like this.

"You've never been restrained before, have you?"

Restrained? Oooh. He was into *those* kinds of things. Kinky sex games. She'd never done any of that stuff. The closest she'd ever gotten was when her old boyfriend insisted on having her use a dildo in his anus before they had sex. But this was different. That guy was looking for her to be the leader while he lay there, enjoying it. She had the distinct impression this man would be the one doing all the leading. He was much more aggressive.

The danger vibe just upped a few dozen degrees. Now she was intrigued and aroused and...a little scared. The tissues between her legs clenched. Wow, she was very aroused. As in, dripping.

"No, never," she whispered.

He forced a bent knee between her thighs, and she began tipping her hips forward and back, forward and back in time to the beating pulse thrumming through her body. A soft whimper slipped from her lips as the heat intensified, thanks to the friction rubbing against her delicate, swollen tissues. "Are you afraid?"

"A little," she admitted.

"Good." He hit a button on the elevator, and it lurched into motion. She hadn't even realized he'd stopped it. As it crawled up, up, up, he turned back around and tormented her neck with his tongue, lips, teeth until she was writhing in agony.

"Come with me," he whispered against her neck.

She opened her eyes, having not realized she'd closed them. The doors made a deep rumbling sound as they opened. He took her hand in his and led her down the hallway to the suite at the very end. Seconds later, he had them locked inside. She glanced around the dark space. It was a small reception area, furnished with a few chairs. At the rear was a narrow corridor, she learned a few seconds later, as he escorted her to the room at the end of the hall. He opened the door and flipped on the light.

It was an office, furnished with the standard desk, chair, bookcases, and file cabinet. More than a little anxious, she stepped aside, turning toward him.

His eyes were like flickering bits of coal. Dark, simmering. He prowled toward her as she back-stepped until her rear struck something hard and low. He angled closer, bracing his hands on the desk behind her. "You don't know what you want, do you? You're not sure you're ready. You'd better make up your mind. Fast. Now."

Like she could think in this position?

Here she was, trapped once again. This time he had her caged between his body and the desk. His eyes were telling her she should run, fast.

His face was telling her she should stay.

And that wicked curl in his lips...it was saying a lot of things.

"Last chance," he whispered. "Leave now. Go. Before I get another taste of you. Because once that happens, I won't be able to stop."

Oooh, did she like the unspoken promise in his voice. Of pleasure far beyond her imagination. Dark pleasure, like nothing she'd ever experienced.

That was it. She couldn't leave. She had to find out what that wicked gleam meant.

10

Unable to speak with all the emotion swirling through her system, Michelle gave him her answer. She lifted her lips into a smile and then closed her eyes and let her head fall back.

He growled. Like a big bear. Or a wolf. A beast. A shudder quaked her.

His lips and tongue teased her tingling skin, sending little tremors buzzing through her body like electrical charges. All those buzzes and zaps arced through her, coiling in her center.

Her hands trembled as she lifted them to fist the crisp, smooth cotton of his shirt. She wanted to tear it open and explore the smooth-skinned body beneath, but she couldn't summon up enough strength. When he nipped her earlobe, she practically melted. It seemed he knew exactly what to do to make her more desperate for his next touch.

Moaning softly, she let her body fall back. He caught her, supporting her with strong but gentle hands as she reclined onto the desktop.

"Look at me," he commanded once she was lying flat on her back.

Look at him? Gladly. It took some effort to drag her heavy eyelids up. But she was very glad she did it once she saw him.

Could there be a more beautiful man alive? She doubted it. His face could have been sculpted by a master. It was utter perfection, from the slight cleft in his chin to the arch of his brows.

"If you want me to stop what I am doing, say the word 'red.'"

Why would he tell me that? She must have looked as confused as she felt because he nodded and angled upright. His face and neck were flushed as he took a visible breath and slowly let it out, mumbling something unintelligible as he exhaled.

He cleared his throat. "Do you remember the question I asked, before we came up here?"

Did she? No, she didn't. Her brain was sort of short-circuited right now. Thinking was hard. Feeling a little foolish, she pushed herself up on bent elbows and shrugged.

"I asked if you'd ever been restrained," he reminded her.

"Oh yes. That. I remember now."

"You said you hadn't."

"That's right." An image flashed through her mind. Him, angled over top of her writhing body, her arms bound together, over her head, his hips wedged between her spread legs. Her heart jumped.

"Say 'red' if you want me to stop, if anything gets too intense. Understand?"

"I understand."

"Do you have any health problems I need to be aware of?"

"No."

"Okay." He took a single step back. It seemed, from the vibe he was giving off, that he'd regained his ability to think, and he was having second thoughts about this.

She wasn't.

He needed to know that.

"Please," she said, her voice small. "I can't believe I'm begging. That's so not me. I've never begged a man for sex. Never. But I am now."

The corners of his lips curled slightly. He wasn't smiling, no. But she could see he was pleased. And for some reason, knowing that made her insides hop around like a pack of wild rabbits.

His hand cupped her cheek, and his gaze drilled into hers. "What is it about you? You're nothing like what I thought I was looking for. Nothing. But I can't..." He dragged his thumb across her lower lip.

"Can't what?" she asked, her heart in her throat.

He shook his head. Then, suddenly, he kissed her. Like the last one, this kiss was fiercely passionate. His tongue swept inside her mouth and filled her with his decadent flavor. One of his arms looped around her back, holding her up while he angled over her. She felt herself slowly easing back again until she was lying on the desk, her burning body trapped under his.

When he broke the kiss, she had to gasp to refill her lungs. His gaze raked down her body, setting every nerve inside her aflame. "I want to see you." He grabbed the lapels of his jacket and tossed them out to the sides. "Beautiful," he murmured, eyes fixed on her lace-covered breasts, which were aching for his touch.

Instinctively, she arched her back, pushing them higher. *Touch them,* her body was telling him.

Answering her unspoken plea, he pulled down one cup, easing her breast out. With finger and thumb, he tugged her nipple, rolling it until sharp blades of need were piercing her insides, shooting straight to the swirling heat burning between her legs.

One thought kept racing through her head as she writhed and burned beneath him. Only one. *Take me. Take me now.* But she didn't speak. She let the pleasure and the torment pulse through her in white-hot bursts. One after another. Hotter. Faster.

He slipped a hand under her back and unhooked her bra. Now she was bare from the waist up. Her skin tingled. Her nipples prickled. Hard little peaks. He pulled one into his warm, wet mouth. His tongue flickered over the tip and a blaze erupted inside her body. She cried out, swung her arms up to hold on to him. He caught them in his fists, pushed them up over her head.

"Hmmm. You can still use your hands. We're going to have to do something about that." Moving away from her, he circled the desk. The scrape of wood echoed through the small room.

She dragged her eyelids up to see what he was doing.

He had a desk drawer open. His gaze lifted, locked to hers. "Remember, 'red.'"

"Red," she repeated.

"Good." Circling back around the end of the desk, he lifted his hands. A dark gray silk tie was draped between them. "We're going to have to improvise tonight." He stopped at the far end of the desk. "Your hands."

Jitters quaked through her. Slowly, and somewhat reluctantly, she sat up and extended her arms in front of her. "Do you always tie your partners up?" Even to her own ears, she sounded scared.

"Pretty much, yes. I'm asking you to trust me, by allowing me to do this. I realize that's no small thing. I promise," he said, meeting her gaze, "I don't take it lightly."

A shudder quaked through her whole body. Deep blue-black flames shimmered in those eyes of his. And hiding in the darkest depths was something else, something she couldn't name yet. She was mesmerized, captivated.

This man, this stranger, was tying her hands. He could do anything to her, rape her, hurt her, kill her. She didn't know him. He could be wanted in all fifty states. If nothing else, he'd proven he was nothing like the men she normally dated. He was different. He was a little dangerous. He was mysterious. And yet something told her he was trustworthy. If she said 'red,' he would stop.

She watched through slightly glazed eyes as he tied a neat knot around her wrists. Once they were bound, he helped her lie down again and pulled on the tie, forcing her arms up, wrists over her head.

"Now, that's better." He dragged the tip of his index finger down the center of her face, between her eyes, down her nose, over her lips, her chin. His gaze followed that finger as it traveled lower, along the sensitive skin of her neck to her collarbone. Lower, between her breasts. Her breathing sped up as she felt the heat of his gaze on her skin. The nerves lying below the surface tingled and zapped, little mini-blazes of heat sparking all over her chest.

How did he do that? How did he ignite so much heat in her with just his eyes and one little fingertip?

"You're breathing very quickly," he said.

"Yes."

"Are you all right?"

"Yes." Better than all right, actually. But she still yearned for more. A lot more.

How much longer would he draw this out? She was in agony. Was it the anticipation that was making her so hot? Or was it the way he looked at her? The way he touched her? The way his perfect lips lifted at the corners when he was pleased?

Her fingers curled into fists as wave upon wave of wanting washed through her. Those waves swelled when he growled, "The rest of these clothes have to go."

They did, oh yes. Most definitely. And his clothes, too. The thought of seeing that body, all of it, sent a shudder quaking through her center.

He unzipped her skirt and tugged it down over her hips. A cool draft of air gusted over her legs as he stepped away, and she shivered slightly. "Are you cold?" he asked as he hooked his fingers in the waistband of her panties.

"Yes and no. Cold and hot."

"Ah, good." He gently eased her lace panties over her hips. As he slid the garment lower, over her thighs, he dragged his blunt fingernails over her skin. The slight scuff felt so good.

A sigh of pleasure slipped from her lips.

She was nude, lying on his desk, wrists bound, semi-defenseless and under his control. And, ohmygod, she was loving it.

"Now that's a picture," he murmured, bending over her. He flicked his tongue across the sensitive skin of her lower stomach, and her spine arched, rocking her hips forward. As a pulse of need rushed to the juncture of her thighs, she squeezed her legs together. But that gave her no relief from the burning. She needed a touch. No, she needed more. She needed a hot, hard, thick cock plunging inside, stroking her to ecstasy.

If this had been either of her former lovers, they would have been done by now. This agonizingly slow, drawn-out foreplay was killing her.

"Please," she mumbled when his deft tongue meandered its way north, toward her breasts.

"Please what?"

"I hurt." She squirmed. She shuddered. She whimpered.

"Where?"

"All over. Everywhere."

"Tell me," he commanded.

"Lower."

His tongue flicked down, toward her belly button. "Here?"

"Lower."

Leaving a cool, damp path, it moved a tiny bit closer to where she hurt the most. Still, it wasn't nearly close enough. "Here?"

"No. Lower. Much lower."

He stepped back, and she practically cried out in frustration. Then he picked up one of her feet and cradled it in his hand. With a fingertip, he traced a line along the arch of her foot. "Here?"

"Higher."

Supporting her leg with his hand, he tickled her ankle with his tongue. "Here?"

"I'm going to die. I swear."

"No, you won't die. I promise." His tongue found a ticklish spot, at the back of her knee. He chuckled when she let out a little squeak. "You just may wish you could die."

"Oh God."

"I tried to warn you. Do you want to leave? You remember your safe word?"

"I remember. And no, I don't want to leave." She squeezed her eyes shut as another blast of erotic heat blazed through her. "Just tell me you won't leave me like this."

"Like what?"

"Burning inside."

"I promise I won't leave you like that." He eased her leg out and a pulse of warmth gushed between her legs. He was moving closer, slowly, too slowly. But he was getting there. Maybe if she kept letting him know how much she was suffering he would speed things up a bit.

"Thank you," she whispered. "It's almost unbearable."

"I'm sorry."

"Please don't apologize. Just help me."

"I am." He nipped a little higher. "You'll see, soon."

She was seeing already. Those little sharp nips were making her heart jerk and the air gust from her lungs in little puffs.

"Oh God," she murmured as she squeezed her inner muscles around aching, pulsing emptiness.

"Patience, sweet. You must learn patience."

She was in no mood for a life lesson at the moment. She whimpered to let him know that.

And then there was a touch. There. Between her legs. Too soft. Too brief. A tiny flick. She jerked, legs, arms, chest tight.

"Easy, sweet." His tongue drew a meandering line up the inside of her thigh. "Damn, you smell good."

"Please," she uttered, unable to say anything else.

He audibly inhaled. "I can't wait to taste you."

She couldn't wait for him to taste her. She couldn't wait for him to do other things, too, like plunge deep inside, stuffing her empty center full of hard cock. She bent her knees and pulled her legs open and back, brazenly exposing her burning center to him. She'd never done anything like that before. In the past, she'd had sex in a dark room with the covers pulled up to her chin. Her partner had climbed on top, shoved his cock inside, and thrust away until he was done.

This wasn't sex. Not the sex she knew. This was torture. This was torment. This was agonizing ecstasy.

The pounding of her heartbeat was almost painful. It sent bursts of heat pulsing through her whole body, from the top of her head to the soles of her feet. She couldn't help clenching her stomach, rocking her hips forward and back, forward and back, in time to the heavy rhythm of her need.

Another soft touch nearly made her crazy with need. A tiny, fleeting touch to her labia. She clenched and relaxed the heated tissues, wishing something would slip inside to stroke away her suffering.

"So wet," he whispered.

"Yes. Wet."

"So hot," he added.

"Burning."

"Mmmm." His fingertip slipped between her labia, delving deeper but not piercing her opening.

Her legs trembled. The air rushed from her lungs. She tensed up, everywhere, soles of her feet, her neck, her face.

"Relax."

Relax? Was he kidding? She whimpered again.

"Is this what you're looking for?" That naughty finger pushed a little deeper, slipping between her nether lips and barely dipping into her tight canal.

In response, a white-hot inferno blazed through her insides. She curled her fingers so tightly her nails dug into her palms. Oh yes, that was what she wanted. But deeper. Harder.

"Yessss," she said, arching her back, willing his invading digit to plunge inside, all the way. It did delve a tiny bit farther before withdrawing. She couldn't help whimpering when it didn't return.

"Damn, you're so wet," Talen murmured as he inhaled deeply, drawing Michelle's scent into his nose. She smelled so good. He imagined she tasted even better. He had to find out.

He touched her again, parted her puffy outer lips to expose her slick tissues. Coated with her juices, they called to him. He licked his lips, saliva filling his mouth at the sight of such sweet temptation.

He hadn't expected her to be like this, so open and willing. While a tie around her wrists was a far cry from the kind of bondage he usually enjoyed, it was enough to satisfy his need to dominate. She was a natural submissive, unaware of it yet, but fully capable of being the kind of partner he craved most.

Her tissues were flushed a deep pink and dripping with her juices. They unfurled for him as he touched them, like petals of a flower, opening, welcoming his exploration. Dipping his head lower, he took his first taste.

Heaven.

Sweet.

Intoxicating.

Her stomach clenched at his brief touch, and she moaned, the sound like a siren's call. There was no denying himself, like he'd initially planned. He wouldn't just play a little, bring her to a climax, and then send her home. He had to have her, had to know how those tight tissues would envelop his cock as it thrust deep inside. Had to feel her thighs wrapped around his waist, the screams of her orgasm echoing in his ears.

Dammit, he'd tried to be good. He knew she didn't take casual lovers. That was all they could be, especially now. She could not be his wife, though she was certainly attractive enough. She was... too delicate. Too sensitive. Between the pressures of his life, and the darker urges compelling him back to the dungeons, he would destroy her if he took her as his wife. No, he needed a woman who would handle the many moves, the occasional dangers, and his constant searching for his next submissive without breaking down.

His cock was hard, painfully pressing against his pants. His balls ached. It was excruciating. But in the end, the pain would be worth it, when they were both soaring high, together, lost in rapture.

And then he would make sure she would never see him again. Even if it meant moving his office to another building.

He was hoping he wouldn't have to go that far.

All of that trouble for a fuck.

But a good fuck. He could tell already. A great fuck.

He worked his tongue over her clit, and she squirmed so prettily. Her thigh muscles and calves clenched, the sinewy lines sculpted. This was a body made for play. In his mind's eye, he could see her bound, arms and legs spread, skin gleaming, muscles taut. Oh yes, if only he'd been able to take her to the club. He could have had a lot of fun with her there.

He drank in her flavor, relishing every nuance. She tasted like no other woman, and he couldn't get enough. He pushed his tongue deeper, plunging it into her opening, where her flavor was its strongest. Still he wasn't satisfied. He couldn't get enough.

And his cock. Damn, he'd probably have a red indentation from the zipper. He was hot, sweat beading on his forehead and along his hairline. His chest felt tight.

It was time to get rid of his clothes. All of them.

Unable to break away from the succulent temptation spread out before him, he kept licking her pussy while he pushed and pulled and tugged and yanked until all of his clothes were gone and he was free.

Ah, what a relief. And yet also torture.

While he continued to lap at Michelle's damp pussy, she squirmed and pleaded and whimpered. He had taken a lot of submissives into his playroom but never had one tempted him as much as this one. She responded to his every touch. And that response was so powerful, he almost lost control. To ease his own suffering, he had to stroke himself. Slow pumps up and down the full length of his cock eased the suffering somewhat. But he knew it wouldn't be enough. The heat pounding through his body told him that.

He was going to force himself to wait, even if it killed him. Not only did he deserve to enjoy every moment of this encounter, but so did the sweet, innocent little submissive writhing on his desk.

11

Oh God. Ohgodohgodohgod. Michelle was in hell. She was in heaven. She was...ohgod.

Her last boyfriend had known a thing or two about how to kiss a woman *down there*. But this guy...what he could do with his tongue should be illegal.

She was hot. Everywhere. Tight. Everywhere. On the verge of release. Trembling. Sweating. Heart pounding. Breathless.

But he wouldn't let her climax. It was as if he could feel her body preparing, could feel that rush of erotic heat pulsing through her center. Every time she reached that pinnacle, he paused. Just long enough for her body to recover a tiny bit.

And then he built up the heat again. Over. And over. She was both energized and exhausted. A part of her wanted to finally be allowed to come. Another wanted this to last forever.

His tongue began dancing over her clit again, and she felt the tendrils of desire coiling through her once again. Surely he would have mercy on her this time. He wouldn't make her suffer anymore.

Tears were streaming down her face, but it wasn't because she was sad. She didn't really know why they were coming, fast and hard. Perhaps she was overwhelmed by emotion. Perhaps she was happy beyond realization.

"I didn't want to...I didn't plan..." He was muttering, his voice so deep she couldn't make out every word.

But she didn't care. All she knew was that he had stopped again. But this time he was holding her hips and pulling her. She slid until her bottom was at the edge of the desk.

Oh, could that mean he was about to plunge that enormous cock inside her at last? *Pleasepleaseplease.*

He pushed her legs back, forcing them wider. She loved how that felt, how he controlled her body, possessed it. His every touch and stroke was masterful.

His plump, swollen member nudged at her opening, and she reflexively tightened the muscles. He pushed harder, against her body's natural resistance. Her body ignited when he slipped inside. She cried out, relieved to have something big and hard in there at last. Before the sound faded, he slammed his hips forward and buried himself to the base.

The sudden invasion took her breath away.

So tight. So wet. Utter perfection.

He never did this. Never. He never fucked them without protection. Not the first time. Not with any submissive. But he couldn't deny himself. He'd tried.

He wasn't sorry. Not yet. That would come later. For now, he couldn't help just enjoying what Michelle had so freely offered. Oh God, this was agony.

After the initial thrust, all he wanted to do was drill her hard, possess her with all the wild fury of a beast. His blood was searing his insides, his heart pounding so hard his chest ached. But he forced himself to withdraw slowly, a fraction of

an inch at a time. For his effort he was rewarded with pure ecstasy.

This was insanity, how great it felt to fuck this woman. He'd
had sex with countless women before. Never had it come even
close to this kind of pleasure. And this was only the beginning.
The first time. The first stroke. If it got any better, he might die
from the pleasure.

It took every bit of willpower he possessed to reenter her
with the same patience as he had withdrawn. But oh, was it
worth it. Especially when her tight canal rippled around his
length, and she gave a little moan. The sound of her voice vibrated through his entire body. How he adored her voice. It
was like music.

"Oh God," she whispered.

As he tunneled deeper into her hot, wet channel, he dipped
down and tasted her lips. It was just a small touch, but it sent a
blaze racing through his body. Damn. So good. So fucking
good.

He kissed her again, and she eagerly opened to him. His
tongue swept inside her mouth, filling his own with her decadent flavor. She was sweet, intoxicating, delicious, and already
he knew he would need many more kisses before he would be
satisfied. In response to her flavor, and the way her body accepted his, his balls tightened, his chest, too. No matter how
hard he tried, he wouldn't be able to hold off for long.

He smoothed his hands up her torso to her breasts. They
were soft, warm, full. Perfect. Her nipples pulled into sweet little pink points. How sexy they would look with some jewelry
on them. Maybe nipple rings with a pretty chain looping between them. A blaze blasted through him. Oh yes, a chain. He
rolled those gorgeous pink peaks and they tightened even
more. His mouth filled with saliva. Damn, her body was so responsive.

She trembled beneath him. Her face was flushed. Her chest, too. And he could feel the heat coming off her skin. She was on the verge of release. He could be kind and let her come. He should. But he couldn't bear the thought of this magical experience ending so soon.

He flicked his tongue over one of her nipples, and she cried out. The sound bounced around the room, hummed through his body, and sent another rush of erotic hunger blasting through his center. "Ssshhh," he whispered before pulling her nipple into his mouth to suckle.

"I...can't..." she muttered, squirming and quaking beneath him.

He slid his arms under her, cradling her, and thrust harder, deeper. That was his undoing. He could no more deny himself than he could deny her. Her slick walls rippled around him, then clenched tight. A gush of wetness washed over him, easing his rough thrusts as he surrendered to his own need. He took her hard. He took her rough. Her screams of ecstasy filled the room. He knew the moment she came, felt her muscles rhythmically contracting around him, massaging him. His balls tightened so hard, it felt as if they were in his chest. The flash of heat followed, like an atomic bomb detonating deep inside. His cum burned down his length, and just before he filled her, he yanked out and spilled his seed on her lower stomach. With each spurt, he gasped. His lungs were so tight, he couldn't breathe.

"Ohmygod," she uttered.

He pulled her flush against him and closed his eyes. Her little body fit so perfectly against his. He finally pulled in a full breath. He could smell her skin, her juices. Even though he'd just had her, his body tightened again. He could take her already. He wanted to take her once more.

He fingered her wet slit, and she shuddered against him. She wanted it, too.

"Ohhhhh," she murmured, writhing, rubbing her mound against him. That was an invitation he couldn't ignore.

But first, he had to wipe away the remains of his cum. He couldn't risk impregnating her. He eased away, and she whimpered.

"Just a minute," he said, his voice light with laughter. "You are insatiable."

"Only with you." She opened her eyes, and their gazes tangled.

She was so beautiful.

Mine.

No. No. Not this one.

Mine.

As if she sensed something, she drew her brows. "Is something wrong?"

"No." He scooped up his pants and shoved his hand in his pocket. Wrong pocket. His phone buzzed against his palm.

Dammit.

Withdrawing his hand with his phone in it, he mumbled, "Someone left a message. Let me check and see who called." He grabbed a handful of tissues out of the box he kept in his desk drawer and handed them to Michelle.

She nodded and wiped her stomach with her bound hands, one knee bent, and her foot resting on the tabletop.

He skimmed his call log. Both brothers had called him. Multiple times. And he had several messages from them. That never happened. Dread wound through him, extinguishing the spark that had been simmering inside. "I think something's wrong."

She curled her abdomen to push herself upright. "I hope it's nothing serious."

He played the first message, tucked the phone between his shoulder and ear, and worked on the knot in the tie.

"Talen, it's Drako. Dammit, where the hell are you? We've

been trying to get you for hours. Lei is in the hospital. She was bleeding. Call me as soon as you get this message—"

Talen's heart stopped. Fighting to breathe, he hit the button, cutting off the rest of the message.

"Shit, I have to go." He bent down, grabbed a handful of clothes, and dumped them on the table.

"Is everything okay?" She discarded the wet tissues in the trash can, pulled one garment from the wadded-up pile, her skirt, then jumped off the table and yanked it up.

"No. It's my sister-in-law. She's in the hospital." Quickly, he found his pants and shirt and stuffed himself into them. He didn't bother with his underclothes. Not waiting for Michelle, he raced toward the exit. "I'm sorry I have to leave you like this," he said as he dashed through the suite. He opened the door, glancing back. She was still in the office.

"It's okay. I understand." Her voice was small, distant. He thought he caught a hint of emotion in it. But he couldn't delay. Not a second. For all he knew, Lei could be bleeding to death. He had to go. Now.

"Would you mind locking the door when you leave?" He was such a bastard.

"No, of course not," she said softly.

Feeling like shit, he slammed the door behind him and sprinted down the hallway.

Wow.

She didn't know what to think, what to feel.

That experience...it had been beyond words. Incredible. Phenomenal. Scorching. Nah, those words didn't come remotely close to describing what she'd felt.

But then there'd been that call, and he'd rushed out, leaving her alone. In his office. In the dark. Without her top. That was still in the car.

Had he told her the truth about his sister-in-law? Or was it a lie?

Her hands trembled as she finished dressing, shrugged into his coat, and slid her feet into her shoes. The discomfort grew as she *click-clacked* through the empty space, the soft glow of the exit sign leading her through the dark stillness.

Although she'd been more or less abandoned after having sex with him, she wasn't sure how she felt yet. There were plenty of emotions tumbling around inside of her. But she was too preoccupied to sort them through. Clasping the coat shut with one hand, she wandered toward the exit, locked and closed the door behind her, and hit the button for the elevator. It wasn't until the door closed that the emotions became overwhelming.

Shaking, she wrapped her arms around herself and waited for the car to make its descent. Leaning back and letting the wall support her, she closed her eyes.

Of course, it was his face she saw. That stunning, breathtaking face. After what she'd just done, and what had happened next, a part of her wished she would never see that face again.

It was a fucking miracle he hadn't been pulled over. He'd ignored every speed limit posted as he'd raced to the hospital. Even with going ten to fifteen miles per hour over the limit, he didn't get there fast enough. He literally sprinted into the building, his phone pressed to his ear as he waited impatiently for Drako to tell him where to go.

No fucking answer.

He shoved his phone in his pocket and went to the information desk. The woman sitting behind it asked with a smile, "May I help you?"

"My sister-in-law is in the hospital somewhere."

"What's her name?" she asked, fingers poised over her computer keyboard.

"Lilly Garner."

Her fingers tapped out the name Lei had taken after they'd moved. "Here she is. She was admitted about an hour ago. Her room is number three-fifteen."

"Thank you." He looked left. He looked right.

"The elevator is that way," the woman said, indicating the left. "Just beyond the wall."

"Thank you." He followed her direction, taking long, swift strides. When he stepped out of the elevator on the third floor, Drako was strolling down the hallway. "Tage!" he called out.

Responding to his new name, Talen turned. Right away, he could see that something had happened. Something terrible.

The air left his lungs, and a wave of dizziness rushed through him. "Is she...?" He thrust an arm out, hand braced on the wall for support.

"Resting," Drako said. "The doctor gave her something to help her sleep."

"She's safe?"

"Yes. Safe, but far from okay." Drako looked left, right, then jerked his head toward a door not far from where he stood. "We can talk in there."

Talen followed his brother into the room. The placard on the wall outside told him it was a family waiting area. Inside the small space were a couple of couches and a television.

Drako closed the door before speaking. "She lost the child, Talen."

"Damn."

"She took it very badly. And she doesn't know the worst of it yet."

Talen couldn't speak. He was too choked up with sadness

for the woman he loved to say a word. Her pain ate at his insides, gnawing like a jaw full of sharp teeth.

"She won't be able to have any children," Drako told him. Talen knew what that meant. The pain in his gut amplified.

"Malek's in there with her. He's in bad shape."

"I would be, too."

"He loves her."

"Yeah," Talen said, his voice breaking. "I know."

"I don't know if he can do it. I don't think he can divorce her."

Talen couldn't let Malek divorce her. The thought of never seeing her again made him want to tear out his hair. "So, he won't."

"But what about—"

"Fuck it. One of us can have an extra kid," Talen said. He had to convince his brother not to pressure Malek. It was too soon to force a divorce. "Look at what happened with our father's generation. He was the only one to produce any children."

"But that wasn't by choice. Our uncles were both married to women who could bear children. They'd both been checked by doctors. It simply happened that once our father had produced three sons, our uncles stopped trying."

"Then perhaps Malek can hold off on divorcing for a while, at least until one or both of us produce a child."

"Son," Drako corrected.

"Son."

"We must produce sons," Drako reminded him. Of course, that was unnecessary. He knew what his duty was. Lately, that was all he thought about. And now, the pressure for him to marry was even greater.

"I know."

"And before we do that, we must be *married*. Me and *you*."

"Yes, yes. I get it. I'm working on it." He dropped onto the couch and shoved his fingers through his hair. "It isn't easy, finding the right woman."

"I know. I've been there. But if you don't want our brother to divorce his wife, you need to work harder on it."

Shit. As if he wasn't feeling enough pressure already. He didn't have a clue who his wife would be.

What about Michelle?

He shoved that thought aside. She was too fragile.

Then again, Lei had been fragile when Malek married her. Even though she'd struggled to get over a major tragedy, she had weathered the danger okay, and had handled their most recent move just fine.

Michelle.

Michelle?

No, she was a bad choice. A dangerous one. He would feel compelled to protect her. Like Lei. He might even put his brothers and The Secret at risk for her.

And then there was his lifestyle. Although she showed a natural submissiveness that drove him crazy, she was completely new to D/s. When he needed something more intense, he would be driven to go elsewhere for that. He had a feeling she wouldn't handle that well, either.

Then again, both of his brothers appeared to be content with their choices. Drako's wife, Rin, hadn't had any experience with D/s when they married. And Lei had been a domme. She'd quickly learned to appreciate the freedom and joy in submitting to a master who was loving and protective and trustworthy.

Why couldn't Michelle learn, as well?

Then again, both brothers had experienced their share of challenges with their wives. It had taken time for them to gain Rin and Lei's complete trust. Not to mention, both brothers had taken some major risks because of their love for their wives.

No, it would be better to choose a woman who was more independent. Stronger. Experienced. And someone who wouldn't expect or want his love.

His heart belonged to someone else.

Michelle wasn't the one. Even though tonight had been intense. Already he was ready to go track her down and do it again.

Drako waved his hands in front of Talen's nose. "Earth to Talen. Are you still with me?"

Talen lifted his head. Drako had sat down next to him. He hadn't even realized it. "Just thinking."

"About...?"

"Life."

Drako flopped an arm over Talen's shoulder. "I know you care about Lei. If you want to help her, then you need to think about finding a wife of your own."

"Dammit, I get it. Stop." He shoved to his feet and charged out into the hall. Feeling as though the weight of the world was resting on his shoulders, he followed the signs to Lei's room.

Three-eleven. Three-thirteen. Three-fifteen. This was it. Moving quietly, he stepped inside.

She looked so frail and vulnerable, lying in the bed, eyes closed, smooth porcelain skin pale.

"She'll be okay," someone said.

Talen jerked around, finding his brother Malek sitting in a chair, in a corner of the room. The shadows hanging over his features made him look tired and weak.

"She'll be okay," Talen repeated, stepping up to the bed. His gaze dropped to her little hand. Her fingers were long and narrow, her bones so fine. Her expression was peaceful although her skin was milky pale. "I know how much she means to you."

"More than I could say."

"I promise I'll be married by the end of the month," Talen vowed, resisting the urge to pull Lei into his arms and hold her.

She didn't need his comforting or protection. She had Malek. Malek loved her at least as much as he did, if not more.

"That doesn't give you much time."

Leaving Lei's side, Talen turned to his grieving brother. "I don't care what it takes. I'll find a wife and I'll get her pregnant. With a son. Lei is yours. For the rest of your life."

"Thank you." A single tear slipped from his brother's eye.

12

Talen had to choose. Between two women. Two very different women. One was world-wise, experienced in D/s, sexy, and intelligent. But also self-centered, aggressive, and manipulative. The other was innocent and inexperienced, but also patient, trusting, and giving.

Seemed like a no-brainer. And it would be, if he'd been any other man. The innocent, inexperienced but trusting woman would win hands-down.

Except his life would never be normal, and there were dangers lurking in the shadows. Not only would his wife need to understand that his first duty would be to protect The Secret. Above all else. Including her. But she would also need to realize he couldn't afford to let his emotions get in the way of his primary obligation. She would have to understand, too, that her child would someday be called to carry a great responsibility.

Not every woman was capable of accepting the realities of his life or what the future might hold.

Angela was a better fit. She wouldn't fall apart at the first sign of danger. The lifestyle he could offer her, the beautiful things he could buy her, would make up for any sacrifices she would have to bear. Michelle wouldn't be so easy to buy.

Yes, it had to be Angela.

Angela.

His gut twisted. *Dammit.* Sitting in the family waiting room again, he dropped his head into his hands.

"What's wrong?" Drako asked.

"How's Lei?" he asked without looking up.

"Resting. Malek's staying there with her. No reason for me to stick around, so I thought I'd head back and get some work done," he explained. "You look...tense."

"I am."

"The marriage?"

Talen nodded.

"Do you remember how freaked out I was before I asked Rin to marry me?"

"It's not the *asking* I'm worried about. It's the *choosing*," Talen admitted.

"Ah." His oldest brother shouldered the wall and smiled. "Afraid you'll make a mistake."

"Sure. Weren't you?"

"No."

"Great." The sigh he heaved was loud enough to be heard for miles.

"I knew Rin was the one. But I kept telling myself I couldn't let myself love her. That's where our problems came from, me being stupid and thinking that if I loved her I wouldn't be able to do my job or protect The Secret or the family."

"What about that situation, with our uncle? He used Rin as bait and almost got The Secret from us. Wouldn't you say that your love for Rin made you vulnerable?"

"Maybe at first. But in the long run her love has made me better, stronger." Drako curled his hands into fists. His gaze dropped to them as he unfurled his fingers. Tiny sparks ignited on his fingertips. "Not to mention the power I have now. I believe it's tied to her love."

"That I don't get, how a woman's love could make you suddenly capable of producing and controlling fire."

Drako merely shrugged. "I know, but it is what it is." He gave Talen a thorough once-over. "You know which woman is right for you. Take a risk. *Love* her." Smiling, Drako shook his head. "Listen to me. I sound like a fucking woman. I never would have thought I would tell you to marry for love. But I've learned a lot since I married Rin. Her love might make our job easier, not more difficult. If you gain a power, too, like me and Malek, then we'll be that much more capable of not only protecting The Secret, but our families, too."

Talen let Drako's words sink in for a few moments before responding.

Take a risk.

Love her.

Whom could he love? Angela? No.

Michelle. Yes. Michelle.

"Have you made a choice?" Drako asked, a smile pulling at his lips.

"Yes. I think I have." His heart jerked. Could he marry Michelle? Yes? Maybe. Yes! "I'll do it. I'll marry for love." For the first time in a while, he actually inhaled a complete breath.

Drako gave his shoulder a slap. "You won't regret it, little brother. I promise."

Michelle's day had been ordinary. Dull. Uneventful. Slightly disappointing.

She hadn't heard a word from Tage. He hadn't called. Hadn't texted. Hadn't been on the elevator this morning. Hadn't even come up to check to make sure she made it home okay. Hadn't even come looking for his coat.

He's blowing you off. Forget him.

By noon, she'd told herself that so many times, she had lost count. By six o'clock that evening, it had become a mantra. *Forget him. Forget him. Forget him.*

She repeated those words over and over as she shut down her computer. She repeated them as she grabbed her purse and headed out into the hallway. She repeated them as she waited for the elevator, rode it down, and walked to her car in the parking structure.

Forget him, forget him, forget him.

Her insides ached. But she had nobody to blame. Hadn't he tried to tell her she was making a mistake? Hadn't he warned her?

I can't forget him.

She couldn't. Not the way he'd touched her. The way he'd kissed her. The way he possessed her body when he'd made love to her. A wave of warmth rushed through her as she remembered him tying her hands.

I did this to myself.

She slumped into the driver's seat, shoved her key into the ignition, and turned it.

Click, click, click.

Dead battery?

"Dammit."

Annoyed, she tried it again. *Click, click, click, click.*

"Just great." Muttering a few cuss words, she thrust her hand into her purse and pulled out her wallet and phone. She had a motor club membership. They would send a service truck out to jump-start it. But she would be sitting here for a while. At least a half hour. She grabbed the card from her wallet and flipped it over to read the number.

Someone knocked on her window. She looked. Hopefully it was someone with jumper cables.

It was him.

Shit. Unable to power down the windows, she opened the

car door. "My car won't start. I think the battery's dead. I don't suppose you have jumper cables."

"Come with me." He extended a hand.

"Where?"

"I'd like to go somewhere and talk."

Talk? He had the world's worst timing. Her car was dead. She needed to take care of that first, or she wouldn't have a way to get to work in the morning. "I can't. Not right now."

He stood there, jaw clenched slightly. Was he frustrated with her? Annoyed, maybe? Good. He deserved a little discomfort after abandoning her last night, and the time before.

He reached into her car, grabbed the hood release, and gave it a pull. Then, without saying a word, he circled around to the front of the car, lifted it. A few seconds later, he said, "Try it now."

Fully expecting nothing but clicks, she twisted the key. The engine started right up. "What?" she exclaimed.

He dropped the hood. "A battery cable was loose."

"Battery cable?" she echoed, her mind spinning. "Thanks. That saved me a lot of trouble tonight."

He thrust his hand at her again. "Now, would you please come with me?"

She looked at his face, then his waiting hand. Did she want to hear his explanation for last night? Maybe. Plus he'd just helped her with her car. She cut off her car and stuffed her keys, phone, and wallet back in her purse. With her purse handles looped over her right elbow, she set her left hand in his. "Okay. Oh, I have your coat."

"Keep it." His expression brightened as he watched her straighten up. His fingers wove between hers. "I'm parked over here." He led her around the corner to his black car and opened her door for her.

She watched him round the front of the car. What would he tell her? As he walked, his expression was fairly intense. He looked a little...nervous.

He opened his door and folded his large frame into the seat. "Thanks for giving me a chance to explain."

"Thank you for helping me with my car."

He flicked a glance at her, then draped an arm over the back of her seat and twisted to look over his shoulder. "It was no big deal."

"It was a big deal to me. I'm lost without my car."

He nodded, shifted into forward, and eased on the accelerator. The car prowled through the narrow lane, toward the exit. His arm didn't move. It stayed right where it was, draped across the gap between their seats. Her nerves along her neck and down her back prickled. She wondered if she would ever get used to him being near her. Or would she always feel warm around him? Hot and tense and tingly. "I get that. We all become so dependent upon cars, phones, conveniences."

"So true. Where are we going?"

"Somewhere quiet." He flicked a glance her way. "It isn't far."

Slightly nervous, she smiled and nodded. Her fingers fiddled with her purse strap. After a few moments of silence, she turned to watch familiar landmarks, streets, and buildings zoom past the passenger-side window. He turned onto Route Fifteen, then into the entry of a state park.

"Okay," he said when he'd parked the car. "We're here. Wait here. I'll get your door."

"Thanks." She glanced down at her feet. She hadn't exactly dressed to go on a hike. She hoped he wasn't expecting her to walk far.

He opened the door for her, and she swung her legs out of the vehicle and straightened up.

Once again, he was standing very close. Just like last night, she was trapped between his bulky, insanely sexy body and the car. Narrow waist. Wide chest. Broad shoulders. That face. Oh God, that face.

His eyes.

Her breath caught in her throat.

"Marry me," he said.

"What?" she blurted. Surely she'd heard wrong. He hadn't said ... he hadn't ...

"Shit. I mean, damn. I mean, shoot. I did this all wrong." He lowered himself to one knee. "Michelle, marry me," he repeated.

What the hell? She felt herself wobbling. She grabbed the car door to steady herself. "Marry you?"

"Yes." He took her hand in his. "Be my wife."

"I ..." Her words trailed off. What the hell was this? A marriage proposal? After one date? Correction, two half-dates. They hadn't even had one full date yet. She didn't know what to say. It had to be a joke. Smiling, she shook her head. "You're funny."

"I'm not trying for funny. To be honest, I was shooting for romantic." He swept his arm in a wide arc, indicating their surroundings, which were sort of romantic. The park was lovely, wooded, and lush. Private. Not far away, in a clearing, she saw a canopy set up, with a table set under it.

"You aren't j-j-joking?" she stuttered.

"No. I wouldn't joke about a thing like this." Standing, he pulled on her hand, tugging her forward, toward the canopy and table.

Once again, she was speechless. Her mind was whirring 'round and 'round like a twirling top, thoughts spinning, nothing sticking, other than, *what the hell?*

"It's so ... sudden."

"I realize that." He ducked under the canopy and released her hand to pull out a chair for her.

Grateful to be able to sit—her knees were as soft as melted marshmallows—she dropped onto the chair. "We don't know each other," she said as her gaze meandered over the table, set for two.

He sat across from her. He grabbed the wine bottle from the

bucket next to him and pulled the cork. "We know a little about each other. I know your name. I know you're sensitive and trusting and a little on the conservative side—at least when it comes to dating. Is there more I should know?" He picked up her glass and poured some wine into it.

"Should you know more before you decide to spend the rest of your life with me? Sure." She accepted her filled glass with what was probably a nervous smile. He poured some wine into his own glass, then set the bottle back in the bucket. "And I should know more about you than how you look naked."

"Are you sure about that?" The twinkle in his eye couldn't be missed as he peered at her over the rim of his glass.

She scrunched up her nose, even though she found that twinkle ridiculously adorable. "Yes, of course I'm sure. I hardly know anything about you." At his unspoken invitation, she lifted the cover off her plate. She was surprised by what she found. There wasn't any fancy food, no little pretty portions of gourmet meats and weird vegetables. There was a big, fat hamburger on the plate and some macaroni salad and chips. She had to giggle a little. The food so did not fit with the atmosphere he'd created, or the wine, which was so smooth and delicious she couldn't get enough. "There's a sequence of events that people generally follow before they marry. You know, like going out on more than two dates."

"Yes, well, I've never been the kind to go with tradition." He picked up his huge burger and took a man-sized bite.

"And this is why I need to know more about you. What exactly does marriage mean to you, since you're not into tradition?" she asked as she munched on a chip.

He swallowed before answering. "It means we live together as partners, lovers, friends. We'll start a family."

"Kids? You want kids? See? That's something I didn't know about you."

He gulped down some wine. "I want children right away. At least two. Twin boys would be perfect."

She couldn't help laughing at that statement, as well as the whole conversation. It was all so crazy, this talk about marriage, children. Like she would be insane enough to run to the altar with a man she'd slept with once. "FYI, a woman doesn't have any control over when she gets pregnant, let alone how many children she has, or the gender of those offspring."

"There are things a doctor can do."

"What kind of things?" A little warning bell started chiming in her head. This was weird. No man, particularly one who looked like Tage, who could sleep with any woman he wanted at the snap of his fingers, and seemed to have enough money to buy whatever he wanted, was in a hurry to get married. Something was up. "Are you in a rush to have children for some reason?"

"I am." He took another bite of burger.

That admission stunned her. First, she'd never met a man who was anxious to have kids. Generally, they took the full term of the pregnancy to get used to the idea of a child. And second, wasn't he the wrong gender to be worried about his biological clock? "Why the rush?"

"It's for . . ." He didn't finish his explanation, which worried her. Instead he filled his mouth with more grilled beef and bun. What was the deal with this man? When she'd first met him, he was the epitome of a player, jumping from her bed (okay, if you wanted to get technical, she didn't sleep with him that first night) to Angela's. He was into bondage games, too, which was very strange. And now, all of a sudden, he had ambitions to become Mr. Perfect Husband and Father?

She couldn't say yes. No matter how attracted to him she was, lust wasn't a solid enough foundation for a marriage.

"No," she said. "I won't marry you."

He visibly swallowed. "No?"

"I can't marry you."

"I have plenty of money. You'd live a good life, have anything you want. You wouldn't have to work if you didn't want to. Our children would get the very best—"

What the hell was up with this guy? "That sounds like a dream, but the answer is still no. For now."

"For how long? A few days? A week?"

She shook her head. "I would say closer to a year."

"That long?" He drained his wineglass. Then he refilled it and took another swallow.

"Marriage isn't something I would ever enter lightly or on a whim. It's a lifelong commitment. I don't want to end up in a bad marriage or the wrong marriage. I won't get divorced, especially if there are children involved."

"I have no intention of getting divorced, either."

"Then you should be glad to wait, to make sure I'm the right wife for you." Unable to eat another bite, she pushed back from the table. "To be honest, this whole thing has me stumped. Men generally don't sprint into a marriage recklessly. They usually have to be dragged into one, kicking and screaming."

"I'm not your average guy," he pointed out.

"That, I wouldn't disagree with."

"So." His brows pulled together. "You won't marry me?"

"No."

He visibly swallowed again. "There's no chance you'll change your mind? What can I say? What can I do—"

"Nothing."

"Okay." He exhaled. Then he stood.

Was he leaving again? Running off once more? What would it be this time? He hadn't even offered an apology for last night, outside of that quick "I'm sorry" yesterday as he was racing out the door.

This man was...too hard to figure out.

"Are you finished?" he asked. "I'll take you back to your car."

So that was it? The end of their romantic date? It was early. Why was he cutting it off so soon? Had she bruised his ego so badly that he needed some time to lick his wounds? Surely he'd get over it with a little time. He might even thank her someday.

She followed him to the car.

When she reached the car, she turned to face him. "Thank you for the delicious dinner."

He reached for her but then pulled his hand away. Shadows darkened his eyes, and his expression went blank, suddenly lacking any hint of life. If she didn't know better, she would swear he was genuinely hurt by her rejection.

"I'm sorry I couldn't agree to marry you right now," she said, her voice soft.

"I'm sorry, too, Michelle."

13

"I'm sorry." Those were the last words Michelle heard from Tage.

The next morning she went to work, expecting to see him in the office. They were scheduled to talk about the layout of his brochure. There was a message on her desk when she arrived. He had cancelled the appointment.

Wow, he'd taken her refusal really bad if he couldn't even set aside his bruised ego for business. She called him to reschedule, but she got his voice mail. After leaving a message, she shoved aside the little twinge of confusion about his reaction and carried on with her day. If he was going to be this broken up over an off-the-wall marriage proposal, then maybe it was a good thing she'd rejected his offer. He had to have some personal issues, some serious ones. By the end of the day, when she hadn't heard back from him, she was convinced he was more troubled than she had guessed.

Something was up with that man. Something serious.

* * *

Plan A had failed. It sucked. But Talen had always believed that things happened for a reason. He'd had some doubts that Michelle could handle the stress of being his wife. Not every woman was willing to make certain sacrifices in exchange for money and all the perks that money could buy.

But, even after over a week had passed since her refusal, there was this little knot of pain in his gut. The thought of being around her, wanting to touch her, but not being able to, had gnawed at him. He hadn't gone to work today. That was the first time he hadn't worked since they'd moved to southern Ohio. He loved his work.

He would not marry Michelle.

Dammit. I want her. I. Want. Her. Nobody else.

He needed to get on with things. Lei was counting on him. His brother was counting on him.

At least he had a Plan B. In the end, he told himself, it would work for the best. He would have chosen the right wife. They would have two boys. Lei's obligation to Malek would be fulfilled, and she would be able to remain married to the man who loved her almost as much as he did.

Plan B.

He picked up his phone and scrolled down to the number. His finger hovered over the screen for several seconds before he summoned up the strength to put the call through. His heart thumped fast and hard as he waited for his future wife to answer the phone. One ring. Two.

Speaking of rings, he needed to get with Drako about the ring. He had something in mind. But he wasn't sure if Drako would have what he wanted. No matter what, he had to return the ring he'd chosen for Michelle. That one had been perfect for her.

Only her.

On the fifth ring, the call bounced to voice mail. He left a message. Hung up. Shoved his fingers through his hair. Lei was coming home soon. Drako had run over to pick Malek and her up. He wouldn't rest easy until she was safe at home, where she belonged.

And until he had a pregnant wife, her belly swollen with his seed.

He'd already done some research. There was one surefire way to make sure his wife gave him sons. He wasn't against using science to make sure she gave him what they all needed. He had a feeling Angela wouldn't mind, especially if it meant she would only have to endure one pregnancy.

Three hours later Talen was parked outside of Angela's condo, wishing he didn't have to be there. Sure, he'd told himself over and over he was making the right choice. In reality, this was his only option. But still.

How would he deal with seeing Michelle the next time? How would he keep himself from grabbing her, hauling her curvy, soft body against him and kissing her until she agreed to marry him? How?

Maybe that wasn't such a bad idea.

No.

He wouldn't coerce her. He wouldn't manipulate her. He knew he'd already hurt Michelle enough already. Dammit, he'd been too wrapped up in the marriage proposal to even offer her a decent apology for leaving her that night in his office.

I'm such an asshole. It's no wonder she shot me down.

If a woman accepted his proposal, it would be of her own free will. And she would know exactly what she was getting into.

He checked his pocket. The ring box was there. He had everything he needed. But he didn't feel particularly good about what he was about to do. Still, Lei and Malek were counting on him.

He pulled in one last deep breath, let it out, and opened his car door. He was on her front porch much too soon.

She clearly had been waiting for him. She answered his knock immediately.

Angela looked very nice, her long hair a tumble of blond sexy waves. Her lips were glossed and plump, curled into a shy smile. "Hello again," she said, stepping aside to let him in. "This is a nice surprise."

If she thought his call was a surprise, she would be shocked to learn what was coming later.

Standing just inside the door, she reached for a jacket that had been draped over the back of a chair nearby. "Is it getting chilly yet?"

"A little." He took the jacket from her and held it up so she could shrug into it. As he stood there, inhaling her sweet scent, memories of Michelle invaded his thoughts, distracting him. Trying to hide his conflicting emotions, he smiled as she turned to thank him.

An awkward silence fell between them.

He combed his fingers through her hair. "You look beautiful tonight."

She smiled up into his eyes. "Thank you." Her gaze flicked to his mouth, and her little tongue darted out, to moisten her lips. Although his gaze focused on that pink bit of flesh, nothing stirred within him. There was no heat. No spark. No desire.

Damn.

Shit.

If only...

"Are you okay?" she asked, head tipped to the side.

"Yeah, I'm fine. Had a rough day."

"We don't have to go out if you're not up to it." She circled around his back, placed her hands on his shoulders, and started rubbing.

Now that felt good. "Mmmmm..." He let his head fall forward.

Appling gentle pressure, she urged him forward. He followed her direction to the couch in her living room. "You're very tense. I know how to take care of that," she whispered. Standing behind him. "I long to serve you, Master. Will you lie down?" Then she kicked off her shoes. "I'll be right back."

For a split second, he was tempted to jump up and leave. Everything about this evening felt wrong. It shouldn't have. This strange, unsettled feeling hadn't been an issue the first time he'd met Angela, when they'd spent the night playing and fucking until they were both too exhausted to move.

She returned a few minutes later with a bottle of some kind. She flipped the lid up and the scent of vanilla filled the air. "This is my favorite oil." The soft sloughing sound of skin against skin filled the silence. "Will you take off your shirt?"

"Sure." About as thrilled as a guy waiting for a root canal, he shucked his pullover, the shirt underneath, and the tank beneath that.

"Master, you are absolutely beautiful," Angela murmured as he lay down on his stomach, face turned toward the couch back.

"Thank you. You are, too," he said.

"Why, thanks. I wasn't fishing for a compliment, but I'll take it anyway." Setting her warm hands on his back, she began working out the tension in his shoulders. It hurt a little, a good pain.

He grunted as her fingers pressed into a knot.

"Sorry. Am I being too rough?" she asked.

"No, not at all."

She swung a knee over his hips, wedging it between him and the couch back and straddling his ass. "Wow, are you tense. You must have had a terrible day."

"No worse than any other."

"I had no idea how stressful being a computer programmer could be."

"It's not so much my work," he said. "It's more...family stuff."

"Ah, now that I get. My family drives me crazy sometimes." Again, she dug her little fingers into that same tender spot on his back. "Do you want to talk about it?"

"No."

"Okay." She worked in silence for a while, which he was grateful for. It made it easier for him to relax a little, forget about why he was there. Every now and then, as her fingertips glided down his spine, he imagined it was Michelle dragging her blunt-tipped fingernails down his back, and a tiny flash of heat would simmer in his veins. But the instant he remembered who was sitting on his ass, the heat of her pussy burning through his pants, the little flicker in his blood would sputter out.

Damn, he might not be able to get it up tonight.

"Okay, I'm done with your back," she said. "Would you like me to massage your chest?"

"Sure." Waiting for her to swing off him, he angled up on his elbows, then pivoted on his hip.

Her gaze went from his face to his stomach, then down to the couch. "What's that? Did you drop something out of your pocket?" She pointed.

He had a feeling he knew what *that* was. He looked. Yep. *What the hell? Here's your chance. Just get it over with.* He palmed the box. "It's the reason why I came over tonight."

Her brows drew together.

"You know how I said I was tense about some family things. Well, that's because I have an obligation, a responsibility." He snapped up the lid, displaying the ring.

Her gaze locked on the ring. Her mouth formed an O.

"I realize we don't know each other very well. I can't promise you that our marriage will be perfect or even loving.

To be honest, I don't know if I'm capable of loving someone. Or being monogamous. But I can promise you that I will respect you and provide you with a good life, a beautiful home, and just about anything your heart desires. Designer clothing, jewelry, cars. You can quit working if you want. Or you can continue if it makes you happy."

"Are you kidding me?" she squeaked.

"I'm not kidding." He forced a smile.

She plucked the ring out of the box. "Is this for real? You're asking me to marry you?"

"I am."

"But you don't love me." She slid the ring on her finger. It wasn't a perfect fit, but it wasn't bad.

He wouldn't lie to her, wouldn't give her any reason to feel manipulated or deceived. "Not at this point I don't."

"So why do it? Why get married?" she asked as she stared at the ring.

"It's a family thing."

"Ah, like in a romance novel. Are you going to inherit a fortune?"

"I don't need to inherit a fortune. I already have a fortune."

Her lips twisted. "Hm...you said you can't be monogamous. So does that mean I'll be your wife in name only? Or will we have an open marriage? Will you continue to go to the club?"

He studied her face for any sign of confusion. She didn't look over-the-moon happy. But she didn't look particularly put off by the idea, either. "No, it won't be in name only. We will have sex. It can't be open, at least not on your end. I will continue to scene with other submissives. I may or may not fuck them. But you cannot. You'll need to provide me with two children. Boys. Their paternity cannot be questioned."

"No sex. Two boys," she repeated, still admiring the ring on her finger. Evidently Drako was right, the ring was a good choice. He'd wanted a colored diamond, blue. But Drako hadn't been able to find him one on such short notice. "This is so weird, like the plot of a novel."

"I assure you it's real."

"Are you a prince?" she asked, twirling the ring around her finger.

"No, I'm no prince."

She pulled the ring off, but she didn't return it to the box. "Can you tell me why you must marry and have two children?"

"Two boys."

"Boys," she said.

"As soon as possible." He enunciated those four words clearly.

One of her brows rose. "You know, those things can take time."

"Do you have any issues—"

"As far as I know, I'm good down there. My mother had twelve kids. If I inherited her fertility, there won't be a problem, though there's the issue of gender. All twelve of us are girls. Then again, you and I both know that has nothing to do with her."

"I'm thinking we'll take no chances," he stated.

Now she lifted both brows. "What does that mean?"

"IVF."

"IVF." She visibly swallowed, and he wondered if she might hand the ring back. "Two boys. And then my childbearing obligation would be done? I'm not too thrilled about being pregnant. To tell you the truth, I hadn't planned on having kids. Ever. Pregnancy does ugly things to a woman's body."

"More the reason to go IVF. You would only have to be pregnant once. Then you would be finished."

"I like that idea." She nodded. "Okay, I will agree to those terms. Two children, conceived by IVF. But there's one issue that we must address first. If you won't be monogamous, then you couldn't expect me to be, either—once the children were born. Right?"

He should have seen that coming, but he hadn't. His wife wished to take other partners. The idea grated. But he recognized the hypocrisy of not allowing her to do what she wished if he was going to. "I would have to think about that."

Her eyes narrowed. "You had better think about it. Think long and hard." She slid the ring back onto her finger. "With a slight adjustment, it will be a perfect fit."

His heart twisted. "Yes, it will be."

Well, that was it.

He had his wife. Soon he would have his boys. Everything would be great.

He hoped.

14

The jerk.

What the heck?

The asshole!

What the hell?

By the following Sunday, over a week and a half later, Michelle wasn't sad anymore. She wasn't disappointed. She wasn't confused, either.

She was mad.

Angry.

Furious.

Tage-the-crazy-guy hadn't called since she'd politely declined his insane marriage proposal. What the hell was up with that? Surely her refusal wasn't grounds for him to never speak to her again.

As she had the last week, this morning she took some extra time on her routine, making sure she looked her absolute best. Instead of pulling her hair back like usual, she left it down and curled it. Fat, sexy waves tumbled around her shoulders. She plucked and primped until she was date-ready. Then she grabbed a granola bar and a diet cola and ran out the door ten minutes earlier than normal.

Her hands trembled as she drove to work. Literally shook. And her heart pounded in her chest, fast and hard. She was a nervous wreck. But she had to find out what the hell was going on with Tage.

She pulled into the parking lot almost fifteen minutes earlier than normal—her nerves had her stomping on the gas a little harder than usual—parked, gathered her purse into her lap, and waited.

Ten minutes later, she'd seen no sign of him.

Fifteen minutes later, still no Tage.

Twenty minutes later, and she couldn't wait any longer. She kept scanning the parking lot for his car as she *click-clacked* into the building. She rode the elevator up to her floor alone. As she waited for the car to slowly climb, she closed her eyes and leaned against the back wall, memories of being in that very car with Tage flashing in her head.

He had to be avoiding her. There could be no other explanation. Why? What was going on?

When the car stopped at her floor, she dragged herself out of it.

Her insides were a jumble.

Her emotions were once again all over the place.

This was crazy.

Before she opened the door to suite 610, she sucked in a deep breath, let it out, and jerked up her chin. She couldn't let this silly crap get in the way of her work. She just couldn't.

Still feeling like shit, she let herself into the suite, greeted Lauren with a wave and a smile.

"You haven't heard the big news yet," Lauren said, eyes glittering with excitement.

"What news?"

"Angela came in this morning with a great big rock on her finger. She's engaged."

Angela? Engaged? Her heart jerked.

"He's that rich guy, Tage Garner."

This time her heart stopped. Literally. The air left her lungs in an audible huff. "Who?" she wheezed.

"Tage Garner. You know him. He's your account. Angela said he showed up at her place last night with a ring, told her he couldn't live another day without her, and begged her to marry him. On the spot. Can you believe it? I don't think they even know each other that well. I guess that's what rich people do, huh? Marry women they don't know on a whim. I'm guessing she'll have to sign a prenup."

Tage?

And Angela?

Married?

Married!

Michelle merely nodded. She couldn't speak. Her insides were being wrung like a twisted shirt through one of those old-fashioned, crank-style laundry wringers. It was absolute agony. But she tried to hold it together. And she did okay. For about ten seconds. Then her stomach lurched.

She ran for the bathroom.

Luckily, for her dignity, and the custodial staff's convenience, she made it there in time. She lost both the granola bar and the diet cola. And the makeup she'd taken such care to apply began running down her face.

She wanted to go home, crawl into bed, pull the covers over her head, and pretend the world didn't exist for a while. But she wouldn't do that. No. She wouldn't let that jackass and that bitch get the better of her.

Nor would she storm upstairs to that asshole's office and give him her idea of a congratulatory hug—a slap across the face.

What the hell was he doing? What the hell?

Determined to regain her composure and get on with her

day, she pulled out her arsenal of beauty products from her bag and began putting herself back together. She was looking pretty decent when she heard the door swing open and the soft *click-click* of heels on tile. Ignoring the newcomer, she picked up her lipstick and pulled off the top. As she was lifting her eyes to look in the mirror, she caught sight of blond hair in the reflection. Her gaze jerked, and she found herself staring at Angela's picture-perfect face.

"Good morning," Angela said as she plopped her handbag on the counter.

Good morning it was not, but Michelle pasted on an expression she hoped would pass for a smile and responded with, "Good morning."

Angela gazed at her reflection in the mirror and sighed. "I am so tired. Just look at the bags under my eyes."

Michelle had absolutely nothing to say in response, so she went back to what she'd been doing.

"What a night," Angela said with a second sigh as she used her left hand to smooth her hair back. The big rock on her finger caught the light and practically blinded Michelle.

Sheesh, could Angela be more obvious? Not succumbing to her coworker's ridiculous nudges, Michelle smoothed on some lipstick, dropped it back into her bag, and left.

God, what a bitch. If Angela had any idea what she was doing by basically gloating about her conquest, she was a bigger bitch than Michelle had ever thought.

She had to blink a few times to clear her eyes as she headed to her cubicle, but that did the job. And before long she was busy with work, her mind occupied, taking calls, responding to e-mails, and otherwise doing her damnedest to make sure she didn't break down again. She was doing a fine job of it until Angela knocked on her cubbie wall and poked her head in to ask, "What are you doing for lunch?"

"I'm not eating lunch today," Michelle said.

"Oh." Angela pouted. "Why?"

"I'm sick." That, at least, was partially true. She felt like crap today, worn out, foggy-headed, and nauseous. She'd caught a stomach virus.

"Oh. I'm sorry. Would you like me to get you some soup or something?" Angela offered, not looking sorry or concerned at all.

"No thanks."

"Okay." Angela's head disappeared. Then it reappeared again. "I'm dying. I need to tell you something. And ask for a favor."

"I'm kind of busy now."

"Okay. Catch me later, before you leave."

"Sure."

That bought Michelle a handful of hours. But only that. At six o'clock, Angela was back at her cubicle, purse in hand, clearly ready to leave for the night. "I'm calling it a day. You?"

Michelle was ready, but she didn't want to walk out with Angela. Because she knew if she did, she would have to listen to Angela talking about Tage. "Well, I still have a few things I need to wrap up."

Instead of leaving, like Michelle had hoped, Angela grabbed a chair from the next cubbie and pulled it up to Michelle's. "Are you mad at me about something?"

"Mad at you?" Maybe.

"Yes. You've been so quiet today."

"I'm always quiet," Michelle said, pretending to be busy.

"Okay, so maybe you are pretty quiet. But I'm getting a different vibe from you today."

Michelle shrugged. "I don't know why that would be. Maybe it's because I don't feel well."

Angela seemed to like that explanation. She smiled, nodded. "Yes, maybe. Anyway, I want to ask you for a favor."

"Oh?"

"I um, know you've heard I'm getting married in a couple of

weeks. Lauren said she told you. I'd like for you to be my maid of honor."

It took a few seconds for Angela's words to sink in. When they did, Michelle's head spun. "Maid of honor? Me?"

"Yes, you," Angela said, giving her a little nudge with an elbow. "Who else would I ask? You're my best friend here."

Best friend? Me? "I am?"

"Yes, you are. You sound shocked."

"Well, yes. We hardly know each other," Michelle pointed out as she tried to think of other, more compelling reasons why she shouldn't be Angela's maid of honor. She couldn't go to this wedding. No way.

"Okay, that's true. We don't know each other that well. But my very best friend lives in DC, and she just had a baby. She can't get away. Not even for a few days. So I was hoping you wouldn't mind..." Angela gave Michelle a wide-eyed, pleading look.

"I don't know..."

"Please, will you do it?"

"I..." She couldn't imagine standing in a chapel, watching Angela marry the man she'd just slept with. "I don't know. What's the date? I..." *Think quick. You need a good excuse.* "I have some family coming in from out of town in the next few weeks."

"We've tentatively set the date for May fourth."

"I'll check my calendar."

"Thank you." Angela literally flung herself at her and gave her a big, squeezy, patty, bear hug. "I hope you can do it."

"I'll see what I can do."

"You're the best." Angela stood, smoothed her skirt with her left hand, making sure to display her big, stupid ring, and then flounced off. At the exit, she called out, "See you tomorrow!"

Unfortunately, she would. "Bye." Michelle powered down

her computer, grabbed her purse, and, making sure Angela was long gone, headed for the door. Being the last one to leave, she cut off the lights and locked up before heading to the elevator.

She hit the button, then started scrolling through her personal e-mail on her cell phone. When the bell rang, signaling the elevator car's arrival, she stepped forward without looking up. The doors rumbled open, and out of the corner of her eye she spied men's shoes in the elevator.

Her gaze climbed higher, following the long line of two well-clad legs, lean torso, broad shoulders.

Oh hell.

It was time to start taking the stairs.

Maybe it was her imagination, but she could swear she saw something flash in his eyes. She didn't step inside right away. She was frozen by surprise. But when the doors started rolling shut, she stuck out her arm to catch it. To hell with him. She wasn't going to let him scare her away from the elevator. Or anything else.

She moved to the front corner of the car and watched the doors close. Then she stared straight ahead and tried not to let him know how intensely she felt his nearness. Nerves in her skin prickled with heat, up and down her back. The short ride was going to be freaking torture. All sixty or ninety seconds of it.

The car remained silent except for the hum of the motor as it slowly descended to the ground floor. She tilted her eyes up to watch the numbers above the doors illuminate, one at a time. Five. Four. Three. Out of the corner of her eye, she caught him poking at one of the buttons. Was he going to get out? Good.

The car stopped.

"Michelle."

Why weren't the doors opening?

She didn't turn around.

"Michelle," he repeated.

A wave of warmth washed through her. A war was raging

inside her mind. One part of her brain was telling her to turn around, to get the answers she'd been aching for since she'd found out about the engagement that morning. The other part was telling her to keep silent and still and let that man marry whomever the hell he wanted, whether she was a coldhearted bitch or not.

The part that wanted answers won. She glanced over her shoulder and her gaze tangled with his. Immediately she saw a dark shadow in his eyes. Something was wrong.

"I owe you an explanation," he said.

"You don't owe me anything."

He pushed away from the back wall. That put him within inches of her. Too close. Within reach. "You don't believe that."

A flare of anger surged through her. "What do you want from me? What do you want me to say? That I'm devastated because you decided to marry someone else? Because that would be a lie. I'm not devastated. You did what you had to do. Life goes on. Whatever."

"You sound angry."

"I am angry. And confused. But what do you care? I'm nothing to you. Nothing." Angling across him, she reached for the button on the panel to get the car started again. There was no point to this conversation. None. And she was starting to lose control. Her nose was burning. Her eyes, too. She couldn't cry in front of him. She couldn't let him see how much she hurt.

He grabbed her wrist. "No, you're definitely not nothing to me."

"Stop it!" She jerked her arm, yanking it from his grasp. "What the hell are you trying to do? Drive me insane? You made it clear from the beginning that sex was just sex to you. I shouldn't expect anything more. I assumed the marriage proposal, which came out of nowhere, was a joke. Evidently I was wrong."

"If you'd realized it was serious, would you have answered differently?"

"Now? No. We don't know each other. I'm not the kind to run off to Vegas and get married, only to divorce a week later."

"I'm not that kind, either."

"Yeah, well, I guess we'll see about that."

He visibly exhaled. His gaze wandered over her face for a moment, searching for something. She wasn't sure what. Then he pushed the button. The car lurched, then began once again to slowly fall toward the ground floor.

Michelle didn't breathe until she was out of that stupid elevator, and far, far away from that infuriating man.

Angela had no idea what she was in for. Whether it ended up being a week of hell or a lifetime, she couldn't possibly know what a screwed-up man she'd agreed to marry.

15

After that little moment Michelle had shared with Tage in the elevator, she had forgotten all about Angela asking her to be her maid of honor...until the next morning when Angela cornered her in the bathroom while she was washing her hands.

"Did you check your calendar? Can you be my maid of honor?" Angela asked, her eyes sparkly.

Oh shit. "I forgot," Michelle confessed. Why she didn't just tell Angela she was busy, she didn't know. Surely she couldn't feel guilty for not wanting to do this. Anyone in her shoes would be looking for a way to get out of it. Right?

Angela looked absolutely deflated. Every single sparkle in her eyes disappeared. "Oh. Okay." She dug in her purse and pulled out her lip gloss. Studying her own reflection in the mirror, she said, "If you don't want to be my maid of honor, I totally understand. It isn't like we're best friends or anything. I just thought you'd like to be there, for both Tage and me. Since you are Tage's friend."

Great way to heap on more guilt. "I promise I'll let you

know tomorrow." She needed to get out of the bathroom pronto, before Angela had her saying yes. She plucked some paper towels out of the holder to dry her hands.

"O-okay."

"Maybe you can ask someone else, just in case?" Michelle added.

"I don't have anyone else to ask."

"Nobody?" Michelle's gaze met Angela's in the mirror. That had to be a lie. A girl like Angela, not having any friends? Sure, she was a little boastful and self-centered, but she was also gorgeous and articulate and educated.

"Nope. Nobody."

Dammit. Could this be any more awkward? Michelle could think of a million things she'd rather do than stand up in Angela's wedding, like have all her fingernails and toenails ripped out by the root. But she didn't have the heart to tell Angela no if it meant she wouldn't have anyone there with her on her wedding day. "No family? Cousins? Aunts? Uncles?"

"No family. At least, none that I would want there."

Clearly there was more going on in Angela's life than she'd ever let on. And for the first time, Michelle saw her as less of a bitch and more of a woman who had problems. Serious ones, if this sudden marriage to a virtual stranger was any indication.

Angela dropped the bottle of lip gloss in her purse and turned around. "I'll be blunt. I realize you were thinking there might be something going on between you and Tage. I'm not blind. Maybe he hurt you. Maybe you wish he was marrying you instead. If things were reversed and you were marrying him, I probably wouldn't be so eager to be your maid of honor, either. This is a strange situation we're in. Both of us."

Michelle didn't know how to respond, other than to nod. She wasn't sure if she wished Tage were marrying her or not. She'd had her chance. She'd turned him down.

Angela asked, "Do you think I'm making a mistake, marrying him?"

"I can't judge—"

"You do. You think it's a mistake."

Michelle shrugged. "I don't know your situation or why you've made that decision. So how can I judge you?"

"True. I'll tell what I think about his proposal. I don't have any silly illusions that the marriage is going to be all roses and romance. It's an arranged marriage, more or less. But hey, arranged marriages and marriages of convenience have been going on for hundreds of years. And not all of them were unhappy."

This was blowing Michelle's mind. A beautiful, educated woman like Angela, marrying a man she didn't love. When she could have anyone. The man of her dreams. Why would she do that? Why would she settle for less? And Tage. Tage. What was he thinking, proposing to one woman and then turning around and proposing to another a week later? Obviously, he didn't care who he married. He just wanted a wife. Why? "Of course not, but—"

"I might be happy, too." Angela didn't sound convinced.

What the hell was going on?

To think she might have said yes to him. And if she had...a little shiver vibrated through Michelle's body. What a mistake that would have been, marrying a man who didn't give a crap about who he was saying those vows to. As much as Michelle didn't want to know all the nitty-gritty details of this so-called arranged marriage, she sort of wanted to understand why he was in such a rush to find a wife. And because she knew, maybe a little better than Angela, how desperate he was to marry anyone, she felt a little torn about keeping her mouth shut and letting Angela go ahead with something she was clearly having some doubts about.

"Why are you doing this?" Michelle asked.

"Because it means I won't ever have to struggle again."

Again?

What was she talking about? As far as Michelle knew, Angela had been raised in an upper-middle-class suburb, had attended private schools all her life, and hadn't ever seen any adversity greater than the occasional ugly breakup with a rich boyfriend.

Angela leaned back against the counter. "Maybe I should level with you. My life hasn't been exactly as wonderful as I might have led everyone here at work to believe. I didn't grow up in Palo Alto. I didn't go to Stanford. Or even community college. And my parents weren't doctors. They were alcoholics and drug addicts. Unemployed. Unemployable. Much of my life we were homeless. I stole food to survive. I stole a lot of things to survive. And I'm not proud of what I've done. I try to pretend that that life wasn't mine, that I didn't do those things."

Michelle was speechless. Not in a million years had she ever imagined this gorgeous, seemingly perfect woman had been homeless, stealing to survive. She was so polished and beautiful. But it did maybe explain her ambition and her drive to succeed.

"So, now maybe you understand?" Angela asked softly. "I've always been afraid of ending up back there, in the gutter. In despair. This marriage is an insurance policy, a guarantee I won't ever be homeless or hungry again."

"Yes, I understand. Now."

Angela continued, "I don't have any childhood friends. Most of the kids I grew up with are in jail. Some are dead. Some are still living in Modesto, but I haven't spoken to them in ages. And my parents...I have no idea where they are anymore. I used to try to stay in touch with them, but it's difficult. I gave them a cell phone once, but they sold it for drug money." She pressed her lips together. They were trembling a tiny bit. "So now that you know the truth, will you be my maid of honor?"

After what she'd just heard, she couldn't let her discomfort and torn emotions get in the way. "Yes. I'll be your maid of honor."

Angela flung her arms around Michelle and literally lifted her off the floor. "Thank you," she whispered. She set Michelle back on her feet. "Sorry about that. I got a little carried away."

"No problem," Michelle said, fake smile in place, but her voice flat.

"You look and sound so enthusiastic. Was it the hug? Or is the arranged marriage part still bothering you?"

"Neither," Michelle lied.

Angela tipped her head to the side. "I'm sorry if Tage's proposal to me hurt you somehow. Please tell me if it does. I'll be more respectful of your feelings if I know the truth."

"Okay, yes. Maybe. Maybe it does hurt a little."

Angela's posture wilted. She looked genuinely regretful. "I'm so sorry. About yesterday. About asking you to be my maid of honor. If it's going to be too difficult, don't feel obligated—"

"No, I said I would do it, and I will."

Angela didn't speak for several seconds. But her eyes teared up. "You're a very generous and kind person. A much better person than me. Tonight he's having a dinner party. I'm meeting his family. Will you come?"

Ugh. "S-s-sure."

"I'm so sorry for dragging you into this. Please tell me the truth, were you dating him? I swear I didn't know. You told me you weren't seeing him, so I took you for your word. But I thought I saw something between you two, chemistry."

"No, I wasn't dating him. But I thought there was something between us, too. I haven't spoken to him in . . . a couple of weeks." Getting anxious to get to work, Michelle fiddled with her purse strap. "Your engagement came as . . . quite a shock."

"It was a shock to me, too." Her expression on the dim side, she stared down at the huge ring on her finger. "I hope I'm doing the right thing."

"I hope so, too." Michelle glanced at her watch. "We'd better get to work. It's almost ten after."

"Oh damn. Sorry. After what I've done to you already, the last thing I need to do is get you in trouble." Angela shoved open the door. "By the way, I'll be dropping to part-time after the wedding."

"You are?"

"Yes. And I'm going to request that all my bigger clients be turned over to you."

"Wow, that would be nice. If it happens."

"Oh, it will. Trust me." Angela gave her head a firm shake. Then she reached out and squeezed Michelle's hand. "At least that's one thing I can do to help you out. We'll work together on the transition. I'm giving notice today."

That was a nice surprise. A great one, actually. Angela had some of the biggest clients in the company. Taking over those accounts would mean she could get a raise, and a promotion to senior account representative. "Thank you."

"Thank *you*."

Absolutely dumbfounded by Angela's shift from coldhearted, selfish client-shark to generous and giving friend, Michelle followed Angela into the office.

If this morning was any indicator, today was going to be an interesting day.

And tonight... probably a total nightmare.

She'd done it, turned things around. Damn, she was good. She'd almost lost control of the situation. But her hard work and dogged determination had paid off. Soon she would be a member of the Gryffon family. The rest would be a cakewalk.

One week. That was it. Seven days. That soon she would have what she wanted. The world would be in her hands.

* * *

Talen's day was shitty. He had woken late, gotten a flat tire on the way to work, and had learned his biggest client was pulling the plug and going to a competitor.

But that was nothing compared to having missed those precious few minutes with Michelle in the elevator. Despite the flat tire, he'd arrived at work in time to watch her walk from her car into the building. Everything in him wanted to follow her in and catch her before it was too late. But he didn't do it. She wanted him to leave her alone. It was the least he could do.

The rest of the day, from that point forward, had gone downhill. And now he was with his future wife. He didn't want to be sitting here with her, Angela. He wished it was Michelle sitting across from him, discussing the plans for their wedding over dinner.

Angela was happy, excited. He could see it in her face, her eyes. "Michelle is going to be my maid of honor," she announced.

Talen's gut twisted. Just the sound of her name sent a wave of regret and despair racing through him. "Really?"

"Yes. She's my closest friend." Angela tipped her head to the side. "I thought you would be happy. You don't look so glad. Don't you want her at the wedding?"

"Yes, of course I do."

"Are you sure?"

"Um-hm."

"Okay. I'm glad you said that because I invited her tonight. She's coming." Angela reached across the table, slipped her hand into his. It felt small and delicate, and a little flicker of protectiveness ignited within him. She sensed he had feelings for Michelle. Perhaps telling her the truth would be the right thing to do.

No, what purpose would it serve? It might make her uneasy.

It might cause a problem with their friendship. Better if he kept his mouth shut.

"We're going dress shopping together, too," his future wife told him as she lifted her glass with her other hand.

"That's good."

"I want to wear a formal gown. White."

"You can wear whatever you want," he said.

"Will you wear a tuxedo?"

Ugh. He didn't give a damn about the details of the wedding. But Drako had warned him that this stuff meant a lot to a woman. He should let her have whatever she wanted. Flowers. Tuxedos. Fancy, frilly dresses. Anything. "I'll wear a tuxedo if it will make you happy." He would be content to keep things simple. Simple was good.

She set down her glass and picked up her fork. "I want this wedding to be everything I dreamed about when I was a little girl." Clearly she wasn't thinking simple.

"Then it will be. Whatever you want."

"Thank you." She beamed a brilliant smile at him.

"No need to thank me. I want you to be happy."

"I believe I will be. I genuinely do."

"Good."

If only he felt the same way.

If only.

He checked his watch.

"She'll be here at seven," Angela said.

Seven o'clock. In less than a half hour, he would see her. Somehow he would have to keep his hands off her, and his head straight.

Drako. He needed Drako to get here pronto.

16

Two blue lines. There were two effing blue lines.

Two.

Not one.

One was good.

Two ... two was soooo not good.

How the hell had this happened?

Technically, Michelle knew how it happened. Everyone over the age of five knew where babies came from. But she didn't understand how Tage's DNA had met with her DNA to produce the little person who was now growing inside her. They had had sex. Once. Unprotected sex. Almost two weeks ago. But he'd pulled out. That should have kept her safe.

Should have.

If it weren't for the fact that she hadn't been touched by another man in ages, she would have sworn he couldn't be the father. But it had to be him.

Two blue lines. *Ohmygod.*

Now what? What the hell was she going to do?

Tage deserved to know he would be a father in roughly nine months. But he was marrying someone else in less than a week. And that someone else didn't deserve to be hurt. Angela had already given notice at work and had already turned over all her big clients, most of them to Michelle. Angela had even talked to an agent about putting her condo up for sale.

Shit, what was she going to do?

Abortion?

No. She just couldn't.

Adoption?

Her stomach lurched.

How could she give away her child?

She wrapped her arms around her waist and slowly sank to the floor. If this child was born, everything would be changed. Everything. Her future. Tage's future—he would be a father. Angela's future—she would be a stepmother.

Dammit.

Abortion.

Adoption.

No.

This was her baby. Her child. She would raise him or her, love him or her.

Tage. Angela. They needed to know. She had to tell them both. Tage first. Then Angela. But wasn't it better if she saw her doctor before she told anyone, just to make sure? Maybe the tests were wrong—all five. Maybe she had something else that mimicked a pregnancy? She could only hope. Wasn't it awfully early for a positive test? And what were the chances that he'd impregnated her when they'd had sex once, and he'd pulled out? A million to one? A billion?

Oh hell, who was she kidding? She was pregnant. The first test hadn't lied. Neither had the second, third, or fourth.

Hands trembling, she picked up her phone and dialed her

doctor's phone number. After she made her appointment, she would go to Angela and Tage's engagement party and pretend nothing was wrong.

By seven o'clock, Talen was in absolute misery. His future wife, on the other hand, seemed to be in heaven. She was engaged in a lively conversation with Rin, Drako's wife. Drako and Malek were at the bar, getting themselves a couple of drinks to ease the tedium. Lei was with Malek, quiet, reserved, and still a little pale.

Michelle was standing next to her, trying to look comfortable when she clearly did not feel that way.

He checked on Angela. She was still jabbering away. Michelle, on the other hand, looked like she wanted to crawl into a hole somewhere and hide.

He went to her.

"I'm sorry about this," he whispered, trying to pretend he didn't want to take her into his arms and kiss her until she couldn't speak.

"I would say it isn't your fault, because my being invited here isn't. But the rest of it is your fault. So, I'll accept your apology. Maybe." She lifted her eyes to his. Dammit, did she have to look so fucking beautiful? Did she?

"I'm glad for that, then," he said.

Her gaze jerking away from his, she whispered, "I needed to speak with you anyway. In private." She nodded toward Angela and Rin. "I don't want Angela to hear what I have to say."

"Okay. I'll call you later and arrange for a time—"

"No," she cut him off. "I need to talk to you tonight. Now. Right now. Before I lose the nerve." She hugged herself, hands grasping her arms tightly.

Could it be she'd had a change of heart? Was she wishing she had accepted his proposal after all? If that were true, what would he do? Breaking his engagement with Angela would no doubt hurt her. She'd told him she had made some changes at work. She was selling her home.

And yet...he could have Michelle as his wife. Sweet little Michelle.

"Please. It won't take more than a minute," she muttered.

He glanced left. He glanced right. Now both his brothers and their wives were clustered around Angela. She probably wouldn't see them leave the room if they were quiet.

He had to hear what Michelle wanted to tell him.

He jerked his head toward the back exit. "This way."

Michelle nodded and followed him. He pushed out the rear exit, stepping into the cool, dimming evening. The sun had already sunk below the western horizon, but streaks of salmon still stained the sky, broken by dark indigo clouds. The dim light made Michelle's skin look silvery, iridescent as she turned to face him.

"I have something I need to tell you." Her eyes dropped to her hands, clasped together in front of her body. She visibly swallowed.

What the hell was going on? "What is it?"

"I'm...Oh God." She staggered back, clapped her hands over her mouth.

"What's wrong? Are you sick?"

"Yes." Whirling around, she staggered several steps away, bent at the waist, and vomited.

He hurried to her side, gathered her hair in his fist, and wrapped an arm around her shuddering body for support as she heaved a second time. From the corner of his eye, he caught sight of the back door opening. A blade of light cut through the darkness to their right. Then the door slammed shut again.

As he held her little quaking, retching body, an almost overwhelming wave of protectiveness crashed through him. She was ill. What was she even doing here? Did she have anyone to care for her? Someone should drive her home and make sure she was okay.

When the gagging and retching stopped, she pushed out of his arms and lifted tear-filled eyes to him. "Sorry."

"No need to apologize. You're ill. You should go home."

"I'm not apologizing for that. I'm apologizing for ruining your wedding, your plans, your marriage."

"What are you talking about?" he asked, not following her. "You haven't ruined anything."

"I'm pregnant."

It took a few moments for the words to strike home, much like it took for pain to set in after taking a hard kick in the gut. But when they did, he was just as dizzy and breathless.

She added, "I thought you would want to know. I'm keeping the child. I'm guessing you'll want me to get an abortion, but... I can't do that. It goes against everything I believe in."

A million thoughts raced through his mind. She was pregnant. Pregnant! With his child. It had to be his child, didn't it?

He didn't want to ask. Only assholes asked that question, but he needed to be sure. How could he put it so he wouldn't sound like a fucking jerk?

"It's yours," she said as if reading his mind. "I haven't had sex with anyone but you in a long, long time." She was shaking even more now, and he ached to gather her into his arms and tell her that he was happy about her news. Ecstatic.

Suddenly a huge weight seemed to lift off his shoulders. He wouldn't have to marry Angela now. Surely this meant Michelle would marry him. She had to. She was carrying his child.

"Michelle." He reached for her.

She scurried away, pressing her back against the brick building. "Tage, I've thought long and hard about this. You shouldn't break your engagement with Angela."

What the hell? He stepped toward her. "But—"

She lifted both hands, holding them palm out, to keep him back. "Angela wants to marry you."

"Yes, but—"

"She's *counting* on marrying you."

Dammit, he knew that, too. He did. But he didn't want to marry Angela. He wanted to marry this beautiful, sweet, wonderful woman in front of him now. This was the woman he wanted to vow to protect and cherish. This was the woman he wanted to wake up next to every morning. This was the woman he wanted to be the mother of his children.

"Michelle, I wanted to marry you from the start. It's you I wanted. It's you I still want now."

Michelle was in hell. There was no other way to describe it. What horrible thing had she done to deserve this?

She was pregnant.

She was alone.

She was terrified and confused.

The father of her child seemed eager to abandon his plans to marry another woman so he could marry her. That was all fine and dandy except for the fact that she wasn't sure she wanted to marry him, and she felt awful about him breaking his engagement to Angela. Angela had very compelling reasons for marrying him. And she knew what she was getting into. And she was okay with marrying a man she didn't love.

Michelle, on the other hand, wasn't sure she could say the same thing.

What the hell was she going to do?

The honorable thing would be for her to have the child and then turn him or her over to the father and his wife to raise. That way Tage would have the child he seemed to be so anxious to have. And she would be free of the burden of raising a child on her own.

Yes, that would be a good and honorable thing to do. But

the thought of turning over her baby to another woman...to not be able to hold and comfort him when he was crying...to miss all those special moments in his life...to hear him call someone else mommy.

Her stomach clenched. She was going to vomit again. She was still in the earliest weeks of pregnancy. If the nausea was from her pregnancy (which she hoped it was not), she didn't want to think about the remaining thirty-something weeks she had ahead.

As bile surged up her throat, she spun away from Tage. He wrapped a protective arm around her middle, supporting her gently as she retched until her eyes were watering. When she was through, she moved away from him again. It was too hard to think when he was touching her. Too hard to be objective.

"Have you seen a doctor?" he asked, sounding worried. He handed her a cloth, and she accepted it.

"Not yet." She dabbed at her mouth. "My appointment is next week."

"Have you been sick like this for long?"

"Just the last couple of days. I think I have a touch of the flu or food poisoning or something."

"But you haven't seen a doctor?"

"I've been eating crackers and drinking lots of fluids."

He grunted. "You'll see my doctor. As soon as possible. Come with me." He grabbed her arm.

"What? Wait." She yanked on her arm, but he didn't let go. "Where are we going?"

He tilted his head toward the parking lot. "I'm taking you home. My home. I don't want you to be alone. My brothers' wives will care for you until we can get a doctor to look at you in the morning."

"That's not necessary. I can go home—"

"I said, you're going to my home."

His tone was like barbs raking over her nerves. How dare he try to tell her what to do after everything he'd put her through? "Now, wait a minute!" She dug in her heels and crossed her arms over her chest.

He took one look at her, growled, literally, and then scooped her off her feet and carried her around the side of the building.

She had a healthy respect for her condition, so she didn't physically fight him. But she called him every curse word she knew. Then she made up a few. But she received absolutely no response. None.

He plopped her in the passenger seat of yet another sleek black car. As he circled around to the driver's side, she hit the power locks, locking him out. But the locks clicked open before he'd reached his door.

Stupid keyless entry.

"You're being an asshole," she yelled as he folded his big frame into the driver's seat.

"Am I?"

"Yes. I said I didn't want to go to your house. This is kidnapping."

"Is it?"

What was with the effing questions? "Yes, and you know it."

He merely shrugged and, ignoring his ringing cell phone, steered out of the parking spot. Within seconds, the car was zooming down the road, toward his house, wherever that was.

His phone rang a second time.

"That's probably Angela," she told him. "You kind of abandoned her. At her party. You seem to make a habit of that kind of thing."

"I'll talk to her later."

Jerk.

Asshole.

Michelle decided to try a new tactic. She clamped her mouth

shut and sat there fuming in silence. Once he took her to his house, she decided, she'd wait for him to leave, and then she'd call a taxi and go home.

If nothing else, tonight gave her a little glimpse into what might have been if she had been foolish enough to marry this man. He took bossy to a whole new level. She wished Angela best of luck dealing with him for the next thirty to forty years.

About twenty minutes after he had dumped her into the car, the vehicle turned down what appeared to be a private drive-way cutting through a patch of dense woods. The drive wound between towering trees and thick shrubs, then curved into an arc in front of a huge stone and wood house.

The place was gorgeous.

But she didn't say a word. Not when he parked. Or when he ran around to get her door just as she was pushing it open. Or when he escorted her up the walk toward the house, acting as if she was about to collapse at any moment.

She had a little touch of the stomach flu, for crying out loud. She was not mortally injured.

His phone rang again. If she were Angela, she'd be really angry by now. He was going to catch it from two women tonight.

Well-deserved.

She almost chuckled as she imagined him getting a tongue lashing from Angela. When she wanted to be, Angela could be a real bitch.

That was probably what he needed in a wife.

"This way. Once I get you settled, I'll deal with everyone else." Placing a hand on her back, he steered her toward the stairs. "Do you feel well enough to climb stairs?"

She didn't speak.

Unfortunately, he took her silence as a no, and once again, she found herself being hauled off her feet and carried like a child.

"I can walk, dammit," she snapped.

"You didn't say so." Was that a little touch of amusement she heard in his voice? Better not be.

"I'm mad. I don't want to talk to you."

He didn't put her down until he reached the top of the staircase. When he did, she whirled around and smacked him. Hard.

"Don't do that again," she yelled.

His lips twitched, and something sparkled in his eyes. He extended an arm, motioning down the hall. "Your room is this way. I'll get you settled and then go get my brothers and the girls."

She had no intention of getting settled. At least, not until she was at home, in her own bed. That sounded really good right now. The stress of being upset and sick had taken its toll. She was starting to feel run-down and weary.

He opened a door and preceded her into a large bedroom furnished with comfortable-looking, solid, well-crafted furnishings. The wood floor was covered with a plush white oriental rug of some kind. It felt very thick under her feet as she tromped to the bed and plopped down.

The mattress was thick, the coverlet smooth. The room looked expensive and luxurious. This was the lifestyle Angela would marry into. She was going to be very happy. No more worries about being poor and hungry for that girl.

She smoothed her hand over the cover.

"Before I leave I'll bring you something to drink and maybe a little snack. You need to keep up your strength and not become dehydrated," Tage said as he hurried about the room, closing drapes and pulling open the closet doors. "Let me see if I can find you something comfortable to sleep in."

"No need for that," she said.

"Oh. Do you prefer sleeping nude?"

Her face heated instantly as his gaze met hers. "No."

In the walk-in closet he plunged his hand into a drawer.

"How about a T-shirt? This one is big enough to reach your thighs." He held up a ginormous shirt. It was big enough to fit two of her in it.

"That's fine."

"Good. Go ahead and change for bed. There are fresh towels in the bathroom and some new toothbrushes on the counter. Then I'll get you something to eat."

She waved him back, before he'd made it to the door. "Maybe the snack could wait until tomorrow? I'm getting tired."

His brows pinched. "I won't keep you up for long. I just want to make sure you don't get dehydrated."

Off he went.

She looked at the shirt in her hands, then at the big, extremely comfortable-looking bed stretched out behind her. And then she glanced at the clock.

It was almost ten. It was no wonder she was tired. Lately, she'd been konking out at nine o'clock. She didn't have to work tomorrow. It was Saturday. Would it be such a bad idea to spend the night here and then go home in the morning?

Maybe not.

As long as he kept his hands to himself.

17

His hand was running up her thigh, and Michelle squirmed as her need grew. She was hot. Burning up. Her need was like a fever, raging through her body, making it tight. Wet. Sighing, she rolled onto her back, offering him full access to every part, her stomach, her breasts, between her legs. His touch was gentle, patient, an exploration. A soft caress. It glided up from her stomach to her breast. She moaned as his hand cupped it, his palm warming her nipple.

Yes. Take me.

His hand moved to her other breast. She felt her spine arching, lifting her breasts up.

"You're mine," she heard him whisper. "Mine. Forever."

Oh shit. She wasn't dreaming.

She blinked open her eyes.

The room was dark, but she could see him. He was lying beside her, his head propped up on one hand, elbow bent, the other resting on her right breast.

"What the hell?" She jerked. When he didn't move his hand, she knocked it away.

"I'm sorry. Did I startle you?" he asked.

Was that a chuckle she heard? He was laughing?

"You were fondling me while I was sleeping, you sicko."

"I thought you were awake."

"Bullshit."

His brows lifted. So did the corners of his mouth. He thought this was funny, eh. She would show him funny.

"You're sick!" Grabbing the covers and holding them against her chest, she sat up and stabbed a finger toward the door. "Get. Out."

"I'd rather not."

"Too bad," she snapped.

"This is my bed."

"Fine. Then I'll leave." Taking the covers with her, she pushed off the mattress and hurried toward the door, tripping over the blankets and sheets as she ran. She made it to within a few feet of the exit before he grabbed her around the waist and yanked her back until her backside was flush to his front side.

She froze. There was a very large, very prominent protuberance poking at her buttocks.

"You...nude?"

"Yes, of course. This is my home. My bed. I don't sleep in my clothes."

Wow, that poke felt kind of good. So did having him hold her like that, feeling his heat seeping in through her pores, flooding her system.

She wriggled, trying to get away from him. He released her, but only after she fought him for several seconds. "You didn't tell me this was your bed. I assumed it was a guest room," she snapped as she stomped toward the door.

"Ah, I understand the confusion then. I couldn't give you a guest room. All of our bedrooms are currently in use. And since you were ill, I didn't think you would want to sleep on a couch. You would have too far to go to get to a bathroom."

At the exit, she whirled around to say, "Well, isn't that kind of you, thinking of my comfort." Her gaze snapped to his groin before jerking up to his face. Even in the dark, he looked magnificent. And his cock...his erect cock...

His lips curled into a wider grin. "Yes, it was kind of me."

Cocky bastard. He caught her looking down there. *Don't do it again. Don't.* She felt her eyes drifting south. "So what stopped you from taking the couch?" she asked his belly button.

He paused, then nodded, his expression sobering. "Selfishness. I came in here to get a blanket, and you looked so warm and soft. I thought I would join you for just a minute, but you cuddled up to me, and it felt so damn good, I didn't want to leave. And to be honest, I did try to get up, but you held on to me."

"I cuddled up to you?" she asked, recalling, with some horror, little bits of her dream. Had she done anything to encourage him? Had she writhed against him, moaned? Opened her legs? Begged him to take her? "You're lying."

"No, I'm not." His gaze flicked to her breasts, which were covered at the moment but still tingling from his touch. "And you know it."

"I do not." Dammit, her face was burning with shame. How could she be such a hussy? "I was asleep. I don't know what I was doing while I was sleeping." The blanket was falling. She yanked it up higher, clutching it in her fists. "The bottom line is, what you did was totally out of line. I am a guest. Do you sneak into the room every time you have a guest and fondle their breasts while they're sleeping?"

"Aha! You remember me fondling your breasts. See? You were awake."

"No, I was not. That was just...a lucky guess." It was a good thing the lights were out. He couldn't see how red her face must be.

"Riiiight. A lucky guess. And if you want to know, I do tend to fondle my guests' breasts. And they generally love it."

"That was a stupid question."

He chuckled.

She didn't want to like the way the deep sound filled the room. Or how it vibrated through her body. But she did. Despite the fact that he was slightly creepy, climbing into bed with her, nude, messing with her while she slept, she couldn't help noticing how glorious his body was, how insanely gorgeous his face was, how his eyes sparkled when she said something that amused him.

He was too sexy. He was dangerous.

Still standing at the door, she cleared her throat. "I'm feeling better. I should go home now."

"No."

"Yes."

She flipped on a light.

Mistake.

There he was, all six feet something of him. Now well illuminated. His chest. That stomach. The shoulders. That... thick, hard cock.

"Like what you see?" he asked, his smile cranked up to full wattage.

"You're an arrogant ass."

"It was an honest question."

"It was not. Besides, it doesn't matter what I like or don't like. You're marrying Angela. I shouldn't be seeing you nude. And you shouldn't be lying in bed with me."

"Well, Michelle, there's a little problem with that plan. Angela broke our engagement last night."

She shook a finger at him. "She probably got mad at you for leaving the party. Those kinds of things tend to piss off a girl. She'll change her mind in the morning."

He shrugged. "Maybe." He wasn't looking very upset about the broken engagement.

"Most definitely."

Their gazes tangled and a suspicion flashed through her mind. "You didn't tell her about the baby."

"Of course I did."

"You asshole." She tossed her hands in the air. The blankets fell to the floor, but she didn't care. She was too furious to give a damn about them. "How could you do that to her?"

"She deserved to know the truth."

"You have no idea how much you've hurt her."

"Would lying to her be better?" He didn't wait for her to answer. Instead, he continued, "You were going to tell her eventually, correct? She would find out. Wasn't it better for her to know that her 'best friend' was pregnant with her husband's child before she said her vows?"

Dammit, he was right. She sagged against the closed door. "But that wasn't how I wanted her to find out."

"I'm sorry if I took that away from you." Moving closer, he reached for her hand. "I apologize for that much. But I won't apologize for giving her the chance to know what the hell she was getting into by marrying me."

"You're happy she broke the engagement."

"Like I said last night, I wanted to marry you from the start." His fingers curled around her hand.

"Well, don't count your chickens yet, buddy. I didn't say I would marry you."

His gaze flicked to her stomach. "But the child. You have thought about the child, haven't you?"

"Yes. The child deserves to grow up in a home that is safe and happy."

He tugged on her hand, coaxing her back toward the bed. "With two parents, a mother and a father," he continued for her.

She planted her feet. There was no way he was going to get her back in that bed. No fricking way. "Safe and happy doesn't necessarily mean with both parents, together. I'm not sure you and I can live together without killing each other."

"Then why don't we give it a trial run?"

She laughed. "That's a stupid idea."

"No, it's not. Millions of couples move in together before they get married, to make sure they can live together."

"Not this girl. I don't shack up with men. No."

Tage audibly sighed. He went to the bed, sat. His dick wasn't at full staff anymore, but even at its current state, it was impressive. "Come here."

"I would rather not."

"Please."

"No."

He tipped his head and gave her a pleading look, and she bit her lip. Damn, did he have some compelling come-hither eyes. "I promise I won't touch you. I just want to talk."

Her willpower was weakening. Not to mention, she was getting tired. It was sometime in the middle of the night. Her internal body clock was reminding her of that fact.

"Fine." She grabbed the blanket before shuffling over to the bed. When she sat, she made sure there was a safe distance between them.

He shoved his fingers through his hair. As he did that, his shoulder and arm muscles flexed. They were really nice. He was a beautiful man. Beautiful, but also more than a little overbearing. Controlling. Could she spend the rest of her life with him? She honestly couldn't say.

"You are pregnant with my child. Maybe I haven't presented myself as the most stable and dependable man to you. I did that because I wanted you to know what to expect. I'm not perfect. Actually I'm as far from perfect as a man can get. But I am trying to do the right thing. For you. For our child."

She pulled the blanket tighter around her. "There are so many things about this situation I don't understand."

"I get that."

"Do you really?" When he nodded, she asked again, "Really?"

"Sure. From your perspective I probably look like a complete ass."

"Well..." At his don't-lie-to-me look, she confessed, "Okay, yes. Why did you ask me to marry you, then turn around and ask Angela practically the next day?"

He stared down at his hands for several minutes. "I need to get married."

"Need to?" That explained him going to Angela after she refused. But it didn't explain everything. "Why?"

"It's a family thing. There are certain expectations my brothers and I must abide by. One of them is to be married. My two brothers have both taken wives. I'm the youngest, the last."

"This sounds like the plot of a fairy tale or a romance novel," she said. "What happens if you don't? Will you lose an inheritance?"

"The consequences are a little more serious than that. To be honest, if they weren't, I would have been willing to wait for you."

She didn't know what to make of this. He had to marry someone for some reason. And quickly. "What consequences?"

"It's complicated."

He wasn't going to explain it all, but she had the gist. "So what you're saying is if I don't marry you, you'll marry someone else."

"No, I'm saying that somehow I have to convince you to marry me. Angela was easy. She wanted money, stability. That was something I could promise her."

"Well, that's going to be one hell of a challenge. Because I won't marry just for stability. I want more. I want everything. Companionship. Friendship. Affection. Love." She yawned, blinked. Her eyes were dry and scratchy, her body heavy.

"That's okay. I'm up for the challenge." He flashed a heart-stopping smile as he scooted back until he was reclined against the headboard. He patted the pillow next to him. "But I think you need some rest. Come here. I promise I won't wake you again."

She sent him a squinty glare. "I don't think I trust you."

He chuckled, and the way her body responded to that sound made her question whether she could trust herself. "I swear I won't lay a hand on you." He yawned. "I'm tired, too." Reaching up, he turned off the lamp. Then, not waiting for her, he slid down under the covers.

She sat there in the dark for a few minutes, listening to his slow, steady breathing. The longer she sat there, the better that bed looked. Finally, she could deny herself no longer. She crawled up to her spot, pulled the covers back, marveled for a moment about the gorgeous hunk of manliness lying next to her, then covered herself up and closed her eyes.

His warmth felt so good. Comforting. The sound of his deep breaths lulled her to sleep.

Yes. At last. He had her where she belonged. His Michelle. His wife. His.

He inhaled deeply, drawing in the sweet scent of her skin. He had promised he wouldn't touch her. Impossible. But he would wait until she was asleep.

She whimpered, and a flash of heat ignited deep inside his body. Damn, he hoped he could wait until she fell asleep. His palms burned. His blood simmered.

She was right there, within reach. Her silken hair. Her smooth, satiny skin. Her soft, warm little body. What man could resist?

His hand stirred. He slid it across the sheet and let a single fingertip graze her arm.

"Do that again, and I'll kick you so hard, you'll be singing soprano for a month," she snapped.

He swallowed a chuckle. His wife was a fiery little thing. If someone had asked him a month ago whether he liked a woman like her, he probably would have denied it. But now that he had gotten to know Michelle, he couldn't imagine her being any other way. She was perfect. The perfect wife. The perfect mother for his children. Stronger than he'd thought. Independent. Determined.

And committed. To her beliefs. To her morals. And soon to him.

When her breathing grew slow and deep, he pulled her little body against his. Yes, she fit there perfectly. His cock hardened. His balls tightened. He bit his lip, closed his eyes, and prayed she would sleep for many hours.

18

Birdsong.

The scent of a man, fresh out of the shower.

The cool, smooth sheets caressing her skin.

The mouthwatering smell of bacon.

Mmmmm, bacon.

Michelle stretched. Her body was still stiff and heavy. She dragged up her eyelids and checked the bed first. Tage was gone. Where he'd been sleeping the sheets were now cool. His pillow still had the indentation where his head had been resting. She grabbed it, pulled it to her chest, and cradled it to herself.

Last night had been so strange. She'd gone to an engagement party, thinking she would be celebrating her friend's marriage to the father of her child. Instead, she'd vomited. In front of him. Then he'd more or less kidnapped her, left her at his place and returned to the party, returned and fondled her as she slept, then somehow convinced her to not only stay the rest of the night but actually consider marrying him.

She'd gone insane.

Hormones. It had to be the hormones.

She needed to touch base with reality.

Her stomach rumbled. Saliva flooded her mouth.

After she ate some bacon.

Once again, she stretched her stiff, sore muscles as she sat up. Then she scooped up her clothes on her way to the bathroom. Ten minutes later, she'd vomited, showered, brushed her teeth, did what she could to make herself presentable, and dressed in last night's clothes, minus the used panties. Those she tucked into her purse.

She headed downstairs feeling pretty decent, well rested... and hungry. She was roughly halfway down the staircase, when Tage rounded the corner. He looked up, saw her, gave her one of those grins that made her knees weak, and bounded up the steps, taking three at a time.

"How are you feeling?" he asked as he caught her arm as if she was about to collapse.

"I'm fine." Her stomach rumbled loudly, and she clapped a hand over it. "Starving."

"Good. I have breakfast." He wrapped an arm around her waist. It was odd, having someone treat her like she was so frail. She halfheartedly tried to move away from him, but he tightened his hold.

Together, they slowly made their way to the kitchen. It was empty.

He motioned to the French doors at the rear of the kitchen. "Your breakfast is waiting for you outside. On the deck. I thought you might enjoy some fresh air."

"That's very thoughtful. Thanks." Letting him steer her with a hand on her waist, she meandered through the spacious kitchen to the doors. Outside, the sky was a brilliant blue, cloudless. Birds chattered in a nearby tree. The deck was large, multilevel. The table sat at one end, covered with a wood gazebo structure. And a wall of trees circled a well-manicured lawn. At the back of the property shimmered a pond.

It was, in one word, gorgeous.

He pulled out her chair for her.

Sitting, she took in the spread as he circled around to sit across from her. Bowls of fruit, platters of bacon, eggs, and toast sat on the table. At her place sat a glass of orange juice and another of water. "This is some breakfast," she said.

"I read that you will feel better if you eat a good breakfast. With lots of protein."

She giggled. He was trying hard to please her. That was for sure. Clearly he was determined to prove that he was good husband material. One breakfast would only go so far. But it was a good start.

He immediately grabbed the platter of scrambled eggs and started loading up her plate. "The doctor will be coming by the house at eleven. And Rin and Lei would like to take you shopping later. I thought you might like to spend some time with them."

There they were again, Rin and Lei. The sisters did seem nice, if a bit reserved. They didn't have a lot to say last night when she'd briefly met them at the party, which made her a little uneasy. "That's very nice, but I don't see any reason why I need to see a doctor this morning. The nausea is nothing, probably a little bug I caught. It's too soon for morning sickness. I'm fine. I have an appointment with my own physician in a week. Plus, I would like to go home, change my clothes, shower."

"You can shower here," he offered. "While you're cleaning up, I can run over to your place and get you some clothes."

"Why would you do that? I mean, that's nice of you to offer, but I was assuming I would be going home this morning. I have things to do—"

"What things?" he asked as he dropped several strips of bacon on her plate.

"I need to do laundry."

"I'll help you. You shouldn't be carrying anything heavy."

"I can manage a laundry basket. It isn't that heavy. I don't own very many clothes. And none of them are made out of plate steel or anything."

"I don't mind helping." He spooned some fruit onto her plate.

She touched his wrist, stopping him from putting any more food on her plate. It was loaded enough. "It isn't necessary, Tage."

"Okay." He dumped some eggs on his own plate, a big mountain of them. "How long will it take for you to finish?"

"Why?"

"Like I said, I thought you might like to go out with the girls. And I wanted to take you to lunch first."

She was feeling a smidge crowded. Holding up her hands, palms facing him, she said, "You're getting too pushy."

"Oh. Damn. Okay. I've got the message." He stared down at his plate for a moment. "I thought you'd appreciate the thought."

Was he pouting? No. Disappointed? Yes, that was it. Disappointed.

"I'm sorry. I have a routine. I like my routine."

"No reason to apologize. I'm the one invading your life," he said to his plate.

"You aren't invading it." Actually, he kind of was, but she couldn't stand seeing him look so sad.

His lips curled slightly. "I'm glad you feel that way." He tipped his head toward the table. "Finish up, and then I'll run you home."

"Thank you." She took another bite of bacon. It was crisp, just the way she liked it. Salty. So good. She took another. And another. And several more until she couldn't eat another bite. Leaning back, she placed her hand on her stomach. "That was insanely delicious. Please tell whoever cooked it I enjoyed everything immensely."

"You just told him yourself."

"You cooked all of this?"

"Yes."

She just might be in love. "Wow, I'm impressed. I never would've thought a man like you would know his way around a kitchen."

"A man like me?" His smile amped up to full wattage. "What kind of man is that? I'm curious."

"A man who works a lot, makes good money, doesn't have to cook for himself."

"Hmmm. You're in for a few surprises, I think."

"Good ones, I hope."

"All good." Standing, he set his hands on the back of her chair. "Ready?"

"Yes. I just need to grab my purse upstairs." As she stood, he pulled her chair out for her. Then he led her through the house and, once she had collected her purse, outside to the car with a hand resting on her back. Like a gentleman, he opened her door for her, then waited until she was seated, before slamming it and rounding the front of the car to take his own seat. The sun was climbing quite high in the eastern sky as their car turned onto the road, roaring toward her house.

She stared out the window most of the drive, watching the world hum by. Businesses, schools, houses. As she sat there, she wondered what her life would be like in a year. By then she would be a mother. A mother. A little quiver of panic raced through her.

She was going to have a child.

Her life was about to change, whether she married Tage or not. And that change was going to be huge. Another wave of panic crashed through her.

What if she wasn't ready? What if she didn't know what to do? What if there was something wrong with her baby?

And what about work? What if she had complications and couldn't work for a while? Disability wouldn't be enough.

"You've been very quiet," he said, glancing her way as they sat at a traffic light. They weren't far from her place now. Within a mile.

"I'm just...a little tired. Someone woke me in the middle of the night," she said, smiling to let him know she was teasing. A part of her couldn't wait to be home, alone. She needed to think, to make plans, to consider all her options.

The other part, the scared part, wanted to tell Tage to turn the car around and take her back to that big house in the woods. It had been so peaceful there.

She'd felt safe. Protected. Cared for.

As he pulled up in her parking lot, she unclipped her seat belt and hugged her purse to her chest. "Thank you," she said. "For breakfast."

"You're welcome." He motioned for her to stay put, then hopped out of the car and jogged around to her side. As she climbed out, she turned to step away from the vehicle, but he moved, blocking her in. Smiling up at him, she repeated, "Thanks again for the delicious breakfast. And for taking care of me last night when I was sick. I wasn't happy you basically kidnapped me, but I can see now that your intentions were genuine. Nobody has ever done anything like that for me before."

He cupped her cheek. "Come back to my place."

"I will. Sometime. Soon."

"No. Today. Now." His gaze flicked to her mouth.

"I can't."

He leaned closer, angling his head until his mouth was so close to hers, his sweet breath warmed her lips and her head spun. If he kissed her, he just might convince her to go back to his place. He might convince her to do a lot of other things, too.

She placed her hands on his chest, intending to push him back. He didn't budge. "Tage, I need some space, some time."

"You need rest," he suggested, his mouth still hovering dangerously close to hers.

"That, too, yes."

"You can rest at my house."

"For some reason, I don't think I would get much rest there."

He looped an arm around her waist and pulled her flush against him. "I guarantee you wouldn't leave my bed."

A blast of heat rocketed through her at the flames she saw flickering in his eyes. "Yes, but that doesn't mean I would get any sleep."

"True. But can you blame me?" He angled his head lower, letting his mouth gently caress hers. The light touch sent another wave of erotic need raging through her. He growled. Literally. The sound was low and rumbly and made her knees wobble. "I want to do things to your sweet little body. So many things. Some things I shouldn't want to do."

The air left her lungs. A flurry of images flashed through her mind, all of them bone-meltingly hot. "Tage," she heard herself mutter.

"Tell me to leave," he said as he sprinkled kisses along her jaw.

She opened her mouth but all that came out was a whimper.

"Tell me to leave now." One of his hands skimmed up her torso, fingertips grazing the side of her breast. Her spine arched, pushing her breast against him.

A growly groan vibrated against her neck as he flicked his tongue over the sensitive skin just below her ear.

Ohmygod, she wanted this man. A moan slipped from her lips, and she felt her bones softening. Heat was pounding through her now, waves of need. She curled her hands into fists, gathering the material of his shirt in them, and tried to summon up the strength to push away.

She couldn't. She couldn't do it.

His arm swept under her legs, and within a heartbeat she was cradled against him. The world bounced as he carried her up to her building. She curled an arm around his neck, handing him her keys when he reached the door. The instant they were inside, he rushed toward her bedroom. He eased her down onto the bed and trapped her between his outstretched arms. Not that she wanted to go anywhere. If anything, she wanted to pull him down, feel his weight on her, feel his heat blazing through her body.

"I want you so damn bad," he muttered, jaw tight, eyes dark. "You have to tell me to leave. Tell me."

"I...can't." Lifting her arms, she hooked them around his neck and pulled. He angled lower and gazed into her eyes for one, two, three heartbeats and then groaned and kissed her.

The kiss was feral, rough, full of raw emotion. His lips were hard as they claimed hers. His tongue pushed into her mouth and stroked hers until she was writhing and whimpering, trembling all over.

Her pelvis rocked back and forth with each thumping beat of her heart, and wave upon wave of need crashed through her. By the time the kiss had ended, she was blind with need, desperate for his touch. Any touch. Anywhere.

When it didn't come, she opened her eyes.

He was propped on one arm, his large frame stretched out on her bed beside her. "If I stay another minute, I'm not going to be able to leave until I've made love to you. And this time when I have you, I won't be able to stop. I'll want you again. And again." The hand that wasn't supporting him was resting on her stomach. It started sliding down, down, until it warmed her mound.

That again-and-again part sounded good. Better than good. "Maybe I want you to make love to me," she muttered, surprised by what she was saying. Hadn't she told him just a few short minutes ago that she needed space? Time to think? And now she was practically begging him to take her.

"Dammit, you're not making this easy."

"Neither are you."

He pushed upright, stared longingly at her. She looked into his eyes, catching a glimpse of the conflict raging inside him. He wanted her like no man had ever wanted her before. And that thrilled her. And scared her. Both.

His hand was still there, on her mound. His fingers tensed. She felt the subtle movement.

She placed her hand over his.

He gritted his teeth. "Goddammit." He grabbed her hand and jerked it over her head. "Don't move those fucking hands."

A thrill buzzed through her like an electrical current. The dangerous edge in his voice made her simmer from head to toe and made every nerve in her body tingle.

Roughly, he shoved her skirt up and pushed her legs wide apart. "No panties," he growled. "No fucking panties." Sliding down her body, he inhaled. "You smell so good. I have to taste you."

A shiver quaked up her spine.

He sounded so dangerous and wild, like a beast on the verge of losing control. Roughly, he shoved her legs wider apart, opening her to his dark eyes. Being so open, so exposed, thrilled her. Heat pounded through her body, coiling deep in her belly. Her inner muscles clenched. She was empty. So empty. How long would he make her suffer?

She quivered as he parted her swollen folds, exposing her clit. And that first touch, a tiny flick of his tongue, sent a raging inferno blazing through her. The first touch was followed by another, and another. With each one, her body burned hotter, the tension winding through her muscles tighter.

Ecstasy. It was pure ecstasy. And agony. Both. She reached

down to tangle her fingers in his hair, but the moment she caught his silky strands in her hands, he grabbed her wrists.

"I am in control. Of your body. Your pleasure. Your everything. Trust me." And then, as if to prove his point, he plunged his tongue into her empty channel.

"Yesssss," she said on a sigh as she surrendered to his possession. She lifted her hands over her head, crossing her arms at the wrist as if they were bound. And eagerly she submitted to him.

Ahhh, how magical his mouth was. His tongue, his lips, his teeth. He kissed her intimately, pushing his tongue inside her wet tissues, lapping away her juices and stirring more heat deep inside her core. Tension pulled at her muscles and quickened her breathing. The faster she inhaled, the deeper she pulled in his scent. Man. Soap. Desire. His cologne. The smell was delicious. Her tongue swiped across her lower lip, catching the lingering flavor of his kiss. That was delicious, too.

Oh God, she was in heaven. But she craved more. A thick rod pumping in and out, stroking away the unbearable ache.

"You are intoxicating," Tage murmured as he nipped at the inside of her thigh.

"Please."

"Please what, Michelle? I love how you beg. Your voice is so pretty when you plead."

"Please," she repeated, unable to say more. She was too lost in need to put two words together. Her fingers curled into fists. Her toes curled, too.

"I want you. I want you so badly I hurt. But I won't take you. Not until you say the words I have been waiting to hear."

"What words?" she somehow managed to whisper. She didn't want to talk. She was dying. From pleasure. Why was he making her suffer so much?

"Tell me you will be mine. All mine. Mine forever." He pushed a finger into her core. His nail grazed the inner wall and she trembled. Her muscles inside tightened as she tried to hold his finger in place.

He wanted her to say what? To say she would be his?

"Tell me you'll marry me. Today."

Today? She couldn't. She didn't love him. She wanted him. She desired him. He amused her. And tormented her. But love? No. Not yet.

She let her head rock from side to side. It was the only answer she could muster up.

He added a second finger. Two fingers. They felt glorious. But they still weren't enough. She needed more. She needed his hips wedged between her thighs, his thick cock pushing deep inside.

"More."

"Say the words," he demanded.

This was insanity. This was blackmail. Torture.

"Tage."

"You will be mine." He added a dampened finger to her anus, stretching her hole. As that third digit pushed deeper, invading her like she'd never been before, she cried out.

He stopped just as an overpowering wave of pleasure crested inside. She didn't climax. She was on the verge. Breathless. Dizzy. Tight. Hot. Trembling.

"Look at me," he commanded.

She opened her eyes, having not even realized she'd closed them. Her gaze locked on his dark eyes. She searched their depths. Did he love her? She couldn't marry him. Not if he didn't love her.

She saw desire. Raw, untamed desire. But no love. "I can't marry you. Not yet."

"You will. I'll bring you to the brink of ecstasy over and over until you can no longer deny me. You will surrender. You will yield to me."

Perhaps. She was on the verge of yielding already. If she gave him the opportunity to do this again, he might get her to say the words he was waiting to hear. But he also was going to suffer, too.

She would make sure of it.

Now that her head was clearing a little, she was determined to make this tormenter get a taste of his own medicine.

He gave her clit one last swipe of the tongue. A slow, languid caress. Then he straightened up and smiled down at her. "I'll be back tomorrow. You'll be ready for me when I call. No clothes. Waiting here, in your room."

A wild thrill raced up her spine. This was a fun game, a naughty, scary, thrilling game. One she might not mind losing. "Or else?"

"You won't like the consequences." Bending over her head, he kissed her, catching her lower lip between his teeth and biting just hard enough to sting a little. When he released her lip, he dragged his thumb across it, making it tingle more. "No touching yourself. If I am going to deny myself, then so are you."

He left.

19

Talen stepped into his private suite at the Gemedess Club expecting it to be empty.

It wasn't.

Oh hell. How did she get in here?

She was kneeling, head lowered in respect, her spine arched perfectly to show off her round, firm ass. Her long blond hair hung down her back, a tumble of glossy waves. Angela was waiting for him. Waiting for his command.

There was no reason why he couldn't spend some time with Angela here. It was what he'd done for years, explore his darker urges with women who were willing and able. Angela was most definitely able. And her presence here, after he'd broken his engagement with her last night, suggested she was willing.

But something made him stop from uttering that first command.

She lifted her head. "Tage? Master?"

"Yes, it's me." He circled her. She was a beautiful woman, everything he'd always thought he wanted in a wife. Sexy. Submissive. Experienced. Open to sharing, and easily motivated.

But she wasn't for him.

He wouldn't play with her. Not today. Not ever again.

Obediently, she tipped her head, lowering her eyes.

"Please stand," he commanded.

She stood, eyes still downcast, hands at her sides.

She was nude, wearing nothing but a pair of shiny black platform pumps. Her body was the picture of perfection, her breasts full and round, stomach flat, hips nicely curved, legs slender and long. But his cock didn't stir. His blood didn't simmer.

"I'm cancelling my membership."

Her gaze jerked to his face. "Cancelling? Why? Would you have done the same thing if we had married?"

He wouldn't have. But he had no need to crush the woman's pride any more than he already had. "Yes."

Her features twisted. "You told me you would continue to scene with other women if we married. You said you might even fuck them."

"I would—will."

"But not today? Not with me?"

"No."

She blinked. An emotion of some kind played over her features for a brief moment, then her expression changed. Her lips curled into a sexy semi-smile. "Are you sure?" Her hips swayed as she took a couple of steps closer. "I've been practicing a few things for you." Stopping directly in front of him, she placed her hands on his shoulders. "Don't you want to see how hard I've been working?" Slowly lowering herself to her knees, she let her hands drag down the front of his body. They stopped at his crotch, cupping the front of his pants.

He clasped her wrists and pulled them out to the sides. "I'm sorry, but you'll have to show your new skills to another dom."

"But you were the one to teach me. Don't you want to reap the rewards of your *hard* work?" She licked her lips, her tongue leaving them glossy and moist.

"No."

Her brows pulled. Her lips curved into a snarl. "What is your deal? First you ask me to fucking marry you, then you dump me for that... that little whiny bitch, break our engagement—"

"Enough!" It would be so easy to curl his fingers around that little throat of hers and shut her up. For good. But he would never touch a woman in anger. Never. "I said I would take care of you. And I will. You wanted money. That's what you'll get." Reaching into his pocket, he pulled out the envelope. He'd put the first of many payments in his pocket, intending to take it to her place later, after he was done packing up his stuff at the club. The envelope held ten thousand dollars. In one-hundred-dollar bills. "Here you go. Like we discussed." He would arrange the rest to go by wire transfer to the overseas bank account she was setting up. The ten thousand would hold her over until then.

He hoped. He had a feeling the woman would have her hand in his pocket for a long time, until he and his brothers moved and took new aliases. With any luck, it would be years before they would have to do that.

She jumped to her feet, ripped open the envelope, and peered inside. "Thank you. This will cover my overdue lease payments for a little while. But I'll need the rest soon."

"You'll have it when your account is open and available to accept payments."

"I'll call you."

"Fine." He motioned toward the door. "Now, if you don't mind, I need to ask you to leave. I have some packing to do. The club is eager to get this suite leased to someone else."

"Sure." Her shoulders lowered somewhat, and as their gazes met, he caught a tiny glimpse of hurt play across her face. Damn. He'd wanted to believe she would be okay with just the money.

She wasn't.

He had to say something to try to ease her pain. "Look, I'm not trying to be a bastard about this. There's a reason why I had to break our engagement, and it has nothing to do with you."

She blinked once, twice, again. By that third time, her eyes were red and watery. "I would have been a good wife to you."

"I know."

"Anything you wanted, I would have done. Anything." Turning, she grabbed the dress that was draped over the chair in the corner. Her handbag was sitting on the chair's seat.

"Yes. I believe that."

A heavy, tense silence fell between them. Her gaze locked on his face as she pulled on the tight sheath and tugged it into place.

She slid the envelope into her bag. "I hope you're happy, Tage. I hope you've made the right choice."

"I believe I have."

She nodded, turned, and left his suite.

That had been awkward, far worse than he'd expected. He'd been wrong when he'd assumed Angela had agreed to marry him for money. It was painfully clear to him now. He hoped the money—it would be a large sum—would ease her burden. A small part of him did care for her. He would be happy to see that she was set for life, would never again have to worry about food, a home, the necessities.

A couple of hours later he had, with the help of his brothers, all of his personal belongings packed into a truck. This whole thing was blowing his mind. Never, not even after watching his brothers fall in love, had he thought he would ever voluntarily give up his suite at the club. Yes, his brothers had given up the lifestyle, and their many lovers, when they'd married. But they had fallen in love with their wives. He didn't think it was possible for him to fall in love with his. Not when he'd never felt an emotion that even vaguely resembled love before.

But here he was, desperate to hear his wife tell him she would be his. And willing to do just about anything to get her to do it.

Didn't she realize how much he loved her? Didn't she know he would surrender his life for her? He would do anything to make her happy. Anything.

But she didn't trust him yet.

A couple of hours later, as he hauled the first load of his bondage gear into the house, his brother Malek slid him a sideways glance. Malek was sitting in the family room, watching football and stuffing his face with chips and dip. "I can't believe you quit the club," he said, crunching. "Must be love."

Talen shrugged. He didn't want to talk about it.

"It's okay, bro. Been there." Malek jumped up, jogged over to Talen, and grabbed a bag from him. "When's the wedding?"

"She hasn't agreed to marry me yet," Talen confessed, heading toward his bedroom.

"Still holding out?" Malek asked behind him. "This one's making you work for it."

"She's worth it." Talen dropped his load on the floor and turned back to get some more. He figured he would bring the smaller stuff to his room and store the bigger things in the basement. With the private dungeon set up in the house, he had no need of those larger pieces.

"I'm sure she is worth every minute of hell she'll put you through. Lei put me through hell, but I wouldn't change a thing." Malek clapped him on the back as he headed through the doorway. "Don't worry. Your woman can't resist you. Not for long. No woman has been able to before."

"She said she won't marry me if she isn't in love with me."

"Damn. Love? I had it easy, compared to that. Lei needed stability, patience. She needed to feel safe."

In the garage now, Talen reached into his Range Rover for his next load. "I wish it were that simple. Originally, I'd thought I would marry a girl who needed money and stability. I found one. She'd accepted my proposal. Then I had to go and be an asshole and turn her down so I could chase this one."

His brother laughed. "That's a Gryffon for you. We can't make it easy on ourselves. Look at Drako. He had it easy getting her to the altar. But it was after that things got crazy. Rin put him through hell for months."

Arms loaded, Talen headed inside the house. "I won't last months," he said to no one in particular.

Malek was right behind him, his hands full, too. "I feel for you, bro. You just gotta make it so she can't live without you. If you can do that, you've got her. But be careful. Love is dangerous. It gave me some crazy power. That was something I hadn't expected. And Drako. But it can work against you, too. You know what happened to our father. In the end, we have a duty. I won't tell you what to do. Nobody told me. But remember, you need to marry as soon as possible. And we need you to be strong. Love makes us vulnerable. I'm vulnerable. Drako's vulnerable. I'd like to say it would be a good thing if you weren't vulnerable, too. But I think it's already too late for that."

Talen nodded.

"As I thought."

In the bedroom, he set load two next to load one. "But there is one thing. A good thing. She's pregnant."

Malek's expression brightened. "Damn, you work fast, little bro! Do you know it's your child? Are you sure?"

"I am." Talen hesitated. He wanted Malek to feel some sense of relief, to know he was thinking of him and Lei. "With Lei losing your child, and knowing she cannot...I wanted to make sure I did everything I could—"

"Yes. If it works out that way, I'm going to owe you big-time." Malek slapped him on the back. "Now, let's get that woman in the family. We want her here, in the house, where she'll be safe. Time to up your game."

"That's exactly what I intend to do, Malek."

What was he doing?

Michelle checked the clock. It was a little after eight. Not terribly late. What was Tage doing tonight? Did he go to that club, the one where he'd met Angela? Was he there now, mixing and mingling with other women?

A tiny bit of jealousy bit at her insides.

What was he doing?

Although he'd said he was determined to convince her to marry him, he hadn't said he wouldn't see other women. To her, it was a no-brainer. If she were a man, she would keep it in her pants. Period. He wouldn't touch another woman.

But she wasn't a man.

Some men were dogs. Some men couldn't go twenty-four hours without sex. Was Tage the kind who would chase women until the day of his wedding? After his wedding?

Right now, right this very minute, was he making love to someone else? Someone like Angela?

Stop it. You don't have any claims to him.

She glanced down at her still flat stomach. *She* didn't have any claims to him, but the tiny person inside her did.

What was he doing now?

She dragged her fingertips across her lips. The memory of his kiss blossomed in her mind. That man knew how to kiss. Did he ever. Never had she been kissed so well or so thoroughly. Never had she been so lost in need that she didn't care about anything but relief.

What was he doing now?

Feeling restless, she grabbed her phone and checked it. He hadn't called. She'd expected him to. At least once today. But he hadn't.

Had he changed his mind? Had he decided she was too much work, not worth the effort?

A twinge of regret buzzed through her, making her realize something. She wanted him to pursue her. She wanted him to convince her. She wanted him to prove to her that he not only wanted her to marry him but that he would love her.

Sighing, she dropped her phone on the table, grabbed the television remote, and powered on the TV. Then she remembered she hadn't paid the cable bill yet.

Maybe a book.

When she was a child, books had been her escape, a doorway into magical, exciting worlds where every girl got her Prince Charming and a happy ending. Lately she hadn't done much reading. She kept telling herself she didn't have the time.

Now, more than ever, she had the time. And she desperately needed the distraction. She grabbed her ebook reader. It was still fully charged. A quick skim of her meager inventory of ebooks convinced her she needed to do some shopping. She wanted to read something new. Exciting. She browsed the store's bestseller list.

There. That one.

It was a romance.

In roughly sixty seconds she had the book downloaded and open. She got herself comfy on her couch and started to read. One page. Then another. Oh yes, this one was going to be good.

She was almost at the end of the third page, when a knock pounded on her door.

Immediately, she imagined it was Tage.

Her nerves jangled.

What if it was him?

Who else would it be if it wasn't?

She was in her sloppy sweats and a tank top. Her hair, oh God, her hair. No makeup. She had showered and was clean, but she hadn't bothered with makeup. Last night she'd been wearing makeup. And this morning, before going down to breakfast, she'd fixed herself up a little. She always carried the essentials in her purse. Some bronzer, lip gloss, eyeliner.

Right now, she was clean-faced except for the healthy-sized glob of moisturizer she'd smoothed on after she'd gotten out of the shower.

Her visitor knocked again.

It might be her neighbor, she reasoned. Every now and then, her neighbor, Mrs. Hebert, came over to ask for some milk or help with her computer.

Or it could be Tage.

She dashed back to her bathroom, brushed on some bronzer to give her face a little color, sloshed some mouthwash in her mouth, and pulled her hair out of the messy knot it had been in and raced back to the door.

It was him.

Oh God.

"Hi," he said when she opened the door. "I didn't wake you, did I?"

She felt her face warming. How embarrassing. He thought she'd been in bed. *I must look worse than I thought.* "Um, no. I was just relaxing."

"Good. I...wanted to check on you, make sure you're feeling okay." He was still standing in the doorway, looking as handsome and sexy as ever. His shoulders were so broad. She swore they hadn't been that wide this morning. And the five o'clock shadow darkening his jaw made him look a little dangerous. He lifted his brows.

"Oh. Yes. Come in." She moved to the side and after he was inside, she closed and locked the door.

He turned to face her fully, and she couldn't help staring. Honestly, he was the most stunning man she'd ever seen. His face was perfectly balanced, with a sharp blade of a nose, angled cheekbones, and a strong jaw. His lips were neither too thin nor too full. And they tended to tilt in a lopsided smile. His white teeth were even and straight, their hue a stark contrast to his olive-toned skin. In one word, he was to-die-for gorgeous.

It was so hard to believe that he not only had sex with her but he wanted to marry her. Never had she attracted the attention of a male who was so incredibly good-looking.

He reached for her hand, caught it. "Did you eat dinner?"

"I did. Thanks."

"What did you have?" he asked as he led her into her own living room.

"The usual, a frozen dinner. I'm not much of a cook."

He scowled. "Those meals are garbage."

"So I've heard. But they are convenient. And I'm taking vitamins."

"If you came to stay at my place, you could eat real meals. Every day." He motioned for her to sit on the couch.

She sat. "If I ate big meals every day, I would probably gain a hundred pounds."

He sat next to her and angled his body so he faced her. His gaze meandered up and down her body, making her feel warm. "It wouldn't bother me if you gained some weight. I like girls with curves."

He had to be just saying that to make her feel better. Angela didn't have any curves, at least none that couldn't be bought from a plastic surgeon.

"Regardless," she said, "I live here. This is my home. I'm not moving in with you just so I can eat better."

He grunted.

"Thanks for the offer, though," she added, wanting him to know she wasn't oblivious to the fact that he was trying to be kind and helpful.

He grunted again, turned, and checked out her place. "I didn't say anything before because . . . well, I didn't take the time. Your home is nice." His gaze focused on the window. He loped over to it, pushed aside the blinds. "But it's not very secure." The window was open. He pushed on the screen. Then he shut the window and fiddled with the lock, which was broken. He discovered it was broken. "Hmmm."

"I've been meaning to call maintenance. I put a board in there when I'm gone. Nobody can break in."

"You live alone. That worries me." Finding the board she used as a lock, he slid it in place and tested it.

"This is a good, safe neighborhood. I've been living here for years. Never had any trouble."

He frowned. Even frowning he was glorious to look at. "I wish you didn't live alone."

"I like living alone. I can do what I want, when I want."

He studied her for a moment, two. "I admire your independence. But now you have more than yourself to think about."

"Okay, I realize that. But I'm done being polite. Why did you come here tonight? Was it to harass me about my eating habits? My unsecure apartment? Is that why?"

He prowled closer, stared into her eyes. The air between them seemed to thin, electrify. Tiny unseen zaps jumped back and forth between their bodies. "No, I came here...for this."

Moving suddenly, he grabbed her, hauled her against him, and smashed his mouth over hers.

20

It was a rough kiss, a kiss that told Michelle there could be no escaping Tage or his fiery passion. There was no choice but to surrender.

His tongue shoved inside her mouth. He tasted so good, minty. Sweet. Man. She could taste him for hours. For days. For years.

She felt her body softening as his tongue stroked hers. She was sinking into him, her body molding to his. He was warm. She couldn't get close enough to that warmth. Lifting her arms, she whimpered into their joined mouths.

Already his kisses were stoking a fire inside her body. Her mind was getting foggy as sensations pummeled her system. The sound of her own quick, raspy breathing, the feel of his hot, hard body pressed against hers, the sensation of his fingers, tangled in her hair, the joy of being in his arms.

Breaking the kiss, he murmured against her neck, "Dammit, I couldn't stop myself."

She let her head fall back. "Stop yourself from what?"

"From kissing you. From holding you. I told myself I would

come here to talk, to prove to you that I'm more than a hard cock."

"I know you're more than that." Her insides were starting to ache. Already pounding, throbbing need was coursing through her veins. "You're definitely more."

He nipped her earlobe, then trailed little kisses along her jaw. The hand holding her head in place moved slightly, easing her head to the right to give him better access to her neck. The other one, which had been pressed flat against her back, smoothed down, over her bottom until it cupped her ass. "Damn, you're sweet. The minute I taste you I want more. I want to lick every inch of your body."

That actually sounded quite scrumptious at the moment. At the tension she heard in his voice, a wave of erotic heat swept through her body.

"Mmmm," she hummed as she let herself just relax and enjoy the moment. Tage knew exactly how to touch her, how to make her body tremble and ache for him. A lick. A touch. A tiny nip and she was lost in need. Absolutely lost.

Within seconds she was writhing in agony. "Please," she muttered. She was burning up with a fever. And only Tage could make it go away.

"Say you'll be mine. Tell me you'll marry me. Now. Right this minute. I'll give you the relief you need."

Bastard.

It would be so easy to give in to his demands right now, tell him what he wanted to hear. She was dying. From the pleasure. Until she had met Tage, she hadn't realized pleasure could be so effing excruciating.

"Can't," she whispered.

"Won't," he corrected. He jerked her top up, and she sucked in a little gasp. When he got rough, it sent a wicked thrill through her. With one hand he unclasped her bra. With the other, he pulled the garment off her arms and threw it. "Nobody else will

ever be enough for me. You've spoiled me. These perfect tits."
He weighed them in his hands, then pinched the nipples between his fingers and thumbs.

Pleasure-pain raced through her, zing. Her spine arched,
pushing her breasts out even more.

"See that? See how you respond? No woman responds to
my touch like that. Only you." Bending down, he flicked his
tongue over the tip of her stinging nipple. White-hot pleasure
raced through her at the tiny touch. Heat pulsed to her center.

"Look at me," he demanded.

She stared into his eyes. Never had she witnessed such torment, or raw, feral need.

She was going to melt.

Her knees buckled.

He swung one of his arms under her, scooped her off her
feet. Seconds later, she was lying on her bed, on her back, staring up into the most beautiful face she had ever seen, and a pair
of haunted, tortured eyes.

Could he really be so desperate? Or was it an act? If it was,
it was worthy of an Academy Award. The darkness in his eyes
tugged at her heart, rivaling the most memorable performances
in movie history.

"I tried to convince myself I would be content with another
woman. But I couldn't do it." Bending over her, he covered her
lips with his, murmuring against them. "It's you I want. Only
you. Always you."

Her heart, it was melting. So was her resolve.

No man had ever said anything like this to her.

She wanted to say yes, she would be his wife. But she was
petrified. The fear tangled her tongue and blocked her throat.

He supported his weight with one hand, flattened against
the pillow, next to her head. The other settled between her legs,
covering her mound.

Her stomach tightened, and her hips rocked forward.

Wouldn't he touch her down there, where she ached the worst? She whimpered.

"Mmmm. How I love to hear that," he said. "Are you suffering, little one?"

She nodded.

His hand inched lower, gliding between her legs. But that wasn't good enough. Her clothes were in the way. "Some suffering is good."

She never would have agreed with that statement before. But, as she lay trembling beneath him, bathed in erotic need, she had to agree with him now. It was good suffering. Very good. Most of her didn't want it to end. The other did. Quickly. Now.

"I will teach you the secrets of pleasure and pain." The hand between her legs moved back up, stopping at the waistband of her yoga pants. He jerked them down, exposing her, and she gasped. "I will teach you the joy of submitting. And the wonder of surrender."

If she hadn't been so enthralled, she might have been scared. But she wasn't. She was captivated. "Teach me."

"I cannot."

"Why?"

"You must trust me first."

"I do."

"Do you?" Straightening up, he curled his fingers in the waist of her panties.

Yes, she wanted him to take them off. If he didn't, she would do it for him. But did she trust him? With her body, sure. But with her heart?

No.

"I want to," she said.

He glanced around her room. Then he went to her dresser and pulled open the top drawer.

"What are you looking for?" she asked.

"Trust me."

She nodded and watched as he sifted through the contents of her drawer. He returned to her bedside a few seconds later, holding a couple of her mother's silk scarves in his hands.

"Trust me," he repeated as he placed one scarf on the bed and gathered the other into a narrow band. When she nodded, he set that one over her eyes. "Lift." She lifted her head and he tied it, adjusting the folds to block off her vision. "There. Now, relax."

She closed her eyes.

He touched her arm, startling her. She felt herself twitch. Then she felt the smooth fabric, gliding over her skin. It was soft and fluid, a gentle caress. She sighed as her insides coiled a tiny bit tighter.

The fabric tightened around her wrists, binding them together. Now she was tied up and blindfolded. Almost completely at his mercy. She was a little uneasy. But she was also excited, too.

Something touched her stomach, and she jerked. Without the benefit of her vision, she didn't know where his next touch would be.

The touch, which was the size of a fingertip, meandered down the center of her belly. Lower it trailed. To her mound. Lower. Her stomach muscles quivered. Warmth pounded through her center.

There was that burn again, between her legs. That glorious, excruciating burn.

She groaned. "Please."

"Please what? Tell me what you need."

"I hurt," she confessed as she tensed her muscles deep inside.

"Where?"

"Everywhere."

"Mmmm. Then I must be doing something right," he said in a low, deep voice.

"You're doing everything right."

"Glad to hear that." He eased her panties down, over her hips. She wriggled, shifting her weight to help him get them off. At last she was bare to him, fully exposed from head to toe. With gentle hands he pushed her legs apart. She felt her swollen folds parting for him. Heat pooled there.

"Touch me," she begged.

He did it. At last. A soft touch. To her outer folds. Her body lurched. It wasn't enough. Not even close.

"More," she demanded.

"You're such an eager girl. Eager and impatient." His finger grazed her slit before delving deeper, between her swollen tissues.

"Ohhhh," she heard herself say.

"Damn, you're wet."

Her empty canal clenched, the muscles pulling tight. Wet and empty.

His fingertip found her clit, and she trembled. He dipped lower, dampening it before returning to her sensitive pearl and stroking it again.

She practically levitated off the bed, the sensation was so intense. Every muscle in her body, even the ones in her fingers and toes, knotted. She needed more. Something big and hard stroking her inside, taking away the agony. She bent her knees and opened wider to him.

"You smell like honey." She felt his breath warming her sensitized flesh. He was going to lick her down there. Oh yesyesyes.

She quivered.

His tongue swirled around the base of her clit. Round and round. Then it flicked gently over it. With each little touch, the fire simmering in her body sparked hotter, brighter.

Oh, this was exquisite. And frustrating. She needed him, his weight resting on top of her, his thick rod stroking away the agony.

"Please," she said on a groan.

His tongue continued to dance over her clit. With each stroke, her body tightened more. Her stomach. Thighs. Feet. Chest. Arms. She felt her hands trembling, heard the rasp of her fast little gasping breaths.

"Please, Tage. I'm begging."

He didn't stop. He had no mercy. She was dying from pure ecstasy.

He gave her not one second of relief. Nor did he shove his cock inside her to allow her to tumble over the edge. No. Instead he cruelly licked and suckled on her clit. When she couldn't take another second, she tried to pull her legs together.

"No." He caught her thighs and shoved them wider apart.

She whimpered, squirmed. "Oh God, Tage. Ah God."

He pressed his mouth to her tissues and suckled her clit.

An inferno blasted through her.

She screamed. She shook. She thrashed. He pulled her against him, smashed his mouth over hers, and kissed her, swallowing her cries of release and stopping her jerky, wild movements. His strong arms cradled her. His heat calmed her.

When it was over, he removed the scarves, gazed down into her hazy eyes, and smiled.

"It's time for me to leave."

"But—"

His smile broadened. "You know what words I'm waiting to hear."

"Tage, you make me feel...you are so...but I can't. Marriage is a huge commitment. I want to, but I can't."

"Maybe next time." He bent down and kissed her again. "Sweet dreams, little one."

He left.

*   *   *

His balls were going to explode.

Teeth gritted against the pain, Talen staggered down the hall. Forget Michelle, this was going to kill *him*.

But it would be worth it. He wouldn't have to wait much longer. And then Michelle would be his.

She'd been close to losing complete control this time. It wouldn't take much more to push her over the edge. He just hoped he didn't tumble over the edge before her.

Formulating a plan, he flopped into his car. His cock was so hard it hurt, and it was caught in his pants. It was effing uncomfortable. In the past he would have taken care of that without a second thought. He'd go to the club, find a willing submissive, invite her back to his suite, and do what needed to be done.

But he couldn't do that anymore. His suite was gone.

And he was done with that lifestyle.

He hadn't taken any vows yet, but it didn't matter. He couldn't lay with another woman. His heart belonged to Michelle.

What the hell was it going to take to make her see that?

21

"Congratulations." That was Angela's less-than-enthusiastic greeting when Michelle dragged herself into work on Monday morning. Angela was holding a large box, a case of paper. She wasn't smiling, and her eyes were cold. "I hear you're getting married soon. Who's the lucky guy? Oh, that's right. I remember now. He was *my* fiancé."

"Angela, I'm so sorry. I swear—"

"Save the lies for someone who might believe them. The fact is, you were the smarter player in our little game. You won the prize."

Michelle didn't really consider Tage a prize to be won. Granted, he was great. But he wasn't a thing. A car. A house. A pile of cash. Those were things one would win in a game. Not a human being.

And she hadn't agreed to marry anyone yet. She would have liked to set the record straight on that one. But because she knew anything she said would be met with rolling eyes and scoffing, she merely shrugged and angled to pass through the door. She made it roughly halfway before Angela grabbed her arm. "It's not over until the vows are said, sweetheart."

It was Monday morning, the start of a new week. The last thing she wanted was trouble. "I don't want to fight with you."

"Then you shouldn't have stolen my fiancé," Angela said through gritted teeth.

"I didn't steal anyone. He made a choice." She threw her hands in the air. "Believe it or not, this wasn't what I wanted. I haven't even agreed to marry him."

"You haven't." Angela laughed. "What the hell is wrong—" She cut herself off. "Never mind. There's a way to make this right then, isn't there? You could tell him you won't marry him, and then he'll come back to me."

She could do that. In fact, she had.

But now a part of her questioned whether that was the right thing to do, and it had nothing to do with what he could offer her—a nice home for her child, stability. Assuming he was the kind of man who would pay his child support, their child would have those things whether she married him or not. The issue was deeper than that.

"You don't care about him at all," Michelle said, thinking aloud.

"Of course I do." There was a dark gleam in Angela's eyes as she spoke. "I care for him."

Like a shark cared about the fat little fish it was about to eat.

"Tell him you won't marry him," Angela insisted.

"I'll think about it."

Moving suddenly, Angela shoved her. She fell back and slammed into the wall. Dazed, she pushed forward, but Angela thrust her arms out, holding her in place. She angled close, too close. "You have no idea what shitstorm you've walked into. Be smart, Michelle. Do what I said. Tell him you won't marry him."

"Back off." Michelle rammed her arms out, but Angela didn't budge.

Angela glanced right, left. "I'm trying to warn you," she whispered.

"Warn me about what?"

"I can't tell you. Let's just say Tage isn't all that he appears. Neither are his brothers."

What was Angela talking about? What could she possibly know about him? Angela didn't know him any better than she did. At least, she'd made it out that way. "What do you mean?"

"I can't tell you anything else." She inched closer and whispered, "I want to tell you but I can't. Please trust me, Michelle. Please."

What the hell was this all about?

"What do you mean not what they appear? Are they criminals?" Michelle muttered back.

Angela glanced around again, as if she was checking to see if anyone was listening. "Not exactly."

"What does that mean?"

"They...terrorists. There. That's all I can say."

Terrorists? Terrorists! What? It had to be a lie. It made no sense. "If that's true, then why are you so eager to marry him?"

"I'm not going to marry him. My cousin is in the CIA. He asked me to help out with his case."

"What?" Michelle's stomach twisted.

Could it be true? Could Tage be a dangerous terrorist, wanted by the federal government? It was so far-fetched, it was hard to believe.

And yet, the sincerity in Angela's voice and expression couldn't be ignored. Whether it was true or not, Michelle was quickly becoming convinced that Angela believed it.

"Why haven't they been arrested, then?" Michelle asked as she tried to wrap her head around what Angela was telling her. "Doesn't the federal government arrest terrorists first and ask questions later?"

Angela took a step back, giving Michelle some much needed

air. "In this case they're trying to collect some information before they're arrested." She wrung her hands.

"I shouldn't be telling you any of this. If my cousin found out, he'd kill me. Whatever you do, you can't say a word to Tage about anything I've told you. He and his brothers will pack up and run off. They've done it before."

"This is crazy." That was an understatement, but Michelle couldn't think of a more descriptive word.

"Are you really pregnant with his kid?" Angela asked, her gaze flicking to her belly.

"I..." Michelle placed her hand there. Her heart twisted in her chest. The pain was agonizing. "I am."

If what Angela said was true, the father of her child was dangerous. The CIA was investigating him. She had to assume that once they had whatever it was they were looking for, they would have him arrested.

Her baby would probably never know his father.

"I'm sorry," Angela said, looking remorseful. "I really am. Maybe if you walk away now, you can find someone else? A decent man who will love the child like his own?" Her eyes lifted to the ceiling. "My stepbrother is a good guy. He's single. I should introduce you two."

Michelle wasn't in the mood to meet a new guy. If what Angela said was true, Tage, if that was even his name, had just destroyed her life, like a bull crashing through a china shop. Everything was shattered, in pieces. Including her heart.

Her stomach lurched.

This was too much. Shoving past Angela, she raced for the bathroom.

Ten minutes later she came out of the bathroom feeling woozy and weak. She wanted to go home, crawl into bed, and bury herself under the covers. She also wanted to check out of reality for a while.

She couldn't do either.

If she wasn't going to marry Tage, then she needed her job. And she needed to be on the top of her game so that if she got sick later, her boss would be a little more forgiving.

Shit, shit, shit.

It took this eye-opening conversation to make her see how much she'd come to expect Tage to provide for her, married or not. Whether what Angela had said was true or not, that was dangerous. The fact was, Michelle knew very little about Tage. Terrorist or not, she would be a fool to marry a man she didn't know.

But.

Standing outside the bathroom, she dropped her face into her hands.

But... if she didn't marry him, and he did disappear or end up in prison, how would she make it on her own? What if she became very ill while she was pregnant and couldn't work for an extended period of time?

Stop. Or you'll think yourself into being sick.

"Didn't you wonder how they had so much money?" Angela asked. She was *click-clacking* down the hall toward her. "I mean, I've never met a computer programmer who lived in a house like theirs."

Michelle had to admit the house had been spectacular. So had the furnishings. And the finishings. Everything in it looked expensive.

Angela continued, "The place is like a fortress, too. There's the wall that circles the whole property, the locked gate, the security system, cameras everywhere. Who has cameras in their home?"

Cameras? There were cameras?

"Where?" Michelle asked, wrapping her arms around herself.

"In practically every room. Look for them. They're small, but they're visible."

Cameras.

Locked gates.

The guy was a computer geek. Not a Hollywood celebrity. Who needed that kind of security?

Terrorists would.

Maybe drug kingpins, too.

Feeling heavy and nauseous, she dragged back to her desk. There was a bouquet of flowers there. Huge. Had to be from Tage. Her insides twisted. She couldn't look at those right now. Because then she would think about him. She couldn't allow herself the luxury of thinking about him here.

She snatched the card off the little plastic clip inside the floral arrangement, then took the vase and headed back to the bathroom.

The pretty arrangement looked very nice in there, sitting on the counter. She left it and returned to her cubicle.

That evening, before Michelle left, Angela poked her head into Michelle's cubicle. "How are you feeling?" she asked, looking and sounding genuinely concerned.

"I don't know. Numb, I guess."

Angela adjusted the strap of her purse. "It's a lot to take in. I get it. It took a while for me to believe it, too."

Michelle had spent all day thinking about what Angela had told her, the whole time trying not to think about it. She'd scoured the Internet, looking for anything she could find on Tage. Nothing came up. Not a single photo, reference, or Facebook page. As much as she didn't want to believe what she'd been told, she couldn't convince herself there wasn't a possibility of it being true. She wanted to know. She needed to know. If only Angela could tell her why the CIA thought he was a terrorist. "Are you sure what you said is true? Absolutely certain?"

"Yes. Unfortunately."

Michelle couldn't hold in the heavy sigh that pushed up her throat. "Can you tell me anything? Please?"

Once again, Angela took a long look around them. Then she stepped into Michelle's cubicle, squatted so she was at eye level with Michelle, and whispered very softly, "I saw proof. They have pictures."

"Pictures of what?"

"Talen meeting with some known members of Al Qaeda."

"Talen? Who's Talen?"

"That's Tage's real name. Talen. The CIA has been trying to capture him and his brothers for years."

"And you're helping them? How?"

"I was working to gain his trust. I'm a spy."

Now that part sounded far-fetched. Angela? A spy? She was an account manager for an advertising company. And she had absolutely no training or qualifications to be a spy. Surely the CIA could do better than her.

Michelle tried to fit the pieces of this puzzle together. They still didn't seem to be snapping in place. "All your talk about wanting to marry him was a lie?"

"Yeah, though I wish it hadn't been. Because I would love to marry a man like him." Angela gave an exaggerated sigh. "He's sexy as hell. And who couldn't get used to that lifestyle? Did you check out the pool?"

"Pool?" Michelle echoed.

"They have an indoor pool. In their freaking house."

"Wow."

"I know." Angela gave her a small smile. "You don't want to believe me, do you? You aren't going to break your engagement?"

Michelle stared down at her left hand. There was no ring on it yet. But she wanted one. She wanted one from him. But not if he was a wanted criminal.

Holy hell. What am I going to do?

"I'm not engaged to him."

Angela set her hand on Michelle's shoulder. "I'm scared for you. I've got to go. See you tomorrow."

After Angela left, Michelle whispered, "I'm scared for me, too." Then she checked the time. It was after seven. Everyone else was gone, home with their children, their spouses. Would she ever have that? A real family?

With tears blurring her vision, she pressed her hand to her flat stomach. There was a child in her. One who deserved to have everything she herself had never had.

At least he'd have one parent. But would that be enough?

She shook herself out of her funk, powered down her computer, and grabbed her purse. There were so many things she needed to figure out. She didn't need to sit around here, in the dark, crying over stuff she couldn't control.

It was time to take her life in her hands again, stop with the silly romantic stuff. Whether Tage, or Talen, or whatever his name was, was a terrorist or not, he was not her Prince Charming. He was no one's Prince Charming.

She held her breath as she waited for the elevator.

He seemed to have her schedule down pat, having timed his departure so they would ride the elevator down together after they'd met that first time. Tonight she'd intentionally waited. She hoped he would be gone by now, on his way to his giant fortress of a house.

The elevator chimed. The doors opened.

Empty. The car was empty.

She breathed a sigh of relief. He hadn't tried to catch her tonight. She would have some time to try to think things through.

Alone, Michelle *click-clacked* through the parking structure toward her car. The distant voices echoing off the concrete walls and screech of tires made her jumpy, like always. It was cool inside the structure, dark. A little chill buzzed up her spine.

As she rounded the corner, she saw a pair of young men walking toward her. Dressed in suits and ties, and carrying briefcases, they chatted with each other as they loped her way. Despite the fact that she didn't feel particularly threatened by them, she felt herself shifting her path to the right a little. They gave her an acknowledging nod and smile as they passed her and continued around the corner. She went to her car, unlocked the door, and dropped her purse on the passenger side seat.

Someone behind her grabbed her arm. She whirled around. Her eyes locked on a face. Something smashed over her mouth and nose.

What?

What was happening? Was someone trying to kill her?

Smell. So sweet. Nauseating. Cold. Ice-cold.

She tried to claw the hand away from her face. But her arms felt so heavy, her fingers numb.

Please help.

Oh God.

Someone.

Please...

Don't breathe. Don't. No. Can't. It's poison.

Oh God.

She needed a breath. Darkness was falling over her, like a heavy blanket, cutting out the light. Instinct was kicking in. Survive. Breathe. One breath. One tiny breath was all she needed. She fought. She kicked.

She inhaled.

Sinking. She was sinking into the darkness.

Confused.

Lying down.

Lying down?

Ohmygod!

Her eyes snapped open.

She was in a room that kind of looked like a hospital. In a bed that looked similar to a hospital bed. She tried to sit up.

Tied down?

Why? What the hell was going on?

The door. Something clicked. It swung open and a man in a suit strolled in. Not a doctor. Not a nurse.

"What happened? Where am I?" she asked, not waiting for him to speak.

"Hello, Miss Linsey. I'm Special Agent Ross. CIA."

"CIA?" She was even more confused. What would the CIA want with her? And since when did they resort to kidnapping innocent civilians? "What's going on? Why am I tied down?"

Ohmygod, did this have to do with Tage?

He strolled closer, and her body tensed. What would he do? Would he hit her? Threaten her? Moving slowly, he reached for her wrists. "We can get rid of those." He unfastened the restraints. "Better?"

"A little. I'm still confused. Where am I?"

"You're in a safe place. No one is going to hurt you. I apologize for having you brought here in such an...unpleasant manner. But sometimes we have to do things quickly."

So she had been kidnapped. By the CIA. The government. Oh God. "Why?"

"We're trying to protect you. Your family. Your friends. The entire country."

"Protect me? From what?" She checked her wrists. Red rings circled them both. The restraints had been tight. The heat of rage sparked inside her. "I can't believe this. I was thrown into a van and taken against my will. By the CIA." A thought flashed in her head. "Ohmygod. My baby."

The agent's brows shot up. "Baby?"

"What did you use? What was that stuff those men made me inhale?"

"I will inform the doctor of your condition as soon as we are finished talking."

She didn't want to talk. She wanted to get the hell out of there and go home. She clamped her lips and folded her arms over her chest. Her eyes were burning, dammit. Why would they do this to someone?

What could she do? What the hell could she do? If the CIA had the power to yank innocent citizens off the street and lock them up, then they could do anything. They could make her disappear forever.

"The doctor will check you thoroughly before you're released," he assured her, as if his words would make up for the horror she'd just been put through. "Again, I apologize for this situation."

His apology meant nothing to her. He wasn't sorry.

"We need your help," he said.

"Me." She scoffed. That was funny.

"You're in a position to assist your country. If you decide to help us, you would be a hero. You would be potentially saving lives."

She felt herself scowling.

"You're skeptical," he said.

"After being kidnapped? Wouldn't you be?"

Agent Ross pulled a small remote from his pocket and hit a button. A screen descended from the ceiling and within seconds she was gazing at an image of Tage. "We believe this is the man you know as Tage Garner."

She didn't respond.

He continued. "His aliases include Trevin Gambrell, Tage Garner, and Talen Gryffon. He and his brothers have been connected to a string of terrorist attacks in several countries." A click of the remote, and she was viewing photos of the two brothers she'd only recently met.

She had no words. Her stomach had a response, however. It wasn't a pleasant one.

"Our agency has chased these men over three states in the last year. We know that they are hiding a weapon that has the potential to kill millions of people." His gaze turned to her. "Miss Linsey, I cannot emphasize how important it is to locate this weapon and disarm it."

Oh God, what Angela said was true. Tage was a terrorist. And he'd dragged her into this...horrific nightmare. "I don't know what you expect from me. I don't know anything about a weapon. I don't know Tage that well."

"You may not know anything about it now, but we know you are about to marry Talen Gryffon. Once you are living on their compound, you will have access to the entire building. You can search in places nobody else can."

"Are you saying the weapon is in their house? That's ridiculous."

"It's on their property."

That made no sense. If the supposed weapon was so dangerous it could kill millions, would anyone hide it in their home? Would they risk their families' safety? The lives of their children and wives?

What the hell was she to think? To believe?

Her head was spinning, her doubts whipping around in her skull, colliding with her fears. "Say what you tell me is true, which I doubt, I wouldn't know where to start to search," she said. She didn't want to be a part of this. She just wanted to go home and live her life and forget she'd ever met Tage and his brothers. She wasn't a spy. She was the world's worst liar. She wasn't good at being sneaky or secretive. "Plus, Tage and his brothers would know what I was up to right away. There are cameras everywhere."

"We can teach you how to handle the cameras."

She didn't want to help this man. She didn't want to believe what he was telling her. Standing, she gave him a glare. "I'm not feeling well. That drug is making me sick, and so help me God, if it hurt my baby, I'll sue. I'm not your spy. Find someone else. I'm not marrying Tage. After this, I don't ever want to speak with him again. Take me home. I want to go home. Now."

"Of course." He clicked his remote again. His gaze lifted to the screen.

She glanced up, expecting to see it roll back up into the ceiling where it belonged.

Instead, she saw a face she hadn't expected to see.

"What?" she blurted as her insides churned. "If you tell me she's involved—"

"No, she isn't. Not in the way you think." He leaned closer and his expression changed. The friendly guy-next-door charm was gone.

She shivered.

"My job is to close our case. Sometimes that means there are hard decisions to make."

Shocked to the point of barely being able to speak, she stuttered, "A-a-a-are you threatening me?"

"I'm providing you with motivation."

"You're blackmailing me?"

He shrugged. "Call it whatever you want."

No. Nonono. "You bastard."

"I've been called worse. But what I do is in the interest of our country. Like I said, millions of lives are at stake."

Her effing eyes were burning, tearing up. "I don't believe you. The whole thing is crazy. People living with bombs in their homes. Come on."

"You would think it was crazy. But it's real."

"I want to go home. I can't do this. I can't."

"You will help us." He clicked that damn remote again, and there was another picture of her mom. "She's a nice lady. I would hate to see anything happen to her."

"Fuck you."

His eyes scanned the full length of Michelle's body. It was a leer. And it made her feel dirty. "I wouldn't mind that."

"You're not worthy of touching a single hair on my head. Or hers." She stabbed a finger in the direction of the screen.

"I won't have to touch her at all. Though it might be fun. For a woman her age, she looks pretty damn good."

Bile surged up Michelle's throat. She couldn't stop it. She vomited.

Her captor smiled. "Now, I think we'll let you go home. You've gotten my message."

She'd gotten his message all right. It was either do what he said or the only person in the world who truly cared for her would die.

22

The next Monday, Michelle made a beeline for Angela's office. She stormed in, slammed the door, and snapped, "I met your cousin."

Seated at her desk, Angela lifted her eyes to Michelle. Her expression was calm, sedate. "He comes off a little rough when he's on the job, but I swear he's a good guy."

Good guy? Was she kidding? "He's a bastard. He threatened to kill my mother."

She shrugged. "He's trying to protect a lot of people. If you do what he asks, your mom will be fine. Trust me."

Ohmygod, she was so furious her whole body was tight. "Trust you? I'm assuming you're the one who told him about me."

"For the record, no, I didn't tell him. I didn't have to. I'm guessing he saw you on surveillance."

She wasn't sure she believed that. But then again, it was possible. Until now, she never would have guessed people were watching Tage. Or her.

Standing, Angela gave her an apologetic frown. "Look, I'm

sorry. I tried to warn you before it was too late and you got dragged into this. I tried to convince you to give him up. I was going to handle it." She gave Michelle's shoulder a rub. "Now... what? What does Ross want you to do?"

Did she believe Angela was sorry?

Kind of. Angela had tried to tell her. But she hadn't believed her story. It had sounded so impossible.

"He wants me to spy on Tage and his brothers. But I don't know how to do what they want. I can't. I'm no spy. I'm scared. I'm terrified." She sank into the chair facing Angela's desk. She gripped the chair's arms with her hands. They were shaking. "Can you please talk to your cousin? Tell him I can't do this. Tell him whatever you have to so he'll leave me alone." She lifted a trembling hand and dragged her thumbs under her burning eyes. The damn hormones, coupled with the stress of the situation, were turning her into such a crybaby. She hated it. "I can't handle this."

Angela gave her shoulder another rub. "I'll see what I can do. But you'll have to break it off with Tage. Completely. Immediately."

That was going to be kind of tough. As much as this situation terrified her, she still longed for his touch. She hadn't heard his voice or seen his face in...two days? More? It seemed like a lifetime.

But she had to protect her child. And her mom. She couldn't think of herself right now. "Yes, I'll do it. I won't speak to him at all. I promise."

"Okay. I'll call Ross and talk to him. Hopefully he'll lay off."

"He has to."

Understanding, Angela nodded. "Break up with Tage tonight. Go see him. Do it in person. Let him know you mean it. You won't marry him. You don't want him in your life. At all." She grabbed a pen and printed a phone number on a sticky note. "Call me when it's done." She pulled the sheet off the notepad and handed it to Michelle.

"Okay. Tonight. I'll do it tonight." Michelle folded the note in half and stuck it in her purse.

"Good." Angela returned to her seat and smiled. "Don't worry. I'll talk to him."

"Thank you." For the first time in hours, Michelle inhaled a full breath as she left Angela's office.

Back in her own cubicle, she powered up her computer and checked her e-mail. As usual, there was a ton of it. Hoping that would keep her mind occupied, she dug in.

Ten hours later, ten *excruciating* hours later, she was standing outside Tage's office door, gazing into his eyes. She'd decided that was the best place to talk to him. She could leave whenever she wanted. Easy escape.

Dammit, this was going to be harder than she thought. His brilliant smile made her heart ache. "Hi, baby." Shouldering the wall, he jerked his head, coaxing her inside. "This is a nice surprise."

"Hi." Her stomach was rumbling and burning. She pressed a hand to it.

His smile vanished and his gaze snapped to her stomach. "Are you okay?"

"I'm okay." She stepped inside, and the door closed behind her. She was trapped now. Face-to-face with a man who made her insides melt.

A man wanted by the United States government for terrorism. *Do it now, before you lose the nerve.*

"We need to—"

The door opened and a couple of women carrying cleaning

supplies strolled in. "Good evening, Mr. Garner," one of them said with a heavy accent of some kind. "Working late again?"

Dammit, she'd almost gotten the words out.

"Yes, working late again." Tage slid Michelle a worried frown. To Michelle he said, "Come with me." He escorted her toward his office with a hand on her lower back. That touch sent a wave of regret and sadness rushing through her.

Her child would never know his father.

This sucked.

How had things gone so wrong?

The cleaning women remained behind, in the reception area.

He closed the door. "What's wrong?"

Almost everything.

Somehow she had to say good-bye to him. Her gaze met his. "I..."

I can't do this.

You have to. Think of your mom. The baby.

No, I can't.

Her heart jerked.

Tage cupped her cheek. "What's wrong?"

Her eyes started burning again. Her chest constricted. "I have to tell you good-bye."

"Good-bye?" A pained expression darkened his face.

"Yes." Her heart literally ripped apart. Her chest burned. She couldn't breathe. She grabbed the door handle. She needed to sit down. She needed to leave. "Marry Angela."

"No. I want you."

She tried to open the door, but he jerked it shut again.

Wedging himself between Michelle and the door, he stared into her eyes. "Why are you doing this?"

"Because I have to. It's best for me and my family. And our child."

"How? How is it best for anyone? You look like you're being tortured."

"I can't explain." She reached across him, trying to pull the door. "Please let me go."

"No." His jaw clenched.

"Please."

His dark, pain-filled eyes searched hers. It was torture seeing him hurt like this. He was confused. Desperate to understand. But explaining would only make things worse and prolong the agony.

"Talk to me," he demanded, thrusting an arm out to hold the door shut.

"No. I need to go. Let me go."

He grabbed her hand. "Michelle."

She slowly shook her head. "I can't marry you. Not ever. But you and I both know someone who will." She forced her gaze from his face, focusing on the doorknob.

"This makes no sense," he growled.

"I'm sorry."

Releasing the door, he grabbed her shoulders. "Please tell me what happened, Michelle. Something's wrong."

"I can't."

"Why?"

"Because. There's no point." Frustration twisted her insides into knots. This wasn't ever going to end. She had to cut it off. *Do it fast, like you're tearing off a bandage.* "Hate me if it'll make it easier. I don't love you. I won't marry you." She gave his chest a shove.

This time he yielded to her touch, falling aside until he was leaning against the wall. His face was a mask of pain, but she forced herself to rip open the door and dive through it before she weakened. She didn't stop there. She ran through his darkened suite, past the cleaning women, past the empty reception desk, through the exit, down the hall, down the stairs, out to her car.

By the time she'd reached her vehicle, her hands were trembling so hard she dropped her keys as she tried to shove them into the ignition. She had to get the hell out of there. Flicking a glance at the entry, looking for Tage, she snatched them up and tried again.

No Tage. Thank God.

Two hands, male hands, smacked against her window as her car's engine started.

His face moved into view. "Michelle."

She shifted the vehicle into reverse. Her gaze met his for an instant before she jerked it away to check her mirror. With her stomach in her throat, she pushed on the gas. The car zoomed back, angling out of the parking spot. She shifted and hit the gas. She didn't take a breath until she'd turned onto the road.

She drove no more than a quarter mile before the tears started flowing, fast and hard. For safety, she pulled into a grocery parking lot. There, she let them go until she was all dried up and exhausted. When she was sure there was nothing left, she grabbed her phone, dialed the number Angela had given her. The line went directly to voice mail. Angela's cheery greeting was almost too much for her. She choked a little, blurted out, "It's done," and cut off the connection. Then she drove the rest of the way home, hurried inside, and flopped onto her couch.

Quiet. Peace.

Solitude.

She was alone.

No, not completely alone. She set her hand on her stomach. No, she would never be completely alone again.

Her phone rang and she checked the number. Tage. It rang again. A third time. She cut off the power.

God, she hoped he wouldn't come over. In case he did, she dragged her worn-out body back to her bedroom, undressed, set her alarm for the next morning, and buried herself under the covers.

Hopefully tomorrow would be a better day.

It couldn't get worse.

23

What the hell?

What the fucking hell?

He was enraged.

He was devastated beyond words.

He wanted to tear something up. No, he wanted to smash something to pieces. And then tear something up.

His insides were being shredded. His heart. Hell couldn't be worse than this. Nothing could.

What had he done wrong? What the fuck? He'd left her alone for a few days, thinking that would make her miss him. And now...

He shoved open the front door. It slammed against the wall. A resounding *bang* echoed through the house.

Footsteps *tap-tap-tapped* on the floor. Little, fast ones.

Lei rounded the corner. Her eyes were wide, her face pale. She was terrified.

Dammit. He grabbed her arms to steady her. "It's okay. You're safe. It's just me."

She tipped her head to look up at him. Her gorgeous, deep

brown eyes met his. "I...I don't know if I'll ever get used to living like this."

"I'm sorry. I shouldn't have pushed the door so hard."

"Was it an accident?" she asked as she stepped back, out of his hold.

"No. I was...am...upset." He circled around her, toward the stairs.

"Why? What's wrong, Talen?"

"It's nothing," he said, not turning back. "Nothing for you to worry about, Lei."

The next morning, she showered and dressed before turning on her phone. There were fifteen (fifteen!) messages. And ten texts. All from Tage.

He wasn't going to make this easy.

Without listening or reading a single one, she deleted them. Then she called her mom as she headed out to her car.

Mom didn't answer.

A sick feeling flashed through her.

She tried Angela. No answer, either.

Surely Ross wouldn't go after her mother already. He hadn't given her a timeline.

Worried, she continued to try her mom until she arrived at work. Her concern mounted as the nerve-grating ring sounded in her ear, over and over and over.

Where the hell was she?

There was no sign of Tage as she boarded the elevator. That was a relief. She didn't need to deal with him on top of everything else.

In suite 610, she checked Angela's office. Empty. She whirled around and scurried to her cubicle and tried her mom's phone again.

She answered.

She answered!

Thank you, Lord!

"Hello?"

"Mom. Where were you?" Michelle plopped into her chair and inhaled a lungful of air. "I've been trying to reach you all morning."

"I'm sorry, honey. I had a doctor's appointment."

"This early?" Michelle checked her watch.

"Yes. I'm always the first appointment. I don't like to wait. You know that. Why do you sound so breathless? Are you exercising?"

"No, I was just worried. That's all."

"Well, there's no reason to get so worked up over me."

If only Mom knew. There was good reason.

"I'm out here, doing my usual thing. My life is a routine. I do the same things at the same time every week. You know that."

Same things at the same time? That was probably bad. How easy would it be for the thugs in the CIA to predict where she would be at any given time? "Mom, maybe you should shake things up a bit. Be the last appointment of the day. Do your shopping on a Tuesday."

"That's crazy." Mom chuckled. "Everyone knows the grocery store discounts their meat on Thursdays."

Discounted meat. Mom planned her week around a twenty-cent discount on chicken.

Michelle opened her laptop and hit the power button. "You live alone. It's dangerous for you to have a very predictable routine. I saw a story about it on the news last night. The reporter said thieves watch your house for a week or so, and if they see a pattern, they'll use that to time when they break in."

"Honey, I live in Sardinia. There aren't any thieves in Sardinia."

"Sure there are. There are bad people everywhere."

"Is there something going on that you're not telling me? I've never heard you talk like this before."

Michelle wanted to tell her everything. She wanted to warn her. But she wasn't sure she needed to yet. She didn't want to scare her unnecessarily.

Where the hell was Angela? She needed to get her butt in here. She needed to tell her what was going on.

Michelle rolled her chair out of her cubbie and leaned to the right to check to see if Angela's office light was on yet. No light. "Like I said, I just saw a story about a woman being attacked in her home last night. She was your age, lived alone."

"Well, if that's what it takes to get you to call me every once in a while, then I hope the news broadcasts more stories like that. When are you coming home?"

"Oh, I don't know. Things are crazy here at work." Scooting her chair back where it belonged, she checked her watch again. It was five after nine. Angela was officially late. She was never late.

Her mother sighed. "You're always so busy."

"Actually, taking a few days off and getting away from here sounds kind of nice. I'll see what I can do."

"I would love that. You know, next weekend is Easter. It would be great to have you home. I could cook a nice dinner."

"Or I could take you out for dinner, so you don't have to spend all day in the kitchen."

"But I don't mind cooking. It's been ages since I've cooked a real meal. All I've been eating lately are those little frozen meals. It makes no sense for me to cook for myself."

The suite's main door clicked. Michelle peered around her partition wall.

Angela.

"Mom, I'm at work, and the boss just walked in. I have to get going. But I'll call you later."

"Okay. I love you."

"I love you, too. Bye." Michelle clicked off and followed Angela to her office. At the door, Angela jerked her head, an invitation to come inside. Michelle shut the door, closing them in. "Did you get my message?"

"I did."

"And...? Will your cousin leave my mom alone now?" Michelle's heart was thumping so hard, it hurt.

"I let him know what happened. Good news." She sat. Her picture-perfect smile stretched from ear to ear. "He's willing to go back to Plan A as long as you stay out of the picture."

"I can do that."

Angela's smile dimmed slightly. "Tage may make that tough for you."

"Why do you say that?"

"Because I talked to him last night. He was a mess."

Michelle's insides clenched. To hear he was hurting was almost as unbearable as seeing the pain in his eyes.

Angela continued, "I wouldn't be surprised if he shows up at your place tonight. He thinks he can change your mind."

"Ugh. Maybe I *should* go away for a few days," she said more to herself than to anyone else.

"That would be an excellent idea. Absolutely perfect."

"I have some vacation days. But I doubt Tom would approve a vacation on such short notice, especially after the screwup..."

"Leave that up to me."

"Okay," Michelle said, doubt thick in her voice as she shuffled toward the door. It wasn't so much that she didn't think Angela could pull some strings for her. That, she knew, was entirely possible. It was that slightly unsettled feeling she had in her belly, that she was making a mistake.

Responding to her tone, Angela looked her in the eye and

said, "I know this is rough. It'll be over soon. The CIA will have what they need from Tage and his brothers and they'll be arrested. Then both of our lives can go back to normal."

Normal.

That wasn't happening. No matter whether Tage ended up in prison or not, her life had changed forever. Her former normal would never be. She only hoped she would be able to handle the new normal once it settled in.

"Thanks," she said over her shoulder as she exited.

"No problem." Smiling again, as if she hadn't a care in the world, Angela picked up her phone.

A half hour later, Angela knocked on Michelle's cubicle wall. "You're all set to go," she whispered. "Your vacation was approved."

"Great." Michelle continued typing. The e-mail to a prospective new client needed to go out ASAP, before they found another agency.

"Power down, girl," Angela said, poking a manicured finger at her screen. "You're out of here for a week."

Out of here? "What?"

"Get going. Shoo." Angela made a shooing motion with her hands. "Hustle, hustle. Your vacation started today."

"Today?" Michelle repeated.

"Yes."

"How did you get Tom to agree to that?"

"I sort of lied." Angela scrunched her nose. "I told him your mom was sick, and you were too afraid to ask for time off."

"Oh. I see." A big lump of guilt collected in her throat. She tried to swallow it. "Um. Maybe that wasn't such a good idea…"

"I promise, you won't get into any trouble."

She nodded, stared at her computer for a moment. What should she do? Take her time off? Go tell her boss the truth?

Angela said, "No one is going to ask for any verification. They aren't like that here. But if you don't get going, they may start to wonder what's up."

Michelle poked a few buttons, bringing up her calendar. She had two meetings scheduled with clients in the next couple of days. She needed to reschedule those appointments. And there were the others, all pending, for later in the week. She should contact those people as well and let them know she would have to push out their appointments into next week. "I have some calls to make first."

"I already told Tom I would cover for you until you get back. It won't be a problem at all."

"Hmm." Still somewhat torn, Michelle nodded.

"I can access your calendar. I'll call everyone today. I promise."

Reluctantly, she hit the power button on her computer. "Okay." What the heck? She had been through hell and back lately, she'd found out she was pregnant and hadn't told her mother yet. That right there was going to require a trip home and a face-to-face conversation. And after that scare with the CIA, she'd definitely been feeling guilty about not seeing her mom lately. "Thanks for taking care of this for me."

"No problem." Angela patted her shoulder. "I hope your mom is feeling better soon."

"I'm sure she will be, especially when she sees me."

At exactly eleven fifty-five he stepped into the elevator and hit the button for the sixth floor. His heart was in his throat. And it was thumping so hard he couldn't breathe.

This had to work. It had to. Michelle had been out of his life for less than twenty-four hours, and already he was on the verge of going mad. He had to talk to her. He had to convince her to change her mind.

The car bounced as it reached her floor. The doors opened.

Angela was standing there, in the hallway, waiting. Her eyes met his. Her lips curved into a smile. "Hi, Tage. Heading out for some lunch?"

"Yes," he said. "Excuse me." He hurried past her, heading toward suite 610.

"If you're looking for Michelle, she's gone for the day."

His heart constricted.

Gone.

Gone?

He checked his watch. It was only noon. Why had she left work early? "Why did she leave?" This was going to mess up his plans. There wasn't much time left. "Where did she go? Home? Is she okay?"

Angela shrugged. "I don't know where she went. She requested some time off, beginning immediately, and headed out. She seemed okay. She wasn't sick."

Digging in his pocket for his cell phone, he whirled around and raced for the stairs. To hell with the elevator. It would take too long.

He had to talk to her. Today. Now.

"I'm sure she's fine," Angela shouted after him. "She probably just needed a few days of rest."

God he hoped that was true, that she'd taken a little time off to rest, relax, take care of herself. If that were the case, that could work perfectly into his plans.

He risked a few traffic citations as he sped over to Michelle's place. His heart was still racing as he jogged up the front walk to the building. It was one of those security buildings, with call buttons. He depressed her button, hoping she would buzz him in. When she didn't, he tried a different one, spoke into the speaker, "UPS delivery," and grabbed the door when it unlocked.

He yanked it open, dashed to the stairs, and stopped.

She was there, a suitcase in her hand. "Tage."

A suitcase.

A surge of emotion blasted through him. She was leaving him. Leaving. "Where are you going?"

"That's none of your business."

That was true. But it hurt like hell, the words slicing through him like a razor. "I'm not here to fight with you."

"Good." She indicated the door with her head. "Excuse me, I need to go."

She sounded so cold. But the pain he saw in her eyes belied the cool detachment he heard in her voice.

"Michelle, what's going on? Please, give me five minutes. Just five."

"I have to leave." She pushed past him, but he caught her wrist. She spun around and glared down at his fist, wrapped tightly around her arm. "Tage, if you don't let me go right now, I'll press charges."

"Michelle."

Her eyes wouldn't lift to his.

He said her name again, letting her hear his anguish. "Michelle."

He waited, his heart thumping against his breastbone. One second, two, three. At last her eyes lifted.

They were filled with confusion, pain.

The urge to pull her into his arms and hold her rushed through him. But he didn't act upon it. From the tension he saw in her body, he knew she would run if he even tried. Or scream. Either way, it wouldn't help. Instead he forced himself to loosen his hold on her. It nearly killed him.

She eased her arm out of his grip. "I'm sorry," she whispered.

Sorry? "For what?" he asked.

"For not being what you needed me to be."

"I don't understand. When did I ask you to be anything but yourself?"

"That's not what I meant." Sighing, she looked left, right. "I have to go."

"Where are you going?"

She opened her mouth, as if to speak, but then closed it. "Away. So you can marry Angela. So you can forget about me." On the move again, she shoved open the main exit door. But he yanked it shut before she'd gotten through it, grabbed her by the shoulders, and pinned her against the wall.

Her eyes jerked to his.

This time he saw fear.

"I won't hurt you," he vowed.

"I know." Her lip trembled.

"Then why are you so afraid?"

She blinked. Once. Again. "I can't tell you."

A chill swept through him. This wasn't about a simple disagreement or misunderstanding. Michelle was terrified. She was running.

She had found out.

"What do you know?" he asked.

"About what?" Her gaze locked on his.

Yes, he'd struck the truth "About me? About my brothers?"

"I don't know anything."

"I don't believe you."

Her chest began rising and falling swiftly. Her eyes reddened. "Please, let me go. If you care at all about me, you'll just let me go."

He took her wrist and pulled her into the building, to her door. "Unlock it. Let's go inside and talk."

"No, I have to leave."

"Five more minutes."

"That's what you said ten minutes ago."

"You exaggerate." He checked his watch. "It's only been eight minutes."

She scoffed, yanked.

He didn't release her.

She swung a little fist at his belly. It didn't hurt.

He didn't release her.

She kicked a knee toward his nuts. He blocked it just before it made contact.

He lifted a foot, slammed it into the door, and it flew open, banged against the wall inside and bounced shut again. With a shoulder, he opened it, dragged her inside, then kicked it closed.

Taking full advantage of their difference in size, he cornered her between the door and the coat closet. "We're alone. Talk to me."

"I can't. I have to go." She ducked and tried to wriggle past him.

He rammed his arms out, caging her body between them. "What are you afraid of?"

She blinked and a big, fat tear dribbled down her cheek. "Please. Let me go. Marry Angela."

"You're safe. I won't let anything happen to you."

"It's not me I'm worried about."

Another chill swept through him.

It was the Chimera. It had to be.

"Who?"

"My mother." She pushed on his chest, weakly. "Please, let me go. They'll kill her if I don't do what they say."

"Damn." The Chimera had already found them? So soon? How? "We can protect her."

Sobbing softly, she dragged her hands across her face. "They know where she lives. They'll get to her before we could."

"Trust me." He caught her hands in his. He pressed a soft kiss to her fingertips. "Please, Michelle."

"I . . . I'm scared." Her little body trembled against his.

Dammit, he had to protect her. "Please, trust me." He cupped her cheek and stared into her eyes. There was so much raw emotion in them, so much terror and worry. All he wanted to do was make it all go away. "Please."

She sobbed. "Tage, I don't know what to believe." She dropped her head onto his chest and wept, and he pulled her into his arms and held her until the tears stopped. Even then, she trembled. "Is what they said true? Are you a terrorist?"

"That's what they want you to believe."

"Do you have some kind of weapon in your house?"

"No, not a weapon."

"What is it?"

"I can't tell you any more until I know if you're willing to trust me completely. You have to trust me with your life. The life of our child. The life of your mother."

That was asking a lot. He knew that. He wasn't sure he would get the response he was hoping for.

This truly was that final moment, the one that would determine which direction his life would take. Michelle now knew some of his secrets. She understood there was danger, risk. What would she do? Would she walk away, find someone else, someone safe who would love her and give her a safe, ordinary life? Or would she choose him?

The agony was almost unbearable.

24

It was true. Oh God, it was true. Michelle was going to pass out.

Little pinpoints of white light were sparkling before her eyes. It felt like the air was thin. No oxygen. Her knees were getting soft.

She was sinking. Falling.

The blackness descended upon her like a heavy blanket tossed from high above. And then she was on her bed. Tage was standing over her, his face tight.

Something was ringing. Her phone?

She started to sit up but he held her in place, hands on her shoulders.

"No, don't move so quickly," he said. "You'll pass out again."

"My phone." Her voice was weak, shaky.

"I'll get it." He jogged out into the living room. Seconds later, he returned, her purse in his hands. "It sounds like it's in here."

"Thanks." She fished her phone out of the pocket and hit

the button to see who had called. It was her mom. She'd left a message.

A few pokes later the message was playing.

"Hi, honey, this is Mom. I can't wait to see you today. Please drive safely. I'll be ready for you when you arrive, with a nice meal. Don't eat any of that junk on the road. I love you." Then there was a bang. *Mom.* "Who are you? What...?" A scream.

Michelle's heart stopped.

The phone slipped from her hand.

"No," she muttered.

"What is it? What's wrong?"

Her stomach flipped. Again. She gagged, tried to jump off the bed, but Tage swept her into his arms.

She vomited on him.

"Oh God," she said between heaves as he hurried her into the bathroom.

"What happened?" he asked as he gently placed her on the floor beside the toilet.

"Someone..." She swallowed hard. "Attacked."

"We'll help her," he said calmly as he gently stroked her hair back from her face. "It's me they want, my brothers and me. Not her. They won't harm her."

She heaved again. And again. Nothing came up. She sputtered and cried and trembled. Behind her, she heard him moving around. Water running. When he returned, he had a soapy washcloth in his hands. And he was shirtless.

He reached out with the washcloth, presumably to wipe her face, but she took it from him.

"Thanks." She blotted her face. "I can handle this myself."

"Okay." Standing upright, he backed toward the door. "I'll wait outside. If you need help, yell."

She nodded and locked herself in her bathroom. She needed this time alone, to sort out what had just happened. It was all too much. Her system simply couldn't handle it. Still trying to sort through the craziness, she cranked on the shower.

Had Tage just admitted to being wanted by the federal government? Had he?

Had her mother just been attacked or taken hostage? Had she?

And now the man who was responsible for all of it expected her to trust him with her life? Her mother's?

This had to be either a really bad joke or she was sleeping and it was a nightmare.

She pinched herself. Hard.

Could she sleep through that?

She checked the water. It was hot. She stripped and stepped under the spray.

It stung.

Could she sleep through that, too?

She soaped up, rinsed off, and finally got out.

She certainly couldn't be sleeping after all of that. She pressed her ear to the door. Maybe she'd sleepwalked into the bathroom and now was awake? Since becoming pregnant, she had had some really vivid dreams.

If Tage was on the other side of the door, then it couldn't be a dream.

She put on her robe and opened the door.

Tage was sitting on the bench at the foot of her bed.

Damn. "Tell me this is a prank," she pleaded.

He visibly swallowed. "I wish I could tell you that. But it isn't."

Reality hit her like a sledgehammer. She staggered.

Within a blink, he was at her side, steadying her. "Let's get you dressed and somewhere safe. Their next move will be to abduct you." He half-carried her to the bench. "Sit down."

She sat. The next step would be to abduct her? That had already happened. But they'd let her go. Maybe the next time... they wouldn't. "I don't understand any of this."

"I'll explain it later. After you're safe." He hurried to her dresser and yanked open her top drawer. Grabbing a pair of panties and a bra with one hand, he pulled the third drawer open with the other. Within seconds, he had a complete outfit picked out, T-shirt, jeans, underwear, socks. He set the clothes down in her lap. "Please hurry." He went to the window and peered through the blinds.

"Are they really CIA?" She pulled on her panties, then shrugged out of her robe so she could put on her bra.

Still staring out the window, he shouldered the wall. "Probably. They've infiltrated just about every organization in the government."

"Who is 'they'?" She hooked her bra.

"The Chimera."

"Chimera?" she echoed, trying hard to comprehend whatever the hell she'd somehow fallen into.

She felt like Alice. She'd tumbled down the rabbit hole and had landed in a scary, dark place. And, the worst part was, she'd dragged her mom down that hole with her. She plopped back down on the bench and grabbed her jeans.

He explained, "They're a secret organization."

"Like...the Masons? But secret?" she asked as she stuffed her feet into her jeans and yanked them up.

"Yes. This group has been trying to kill me and my brothers since the day we were born."

She grabbed her shirt, hugged it to her chest. "When you were children?"

"Yes."

A chill buzzed up her spine. "They wanted to kill children? Why?" She pulled on her shirt.

"I can't tell you yet."

Rage blazed through her.

What?

Why couldn't he tell her? Wasn't she in deep enough? Didn't he owe her an explanation? Didn't he owe her something?

Her hand went to her stomach. "If those people wanted you dead when you were young, then...then..." Her stomach roiled again.

Still standing at the window, he flicked a look her way. "Yes. That's why I was trying so hard to convince you to marry me. I need to protect you."

Her child? They would try to kill her child? No. No one would want to kill an innocent child. That was inhumane. "This is crazy. It can't be real."

"It is. I'm sorry." He turned to face her. "Are you ready?"

"I don't have my shoes."

"Where are they?"

"There." She pointed toward her closet.

"Get them on. Let's go."

"Where are we going?" She grabbed the first pair she found, pulled them on, and tied them.

"To get the rest of the family. We have to relocate. As soon as possible."

Her head was spinning so fast she could barely comprehend a single word he said. "Relocate? Like, move?"

"Yes. That's the only way we can protect you." He waved her toward the door.

She hesitated. Words were sinking in now. And those words were scary. "You're a fugitive. If I go with you, I'll be one, too. That's no way to live."

He caught her arms in his and looked into her eyes. "Michelle, I'm sorry I dragged you into this. I tried to stay away from you. I knew you weren't the kind of woman who would choose a life like this for yourself. I hope someday you'll be able to forgive me. Running is the only way for us to live. If they catch us, they'll kill us. All of us."

His gaze locked on her stomach.

* * *

A half hour later, Michelle was standing in the center of a whirlwind. It wasn't a literal one, but it was no less terrifying. There were bags stacked up next to the back door. Rin and Lei would dump a couple more every few minutes, then scurry back upstairs. Tage, whom they called Talen, had left her in the midst of the melee, promising to return as soon as he could. She guessed he and his brothers were somewhere making plans for their big escape.

More than once she considered dashing out the door and never coming back. But when her mom's face flashed through her mind, she couldn't do it. For one thing, it was too late for that. If the CIA had gone after her mom, then Plan A, in which Angela married Tage and seduced him into giving her the information the CIA wanted, had been abandoned.

Her phone chimed.

Speak of the devil.

It was a text.

Your mother is safe. For now. Get us the information we want.

She texted back, *I don't know how.*

Photos. Send us photographs.

She snapped a picture of the room in which she was standing and sent it to him.

Good. Photograph every room. Look for things that seem out of place.

Every room? How would she do that without getting caught? Her palms started sweating. She didn't want to do this. Although she felt Tage wouldn't hurt her, even for helping the people they called the enemy, she couldn't be so sure about his brothers.

She glanced back toward the stairs. The sisters seemed to have stopped hauling stuff down for the moment. She headed toward the back of the house, where less action was going on.

There she found the room with the indoor swimming pool. Visually scanning the space for anything out of place, she lifted her camera and took a shot. Everything seemed to be in order there. She sent the photo, then moved to the next room.

It was a bathroom. Sink, toilet, shower. She snapped a couple of shots but didn't send them. This was silly. Surely nobody would hide a super-secret weapon of mass destruction in a bathroom. She quietly crept to the next room.

A library. She scanned the shelves of books. All the classics were there. Dickens, Twain, Austen.

She pulled out *Persuasion*. Jane Austen was one of her all-time favorite authors. How long had it been since she'd last read it? Ages. She flipped to the first page.

Sir Walter Elliot, of Kellynch Hall, in Somersetshire, was a man who, for his own amusement, never took up any book but the Baronetage; there he found occupation for an idle hour, and consolation in a distressed one....

"Did you find something interesting?"

The book jostled in her hands, then dropped to the floor. It landed with a *thump*. She turned to face the speaker, standing somewhere near the door.

It was Tage.

"I apologize if I startled you," he said from the doorway.

"I...guess all this has me a little jumpy." If she hadn't stopped to read, he might have caught her taking pictures. Moving her hand slowly, she slipped her phone into her pocket.

"That's not surprising." He stepped closer. His gaze meandered over her face, which was getting warm as her heart rate kicked higher. "You're flushed. Are you feeling ill again?"

"Maybe a little."

He stooped down, picked up the book. Straightening up, he handed it to her. "You should sit down. Rest."

"I was. But then I got restless." She lifted the book to return it to the shelf.

"Didn't you want to read it? You'll need a diversion while we're traveling. Maybe it'll take your mind off things."

"I suppose." She tucked the volume in her folded arm and nodded. "What's happening?"

"We're almost ready to go."

"Where will we go?"

"I can't tell you that yet." He took her hands in his and led her to the big, cushy, oversized chair in the room's corner. "Sit down. Please. I don't want you passing out again." After she sat, he knelt on the floor in front of her. "I know you're terrified right now. Your mother is being held captive by people you don't trust. You've learned I'm not exactly who or what you thought. And now I'm asking you to trust me to keep your mother safe."

Yes, that pretty much summed things up. "I don't understand what's happening."

He nodded. "I know. You'll learn everything soon."

"How are you going to save my mom?"

"We know whom we are dealing with. She won't be harmed." He was being so vague. Was it any wonder she was having doubts? "You aren't convinced yet that you can trust us, I sense."

"Wouldn't you be dubious, too, if you were in my shoes? I'm terrified. I'm pregnant. Somehow I've dragged my mother into something bigger than either of us. I don't know who the father of my child really is. What is your real name? Who are you? I'm watching you all prepare for whatever is happening as if it's a regular thing…" Eyes burning, she blinked, sniffled. "I don't know."

"Not to add any pressure, but I need you to make a choice. Either you come with us, leave everything behind, and start new somewhere else, or you go home and live your life like we were never a part of it."

Not to add any pressure.

She couldn't think as it was. Her brain was short-circuited. How could she make a choice like this now?

"What about my mother?" she asked.

"If you stay behind, I believe they'll release her the minute they learn you've lost contact with us."

"I'm not so sure it'll be that easy." That sounded so simple. Let him go, and they would both be safe?

She could do that.

Couldn't she?

Her insides twisted into a knot.

"I'm sure it'll work," he reassured her.

Could she say good-bye? Right now?

Sure, she could. She could say good-bye.

But what if it didn't work? What if? "If that's the case, and you know she'll be safe, why did you bring me here, knowing you would keep her in danger? Why?"

His gaze dropped to the floor. He shoved his fingers through his hair. "I was—am—being selfish." He lifted his eyes to hers. They were full of raw emotion. Sadness. Longing. Guilt. "I want you. I want our child."

"And you're willing to risk my mother's life to keep me?"

"I'm willing to risk my life, and the lives of my brothers to keep you," he said softly. "If you come with us, we will go after your mother. And we'll be taking a huge risk to do it. That risk, we're taking for your sake."

"I don't know." She glanced down at the book, now resting in her lap. *Persuasion.* Wasn't that title fitting right now?

He cupped her chin and lifted it, supporting it as her gaze wandered up, up, up to his eyes. They were dark, emotion still swirling in their depths. "If you don't come with us, I will never see you again. I will never hold my child."

Her heart jerked.

If she went with him, her mother might not be released

safely. And yet, if she didn't, who knew? Maybe the CIA or Chimera or whoever would kill her anyway?

Then she'd be alone, with no one to turn to for help.

Either way, she was going to be terrified.

Either way, she might lose her mom.

This was an impossible choice. How would she decide what to do?

25

What the hell am I doing?

There sat the most important woman in his life. Michelle meant more to Talen than anything, anyone. She was carrying his child, a child he needed. A child who might spare Lei from the pain of being tossed away.

And she held his heart in her hands.

Yet, he was about to set her free.

It was the right thing to do, the only choice he could make. He loved her too much to watch her go through another moment of pain.

He'd suffered a weak moment. That was why he'd brought her here. He'd thought for a short time that he might be able to go through with it, take her with him, marry her, despite the risk to her mother's life.

But now that the moment was at hand, he couldn't get himself to do it.

He studied each of her features, trying desperately to commit them to memory. Those full, plump lips, curved ever so slightly up as if she were hiding a naughty secret. The elegant curve of her cheekbone. The straight, narrow line of her little nose. The cool blue of her eyes. Still cupping her chin, he leaned closer, wanting to draw in the scent of her skin one last time. After today, the only thing he would have of her would be memories. He wanted them to be as vivid as possible.

Closer.

He inhaled deeply, listening to the soft sound of her little gasping breaths. She responded so strongly to him. Was that why he'd been so drawn to her?

One taste. Couldn't he have one last kiss?

He drew closer yet. Now her sweet breath caressed his face. It felt as if a magnetic force was pulling him even closer. He couldn't fight it. He wasn't strong enough.

He had never been strong enough.

His lips made contact with hers, and he was swept away from the dark, depressing world of reality into a brilliant, beautiful place. There he was warm and alive. He didn't want to leave. He didn't want the kiss to end.

Gathering his sweet temptress into his arms, he deepened the kiss. His tongue stroked inside her mouth. She tasted decadent, like some kind of rare, luscious fruit. She sighed, trembled, then wrapped her arms around his neck and pressed her soft body against his.

Ah, this was the woman who fit in his arms perfectly. No other woman would ever feel so right. He didn't want to let her go. It was killing him to do it.

You must.

His hand slid down her back, over her round derriere. She whimpered and tipped her hips, pressing against his leg. A blaze swept through his body.

If he didn't cut this off in the next second or two, it would be too late. He caressed her tongue with his once, twice. The hand not resting on her ass supported her head, fingers tangled in silken tresses. He could hold her there, kiss her until she couldn't think anymore. He might even be able to convince her to go with him.

But he wouldn't do it. He loved her too much.

He would let her go.

But first, there was one last thing he had to do.

He pulled the scarf from his pocket. It just about killed him to break the kiss. It felt as if his heart had been ripped from his chest. He lifted the scarf.

"What's that?" Her cheeks were flushed a pretty pink, her lips swollen.

"I need to blindfold you."

"Why?"

"I don't want you to see where we're going." He caressed one of her silken cheeks with a thumb. "Will you trust me? I'm thinking only of you. No one else. Especially not myself."

She searched his eyes for a few heartbeats, then slowly nodded. "Yes, I will trust you." She pivoted, turning her back to him, allowing him to tie the blindfold.

Once he had the blindfold in place, he brushed one last kiss across her lips. His eyes burned as he carefully led her to his car and helped her into it. As he was circling the front of the vehicle, Drako came out into the garage. They exchanged knowing glances. Drako mouthed, "I'm sorry," to his brother. Talen nodded.

Off he went, speeding toward her home. He held her hand the entire drive, wishing he would never have to let it go. Tears gathered in his eyes, and he had to keep blinking them away. Who would have thought he'd ever feel so strongly for a woman? That he would ever shed a tear at the thought of losing one? Over the last five years, he'd walked away from so many. Never, not once, had he regretted it.

As much as he wished the drive would take a lifetime, it didn't. It was over too soon, and he was parking his car, dreading the next moment. He'd prepared for this. Earlier, while she'd been waiting, wondering what was happening, he had put together a note, and a little something that he hoped would ease the pain and burden of raising their child alone. It probably wouldn't be enough. But it was all he could offer.

This was it, the last time he would see her.

Twisting in his seat, he faced her. She was sitting there looking so beautiful. Although she said she trusted him, she was nervous. He could see the swift rise and fall of her chest. The hand he wasn't holding was curled into a tight fist.

He leaned toward her and closed his eyes, his lips not quite touching hers. This time he couldn't allow himself to kiss her. If he did, he knew he wouldn't be able to go through with this.

I love you, Michelle. I love you more than I should.

"Tage?" she whispered.

"We're here. I'll help you out of the car. Once I get you inside, you have to promise me you won't move for five minutes. Not a finger. Not a toe. Nothing. It's important."

"Okay."

He dragged in a deep breath. "All right. Wait here."

She nodded.

He handed her bag to her, then left the car, circled around to her door, and helped her out and up to the door. It was locked, but he'd taken her keys out of her bag before giving it to her. After unlocking the door, he led her inside, set her keys on the table next to the door. Then he pulled the small package from his pocket and left it next to her keys.

She was standing stiffly, her lips parted slightly, her chest rising and falling rapidly.

"It's going to be okay now. I promise." A strand of hair fluttered in front of her face. He tucked it behind her ear, then smoothed his hand down the side of her head. "Thank you for trusting me."

She visibly swallowed. Her hand lifted to his, resting on top of it. She was shaking now, worse than before. "I'm sorry for being so weak—"

"Shhhhh. There's no reason for you to apologize. You're perfect. Always perfect." He ached to kiss her. His arms burned to hold her. One more time. Only once.

No. You can't. You won't let her go.

He let his fingers trail down the curve of her jaw. Then he let her go. "Don't move," he warned.

"I won't."

"I don't want you to be hurt."

"I promise I'll stay right here. What's going on? Am I hiding for a little while? When will you be back?"

"Everything is okay. You can trust me."

Somehow, he made it out the door and into his car. Without looking to see if she'd listened, he pulled out onto the road and hit the gas.

It was done.

She was free.

Her life was her own again.

Four fifty-seven Mississippi, four fifty-eight Mississippi, four fifty-nine Mississippi...five.

Michelle pulled the blindfold down.

Her apartment. She was back in her apartment.

That meant...oh God, that meant he'd decided he didn't want her. He didn't want their child. He had told her he would be taking a risk by keeping them in his life. Clearly they weren't worth that risk.

Her heart shattered.

From the moment he had taken her to his place today, she'd kept telling herself it would be better if he would walk away, go without her. At least then she wouldn't be forced to live the rest of her life as a fugitive.

But somehow knowing that wasn't easing the pain.

She hurt. Everywhere. Inside. Outside. Head. Chest. Stomach. Legs.

She staggered to the couch and fell onto it.

He didn't say good-bye. Nor did he give her the chance to tell him how she felt. Maybe that was why it hurt so much. She would never have closure.

"I loved you," she shouted as she surged to her feet. He wouldn't hear her, but she had to say it anyway. And although she felt as if the world was tipping and rocking, she couldn't sit. Too much adrenaline was charging through her veins. "I loved you so much I would have gone with you. Willingly. Despite the danger."

She staggered to the window and jerked open the shades. The car was gone.

How could he leave without saying good-bye? Without giving her the chance to say good-bye to him? How?

He had stolen her choice. He hadn't let her decide what was best for herself.

"You bastard!"

Tears burned her eyes. She didn't try to stop them. They flowed until there were none left.

What would she do now?

Her phone. She could call him. He had to give her a chance to at least tell him how she felt. Surely he would answer when he saw her number.

She stumbled to the table where her purse was sitting.

There was a small package sitting next to her keys, roughly the size of her wallet.

What's this?

She grabbed it and wasted no time tearing it open.

Inside she found a letter and a key.

> *Dear Michelle,*
> *This wasn't the way I wanted this to go. I*
> *dreamed of sharing the rest of my life with you,*
> *raising our children together, spending our days*
> *laughing and crying, sharing joys and sorrows.*
> *Not this.*
> *But I couldn't put you through the pain I*
> *knew would come. There is so much you don't*
> *know. I doubt you'll ever forgive me for what*
> *I've done. But I still wanted to tell you I love*
> *you. I love you more than I ever thought I could*
> *love a human being. I love you too much to*
> *cause any pain, even the slightest.*
> *Take the key to Sprint Fitness. Locker number*
> *105. Inside you'll find something that will*
> *hopefully help you and our child have a little*
> *better life. It is the least I could do. I wish I*
> *could have done more.*
> *Love, Talen Gryffon*

Fury charged through her. Oh, so he got his closure. He made sure of that. But she... she hadn't... oh hell. A sob ripped through her chest. He loved her. This was his way of showing her. It was a horrible way, but it was something.

"I love you, too. I don't know how I'll live without you," she whispered as she fingered the key.

After giving herself some time to settle down, she put the key in the zippered pocket of her wallet, dropped it into her purse, and checked her phone.

Mom. Mom had called? She checked the time. Ten minutes ago.

Holding her breath, she dialed her mother's number. It rang once. Twice.

A click.

"Hello?"

It was Mom? Mom!

Michelle swallowed a sob. "Mom! You're okay? Where are you?"

"I'm at home, honey. Why? Where did you think I was?"

What did she mean by that? "Mom, you called and there was a scream. The call cut off, and I thought... I thought something had happened."

"Nothing happened. What would happen? Honey, are you okay?"

What the hell? "Yes. I'm fine."

"You said you were coming for a few days. Why did you change your plans?"

This was so weird. It was as if nothing had happened, nothing at all. Had she jumped to the wrong conclusion? Had she let her imagination get the better of her?

No. She'd received that call. About the photographs. It had to be what Tage had said, they'd abducted her but then released her, wiping out her memory somehow. And they'd done it quickly. That meant they must have watched Tage bring her home and knew he wouldn't be returning.

She checked the clock. It was after seven already.

If she had left on time this morning, she would have been at her mom's hours ago. It was getting late now. She wasn't really in the frame of mind to drive for hours in the dark. And she was out of danger now. They both were. There was no reason to hurry.

"I'll leave tomorrow morning," she said. "I have to run an errand first and then I'll head out."

"Are you sure you're all right?" Mom asked.

"Yes, Mom. I'm fine. I... just had a few surprises today. Unfortunately, I couldn't get going like I'd planned."

"All right. I'll see you tomorrow, then. Please call me when you set off, so I know when to expect you."

"I will. I'm sorry I was held up for a day."

"That's okay. I'm just glad I'll see you tomorrow. Drive carefully."

"You know I always do. Love you, Mom," she said before saying good-bye and hanging up. Then she headed for her bedroom.

What a crazy day. So full of twists and turns she felt as if she'd been riding on the world's worst roller coaster.

Or lived the most bizarre nightmare of her life.

Tomorrow, she hoped, would be more normal.

More normal, except for the huge hole in her heart. The one she suspected would never heal.

"What are you doing here? You let her go. That was your choice." In the passenger seat of Talen's loaded-up Range Rover, Malek gave Talen an impatient glare. "We need to get going."

"I know." Talen's fingers tightened around the steering wheel. He shouldn't be here. He knew that. It was dangerous. Stupid. Pathetic, too. But he couldn't help himself. He wanted to see her one last time. Just once more. "Give me five more minutes."

Malek's sigh could be heard in Utah. "We're wasting time."

"I know. Just one more minute." Talen squinted at her window. There. That shadow. Was that her? His heart jerked.

"We've been here long enough. The girls are ready. Drako's waiting." Malek gave Talen's shoulder a shake. "Talen, we have to go."

"Fuck." Talen dropped his head until his forehead struck the steering wheel. Malek didn't understand. He had the woman he loved. He didn't know what it was like losing the biggest, best part of his soul.

"Look, I know what you're going through. Been there."

"No, you haven't. You married her. You married Lei." Talen closed his eyes. At least then he could see her. That sweet face, those eyes.

"Did you forget the hell I went through before Lei agreed to marry me?"

"Maybe I did. Because I don't recall you leaving her behind. When it came time to move, she was on board. She was yours." Unable to sit for another fucking second, Talen got out of the truck and ambled down the sidewalk, toward Michelle's apartment.

Malek followed him. "Yeah, well, there was a time when I was sure I would be losing her forever. And it hurt like hell. Worse than hell."

Talen didn't respond. His guts were being crushed and wrung and ripped. Since he had left last night, he'd been in agony. It was wrong, living without her. Nothing felt like it should. But still he knew she would be better off without him and without all the danger that came with him.

"This was your choice, Talen," his brother reminded him as he stopped next to a tree. "Nobody told you what to do." Malek's phone rang. "It's Drako," he said. "He's probably wondering where the hell we are." His fingers tapped out a message as he spoke. "We don't want him thinking the Chimera got us. And we don't want him and the girls sitting around, waiting, targets."

"Yeah, I get it."

Malek shook his shoulder. "Come on. Are you going to take the other one? What was her name?"

"No. She's Chimera," he said, staring down at the lumpy ground at the base of the tree. "She has to be."

"They found us in a hurry this time. We'd better go."

That much was true. They hadn't been in southern Ohio for long at all. That was part of the reason why he'd made the decision he had about Michelle. If they weren't able to shake the Chimera this time, their lives could become very different. What little peace they had known might be lost for good. That was not what he wanted for her, or their child.

"Come on, bro. You love her too much to make her go through hell with us. I get that. Sometimes I wish I'd been strong enough to do the same for Lei. And sometimes I think her problems having a child might have been for the best. If I divorce her..." Malek visibly swallowed. "Then she wouldn't have to be afraid anymore. You know what I mean?"

Understanding exactly what Malek was thinking, Talen nodded. "Yeah. It's tough." He turned, gazing at her window again. "I want Michelle. I want her more than anything. But it wouldn't be right."

"We weren't prepared for this. We should have been. But we weren't." Malek jerked his head toward the truck. "Come on. It's time to go."

Talen turned and took a couple of steps toward the Range Rover before swiveling to steal a glance over his shoulder.

There she was.

It was her. His Michelle. Strolling to her car as if she hadn't a care in the world.

As it should be.

26

Sprint Fitness.

Women's locker room.

Locker number 105.

She pushed the key into the lock and twisted. Inside she found a duffel bag. There was a tag. Feeling a little unsure if she was doing something wrong, she checked the tag.

Michelle Linsey.

Okay. He'd made sure she would know this bag was intended for her. She pulled it out, and, leaving the key in the lock, headed out to her car. The minute she was locked in her car, she unzipped the bag. Inside she found several large plastic bags full of cash and a white envelope. Stuffing the cash back in the bag, she left the envelope out, then zipped the bag back up and started her car.

Her hands were trembling.

She had no idea how much money was in that bag. She'd never seen so much cash in one place. Just from that one glance, she'd noticed that there were bills of different denominations.

Fifties. Twenties. Hundreds. There was no way to know how much money was actually there until she sat down and counted it.

It would take a while. As curious as she was, she didn't want to take the time now. But it was terrifying, driving around with so much cash.

Should she hide it somewhere? Take it back to the gym and lock it up where it would be safe?

A tremor quaked through her as the reality of what she had in her possession hit her.

That was a lot of money—cash meant to provide for her baby. Cash that meant the difference between them struggling to make ends meet and living a comfortable life.

She needed that money. Desperately.

And she had Talen Gryffon to thank for it. Talen. That was his real name. She would use that name from this point on. Talen Gryffon.

But driving around with it, that was foolish. What if she stopped somewhere to go to the bathroom and someone broke into her car? She needed to put it somewhere safe.

A bank was the safest place she could think of.

She turned her car back on the road, but headed in the opposite direction. As she drove, she checked the clock. Her bank would be open by the time she got there. She'd get a bank deposit box, put the bag in there, and then rest easy knowing it was safe.

As she drove the rest of the way, all she could do was silently thank Talen for thinking of her and their child, of wanting to make sure they wouldn't struggle for the rest of their lives.

And for loving her so much he let her go.

That was the kind of love she'd always dreamed of. Selfless love. Giving love. Little had she known how painful that kind of love could be.

* * *

Her stop at the bank went over without a hitch. And once she knew her money was safe, it was easier for her to relax and enjoy the drive out to her mother's place. It wasn't a long trip, just lengthy enough for her to do a little reflecting. But not long enough for her to mentally prepare herself to give her mom the shocking news, that she was pregnant and unmarried. Her mother would be devastated.

Thus, her reunion with her mother wasn't as joyful as she'd hoped. The woman was extremely astute. She sensed something was wrong from the moment she laid eyes on Michelle.

"What is it?" her mother asked, after giving Michelle a big, squeezy hug. "What's wrong?"

Something inside Michelle snapped. A sob ripped up her throat. Clinging to the one human being she knew she could count on, she let all her tears of frustration and loss and terror go.

Her mother gently pulled her into the house and held her until all her tears had dried up and there was nothing left. "Is it a man?" her mom asked as she handed Michelle a tissue.

Michelle dabbed at her soggy, swollen face and nodded. "Yes."

"Love hurts," her mother said.

"Yes, it does. More than I ever imagined."

"Where is he?" Mom asked, handing her another tissue.

"I don't know. Gone."

"He'll come back."

"No. That won't happen. He can't come back. It's all so complicated."

"If he loves you, as much as you love him, he will. Nothing else will matter. He won't be able to stay away."

"This is different." Michelle's insides twisted. "It's because he loves me that he won't come back."

"We'll see about that." Her mom's gaze searched her face as she smoothed Michelle's flyaway hair back from her face. "We'll just see about that."

"Mom, there's more." Michelle swallowed hard, knowing she was about to break her mother's heart. How many times had her mom told her she didn't want to ever see Michelle struggle to raise a child by herself? How many times had she warned her not to get herself into that position? "I...I..." She couldn't do it. She couldn't say the words. A tear seeped from the corner of her eye.

Her mother pulled Michelle into her arms again and kissed the top of her head. "He'll be back if he's worth anything."

Hours passed. No Talen.

Michelle tried not to let her heartache ruin her time with her mother. But it was difficult. She didn't have a lot to say. She couldn't enjoy the things she used to, like walks down dirt country roads, or watching her mother's favorite television shows with her. Or even eating.

Days passed. Still no Talen, not that she expected him. He had no idea where she was, where her mother lived.

The more time went by, the more Michelle came to accept that she would never see Talen again. But even though she accepted it, the pain still gnawed at her. By the time her final day with her mother had arrived, Michelle had found a small measure of peace. She would carry on alone. She would make a happy home for her child. A nurturing family. And she would do it here, with her mother. She'd find a job and move. Any job. This was the kind of environment she wanted her child to grow up in. Safe. Beautiful. Full of nature and clean air and dirt and space to run.

This was her past. And it would be her future, too.

She walked down a winding dirt drive that meandered along a line of trees. At the end of a long driveway sat a beautiful farmhouse, nestled in a clearing circled by tall oaks. She'd always loved that house. It was set far back from the road. There was a barn. Fields. A pond with ducks.

And a *For Sale* sign.

It was for sale.

If only she had enough to buy that place. It was perfect. She hurried her pace, tromping down the road. Gravel crunched under her feet.

Gravel crunched behind her. Was it a car? A child on a bike? She glanced over her shoulder.

Her heart jerked.

"Michelle."

Talen. He had found her. Her gaze snapped to his eyes. What was he doing here? Her heart literally stalled for one, two, three seconds.

"Talen." She glanced left, right. They were alone...she thought. "Is it safe?"

"Probably not. But I had to come find you." Moving swiftly, he grabbed her wrist and tugged her into the deep shadows along the tree line. Once they were obscured, he set both hands on her shoulders and held her in place. "Did you get my package?"

Was that why he'd come? Just to make sure she had the money? Or had he come for something else? "I did," she whispered. "Thank you. I have no idea how much is there, but anything will be a help. I may not be able to work."

"There's enough for you to quit working. Permanently. And...I can send more from time to time."

So, it was the money. "That's very generous. Thank you."

"You're carrying my child. I want to help. I'd rather be a part of his life, but...if that isn't possible..." He stared into her eyes. "I can't stop thinking about you."

"Me, either."

His hand cupped her cheek, and she tilted her head, resting it against his palm. Her eyelids lowered as she focused on that small touch, the heat, the soft caress, the ache of wanting more.

Why couldn't things be simple? Why did loving this man have to be so painful and complicated?

"When you aren't near, all I can think about is you," he said. "Where you are. Whether you're safe."

She placed her hand over his. "Talen." She could hear the turmoil in her own voice.

"I want you to be happy," he told her.

"I know."

His gaze dragged across her face. His eyes were so dark, so full of confusion and turmoil. "Tell me what to do."

"I don't know. I really don't know."

"I haven't married anyone yet. My brother is putting pressure on me to find someone."

"You didn't marry Angela?" Just imagining him married to another woman made her insides feel like they were being thrashed.

"No. She's...she is working for them."

"You know about her?"

He nodded.

"I wish I knew what to do," she whispered.

"Being with me...it isn't easy. We have to move often, take new identities. We have to stay to ourselves, can't trust people."

She pressed against his hand, holding it to her cheek. "It must be a very lonely life."

"It is if you don't have someone...you love."

"I think any life is a lonely life if you don't have someone you love," she confessed.

"I've never loved anyone like I love you." His thumb grazed her lip.

"Me, either," she whispered, blinking. Her eyes were burning again. Her nose, too. Dammit, she was going to cry. "If only things could be simple. Normal."

"I wish that could be, too. You have no idea how much I wish for that. But it can't ever be. Not for me or my brothers. Not for anyone who is in our lives." He tugged on his hand.

She let it go. "Have you moved already?"

"My brothers and their wives are on their way to our next home."

"Is it far?"

"Yes. I won't ever see you again."

She blinked a few times. Never was a long time. Never was a lifetime.

She glanced around. This was home. A place that made her feel safe. At peace.

But it wasn't enough. Not even having that house, the perfect house with the pond and the ducks and the barn, would be enough if she had to live in it without Talen.

"If I knew my mother was safe..." she thought aloud, not really knowing where it might lead.

"If we took her with us, she'd have to understand she can't contact anyone from her past," he warned.

"She doesn't have anyone but me." Michelle's heart started thumping fast, hard.

"And she'd have to leave everything behind. Her home. Her possessions. Everything."

"My mother has never been fond of things. Could she really go with us? Would my mother be safe?"

"As safe as the rest of us. There would always be a risk. For all of us."

"But at least we would be together."

"Yes." He leaned closer, until his mouth was hovering over hers. "I want you, Michelle. More than I want to take my next breath. But not if you'll be unhappy. It'll kill me if you come and then regret it."

She closed the distance between them, sealing her mouth to his and letting her kiss tell him everything her heart was feeling. Would she regret this decision? She hoped not. All she knew was that the world was too empty without him. She had to take the risk.

His tongue stroked the seam of her mouth and she opened to him, welcoming his intimate caress. Her mouth filled with his sweet flavor, and her body filled with pounding heat. She wrapped her arms around his neck and kissed him back until her legs were so wobbly they could barely hold her weight.

When the kiss ended, she was dizzy and breathless and shaky. She inhaled, pulling in a lung full of air, then let it out in a long sigh.

He rested his forehead against hers. "Are you sure?"

"Yes. I'm sure. I want to be with you, Talen. No matter what."

The craziest impulse flashed through her head. Acting upon it, she reached for his hands and placed them on her breasts. "I need you."

A low growl vibrated in the air between them. His eyes turned dark. "Now?" His hands slid down her stomach.

Her breath caught in her throat. "Yes. Please."

"Michelle." He pushed her top up, exposing her bra.

Her heart rate kicked up to double-time. "Take me."

His fingers hooked over the top of her bra cup. His gaze raked over her body, making her skin sizzle.

God, this man could make her melt with just a look. Her empty pussy clenched. Reaching around her back, she unclasped her bra.

He pushed the cups up, exposing her breasts. Her nipples were already hard, tight little peaks. "Beautiful," he uttered as he lowered his head. His tongue flicked over one aching bud, and her back arched. More, she needed more. "Say it again," he whispered. Then he pulled her nipple into his warm mouth and suckled hard.

Little blades of pleasure pierced her insides. Her knees wobbled. "Take me, Talen. I'm yours," she muttered as she slowly sank. Strong arms cradled her, eased her to the ground. She lay on a blanket of earth and cool grass, the brilliant blue sky poking through a thick woven blanket of tree branches overhead.

Heaven.

He kissed his way down her body, stopping at the waist of her pants. Within seconds, he had them off. Her panties, too. He knelt above her, gazing down at her as if she were something priceless, precious.

"Talen." She lifted her arms to him.

He unzipped his pants, pulled his thick rod out, and settled between her thighs. "You're mine, Michelle. I won't ever take another woman again." His rod plunged deep inside her, filling her completely.

Immediately lost in the ecstasy of his claiming, she wrapped her legs around his waist. Deep. Deeper. She wanted him to take her hard and fast, then slowly, sweetly. She rocked her hips, meeting each of his hard thrusts. With each stroke, her body burned hotter, her senses grew sharper. The sounds of their lovemaking filled her ears and heightened her pleasure. The husk of their hard breaths. The crackle of twigs snapping beneath her. The scent of earth and man filled her nose, blending into a perfect perfume. She closed her eyes and moistened her lips, tasting his kiss still lingering on them.

This was where she belonged. In this man's arms. In his bed. She relinquished her body to him, eagerly welcoming him to take his pleasure. But instead of taking, he eased back on his knees and pressed a moistened thumb to her clit. With his cock buried deep inside, he started stroking her sensitive pearl.

Ah, it was glorious.

"You crave domination," he uttered as he stroked her to paradise. "You long to learn how to serve your master."

Her body's temperature spiked. "Yes," she said, writhing beneath him. "Oh yes."

"I will teach you. I'll teach you the joy of submission."

"Please."

That thumb moved faster, drawing swift circles. She was so hot, so tight. Everywhere. On the verge. Oh, almost there.

Her chest constricted. A flare of heat blazed deep in her center.

"Come for me. Now," he demanded.

It felt like a white-hot ball of fire exploded inside her. She was overpowered. Lost in pleasure so intense she thought she might die from it.

He angled over her and slammed his cock into her spasming center.

"Yes," he said, pressing his lips to her neck. His cock rammed in and out, in and out, drawing out her pleasure, making it last and last. Oh, she hoped it would never end. The wave of a second climax rolled over her, and she cried out. His joined hers as he orgasmed deep inside her, filling her.

Then, with their bodies still joined, he rolled onto his side, taking her with him, cradling her in his arms.

She smiled into his dark eyes.

He smiled back, and she knew without any doubts that she had made the right choice. She would rather give up everything she had than let this man walk out of her life.

Tipping his head, he kissed her forehead. "As much as I'd love to stay here and do that again, we need to move quickly. The sooner we get your mother safe, the better."

"Okay." Reluctantly, she pulled out of his hold. It was hard. It was painful. With gentle hands, he helped her dress. Together they walked to a black vehicle she hadn't seen before, parked on the road. Within minutes, they were bouncing down the potholed street toward her mother's house, talking about what needed to happen as they drove. The second Talen had the vehicle parked in her mom's driveway, she scrambled out of the car and hurried up to the door. She let herself in, shouting, "Mom?" as she rushed toward the kitchen where she suspected her mother would be.

She found her there.

But she wasn't alone.

27

Surprised there was a visitor standing in her mother's kitchen, Michelle clamped her lips shut.

What was *she* doing here? Had she followed Talen?

"Hi, Michelle. Talen," Angela said, smiling. "Susan made us tuna salad sandwiches and homemade soup for lunch. Doesn't that sound delicious?"

Michelle's gaze jerked from Angela to her mother, who was busy at the stove. Her mom glanced over her shoulder. "Honey, I wish you'd told me you were bringing friends for lunch. I would have made more sandwiches."

"I...didn't know they were coming," she said, her gaze jumping back and forth between Angela and Talen. Angela looked extremely pleased. Talen, tense.

Cranking up her smile to full wattage, Angela said, "Talen, it's so good seeing you again. When I heard you had moved without saying good-bye, I was disappointed."

"It wasn't an intentional slight," he said, voice cold.

"Honey, why don't you set the table for lunch?" Susan asked as she stirred the soup.

"Um…" Michelle stole a glance at Talen. He nodded. "Okay." Extremely nervous, she went to the cupboard and pulled out plates, bowls, and cups. If Angela was here, then she had to assume Angela's cousin was skulking around somewhere close by.

Talen wandered toward the front of the house. Angela hopped up from her seat at the kitchen table and followed him.

"Isn't it a total surprise, seeing you here?" she said, trailing behind him.

"I suppose it is."

While keeping an eye on the quiet exchange between her coworker and Talen, Michelle set the plates, bowls, and cups on the table, then went to the drawer for silverware.

"Angela told me you work together," Michelle's mother said, still stirring soup at the stove. "I'm so proud of you. You've done so well."

"Mom," she whispered. "We need to talk."

"Okay. What is it, honey?" she asked, much too loudly.

Michelle pressed an index finger to her lips and flicked a glance at Talen and Angela. "In private."

"Now?"

"Yes." Reaching past her mother, Michelle clicked off the stove's burner. Her heart was racing so fast, Michelle felt a little light-headed. She grabbed her mother's hand and dragged her out onto the back porch. "Mom, we have to leave here. Now."

"Leave? Why? Where are we going?"

"I want you to go grab anything important, pictures, keepsakes, anything you can't live without."

"I don't understand—"

"I'll explain later. Just please, go now." Adrenaline pounding through her system as her fear escalated, Michelle gave her confused mother a gentle shove toward the door. "Hurry. Or you'll have to leave everything behind."

Her mom stared at her for several seconds, as if she were

frozen. Desperate to wake her up, Michelle shook her softly by the shoulders until she seemed a little more with it. "Mom?"

"We're leaving?" She wandered back into the kitchen, just as a loud *bang* blasted through the living room.

Michelle whirled around and sprinted toward the front of the house.

Angela was standing in the middle of the room, a gun gripped in her hands. That gun, the weapon that could end all of their lives at any moment, was shaking. A lot.

Talen was sitting on the floor, his head hanging low.

Was he hurt? Shot?

Ohmygod! Panic blasted through her like an electric current. She dashed toward him.

"Stop!" Angela yelled.

She didn't stop. She couldn't. She ran to him, colliding with a rocking chair on the way. She staggered, stumbled. He caught her as she was falling. They landed together on the floor, his body cushioning her.

"Don't move!" Angela shouted.

"Are you hurt?" Michelle wheezed. She couldn't breathe. She was dizzy. Where had all the freaking air gone? Her gaze jerked from one part of his body to another. Head. Looked okay. No blood. Neck, okay. Chest, okay. Thank God it was okay. Stomach, no blood.

"I'm fine." He reached for her face.

Red.

She saw red.

Blood. Blood!

She started clawing at his sleeve, trying to see the wound. "You've been shot." She blinked as little patches of black started obscuring her vision.

"Michelle."

She had to see the wound. She had to help him.

"Michelle." He caught her chin in his hand and lifted. Her gaze snapped to his eyes. "I'm fine. It's nothing. A scratch. It doesn't even hurt."

"You're shot," she yelled.

"I'm fine."

She felt a nudge and looked. Her mother was sitting next to her now, her eyes wide with terror. "Mom, are you okay?"

"What's happening?" she asked.

"What's happening is you're going for a little ride, Susan," Angela said, still holding the gun, which was now pointed at Talen's head. She held a cell phone with the other hand.

"Me?"

"Harboring a fugitive is a crime." Angela poked at the phone buttons with her thumb.

Susan looked at Michelle and then Talen. "Who is the fugitive?"

"She doesn't know anything," Talen said calmly. "Let her go."

"I'm not letting anyone go until backup is here. And that should be any minute now."

"Why are you doing this?" Michelle glared at her ex-coworker. She was so enraged, she could barely put two words together.

"Why? I have my reasons. But there's really no point in explaining them to you. You've been brainwashed by that man." Angela flicked the gun.

"I haven't been brainwashed by anyone."

Looking at her with pity, Angela merely shook her head and poked at her phone with her thumb some more. "It's sad. I do feel a little bad for you. A little." She lifted her phone to her ear and said, "I have them." Then she focused on her phone as she ended the call.

Talen didn't give a single warning. The second Angela looked away, he lunged toward her, slamming her off her feet. She sailed backward. The gun flew from her hand. He scrambled to grab it as it landed with a thud. Everything seemed to move in slow motion.

Michelle sat there in shock and tried to comprehend what was happening. Her mind couldn't quite keep up with events as they were unfolding. Talen was on top of Angela now. He had her pinned to the floor, but she was kicking, screaming.

"Go get in the car," he shouted. "Move! Now!"

Suddenly, as if jarred from a dream, Michelle could react. She grabbed her mom's hand and jumped to her feet. "Come on!" She pulled. Slowly her mother stood. She raced toward the door, remembering she needed her purse, her keys. They were in her room. Leaving Mom at the door, she veered off, down the hallway. She ran as hard as she could, bouncing off walls and door frames and furniture. Purse. On the dresser. She snatched it, turned around, and slammed into Talen.

"They're out front," he said. "Is there a back exit?"

"Yes. This way." She ran past him, sprinted toward the front of the house where she'd left Mom, and then, catching her hand again, led all three to the patio door. They slid it open just as the first few armed agents came around the corner of the house.

She hesitated.

Talen pushed on her back and yelled, "Run!"

Refusing to release her mother's hand, Michelle ran as fast and as hard as she could. Mom kept up with her as their feet pounded over grass. They made it to the small creek at the back of the property. Without slowing, she leapt over it. Mom's hand slipped from hers as she sailed through the air. On the other side, she turned back to see where her mom was.

She had stopped, was looking back toward the house.

Talen. Where was Talen?

Michelle's gaze hopped from her mom to the horde of men in black gathered at the rear of the house.

Something was happening.

Did they capture him?

Her mother turned toward her, her expression a mixture of fear and worry. "What's happening? Who is that man?"

"Mom, that's the father of my child."

Everything was fucked up. Everything.

Talen was on the ground, facedown, hands and legs bound. His arm felt as if it was on fire, thanks to the fucking gunshot.

He needed to get to his phone and turn off the GPS. If he was going down, he didn't want his brothers going with him. They would track them down if he didn't. Right now, they were safe. The Secret was safe. Rin and Lei were safe. It was better for everyone if things stayed that way.

A couple of guys caught him by the arms. Another one grabbed his legs, and he was lifted. They would take him in and torture him, try to get the location of The Secret. He'd prepared for this day his whole life. It was here now. He prayed he was ready.

He was surrounded by black uniforms. FBI agents. Undercover Chimera. He couldn't see Michelle. She had to have gotten away. She had to be safe. She was his weakness, the one person he might risk The Secret for. If they knew that... if they used that...

They dumped him into the back of an armored truck. He landed hard. The air left his lungs, and for a few seconds he struggled to draw in a breath. It hurt, but he knew it was nothing compared to the pain that would be coming.

"Child, Michelle? *Your* child?" Her mom's face was the color of bleached flour.

"Yes. I'm pregnant, Mom." Michelle held her breath, waiting for her mother's reaction. Would she be angry? Worse, would she cry?

"Oh honey." Her hands trembled as she smoothed Michelle's hair back from her face.

"It's okay. I'm set. I have everything I need. I've decided—"

"Except a husband. You don't have a husband. Your child won't have a father."

"You're right." Turning, Michelle looked up at the back of the house. Her mother's words stung, but not nearly as bad as the horrific sight Michelle was watching now. They were carrying Talen away, hog-tied. "He wanted to marry me."

"What did he do? Where are those men taking him?"

"I don't know exactly. They say he's a terrorist, but I don't believe them." Her nose and eyes were burning. Dammit, she was going to cry. She hated crying. Crying was weak.

"A terrorist?" her mother shot back. "Like...like the kind who blows up buildings?"

"He's not a terrorist." Michelle dragged her index fingers under her eyes. They came away damp.

"Oh honey. Oh."

"He's not. I know it. He's a good man. A kind man. A strong man. Brave. Sweet." Tears were flowing freely now. She couldn't hold them back.

"Honey." Her mom gathered her into her arms and held her as the sobs ripped through her chest. She couldn't stop crying. She tried. The sobbing hurt so badly. Her insides felt as if they were being crushed under the weight of a hundred cars. Just as she had when Michelle had been little, her mom held her and smoothed her hand down her hair. "I don't know how you got tangled up in this mess, but it's over now. It's over."

"It won't ever be over for me. Or the baby."

"Yes, the child. I'll help you. Come home. We can raise the baby together."

"That's not what I mean." Michelle sniffled and hiccupped between words. "I can take care of the baby. But I don't know if I can live without him. I love him, Mom. I love him so much

I hurt everywhere when we're apart. I can't breathe when he's away. I can't sleep. I can't eat. I have been trying all week to convince myself I didn't need him. But I failed. I still hurt as much today as I did the first day."

"It's going to take time. Time will heal your heart."

Michelle didn't believe that. Nothing would heal her heart. Because it had been ripped out of her chest. She didn't have a heart anymore. It was gone.

Surrendered to Talen.

Her mom slid her hand down Michelle's arm. When it reached her hand, she gripped it. "Come on. Let's go back to the house. It's safe now."

"I don't know."

"They took him away. It looks like they're all leaving. Come on now. We can't hide out here forever. I'll make you some tea, and later, when you feel more up to it, we'll talk about what we'll do next."

This wasn't the end she had hoped for. No. Not after talking to Talen earlier today. But it had been the one she'd planned for. So why did she feel so awful? So...hopeless?

Unable to speak, she merely nodded. Together, she and her mom walked up to the house. With each step, her racing heartbeat slowed a little, the adrenaline easing. By the time they reached the house, she was feeling wrung out and exhausted.

Her mom opened the door and stepped inside. Michelle followed. But before she'd made it one step, two men grabbed her, jerking her arms behind her back.

Her mom wailed, "Nooooo! They promised! Leave my daughter alone!"

Promised?

What?

"Mom?"

Her mother's eyes were dilated with terror. Her face was the shade of milk. "I called them when you arrived. They were supposed to leave you alone. I trusted them." She sobbed. "Let my daughter go!" she screeched.

"Sorry, ma'am. We can't do that yet," one of the officers said as he yanked Michelle toward the door.

She was going to be arrested? Then what?

"Mom, I'll be okay. I don't know anything," she said to her distraught mother as she was tugged toward the exit. In truth, she didn't know whether she would be okay or not. It was against the law to torture people, but she had to wonder whether that mattered behind closed doors. And if these men were really members of some secret society, then who knew what they might do to her to motivate Talen to talk.

Her blood turned to ice.

As they shoved her into the back of a black van, she turned pleading eyes to one of her captors and said, "Please. I'm pregnant."

He looked at the man next to him.

They smiled.

"Isn't that convenient?" the first man said, his voice a frightening, low growl.

Stars glittered in Michelle's vision, and the air thinned. She gagged as a wave of nausea blasted through her. They gave her one last look, then slammed the door, locking her inside the cargo area.

Oh God, what were they going to do to her?

28

Pain. Throbbing.

Sharp, shooting.

His head. Chest. Leg. Face.

Talen eased onto his back. Light seeped through his closed eyelids. Bright light.

Where the fuck was he?

Hospital?

Prison?

That fucking light was so intense.

He lifted one hand to shade his face. The fingers of his other one moved. They scratched into something soft, gritty.

That wasn't cotton beneath him. It was earth.

Where the hell?

Ever so carefully, he inhaled. It smelled like outside. Like wildlife. Dirt and sunshine and plants.

He fought to think, to remember. What happened? A flashback shot through his mind. A truck. He'd been in a truck. Then...nothing.

Had they dumped him out? Why?

Keeping his hand over his eyes, he slowly opened his eyelids.

Blue sky. White clouds. Treetops.

He rocked his head to the side. There was the road. And roughly thirty feet from the road was the truck. It had veered off, rolled down an embankment, but it hadn't flipped over. The doors were all open.

Stretching his neck, he looked around. He saw nobody. No men.

What the hell?

Moving carefully, he pushed upright. His head pounded. His stomach turned. He swallowed hard. His throat was dry, and his mouth. He ached. Muscles. Bones.

Damn. He wanted to lie back down. Close his eyes. For just a minute. One minute.

No.

Going against everything his body demanded, he climbed onto hands and knees. It hurt like hell to move. He continued, pushing up onto his feet. He staggered a couple of steps forward, a couple more. His sight narrowed. Blackness obscured his peripheral vision. He focused on the vehicle and took another step, then another. When he made it, he collapsed into the empty driver's seat.

Nobody was in the truck.

What happened?

He checked the vehicle. The key was in the ignition. He turned it, and the engine started up.

He had transportation. Where would he go?

He pulled the door shut, but left the window open for fresh air.

Where would he go?

Michelle. He had to check on her first.

Phone.

His pocket.

It wasn't there. *Damn.*

He leaned back in the seat, closed his eyes. He needed to rest for a minute, and to think. His head was so fucking muddy.

"Hey, buddy. You okay?"

It was a voice. Male. Someone was speaking to him.

With difficulty he opened his eyes.

There was man, a stranger, standing next to his door, peering through the open window. White hair. Pale blue eyes. Face that had seen a lot of weather. "Are you hurt?"

"I think I'm all right."

The old man's eyes narrowed. "You don't look all right. Maybe I should call nine-one-one."

"No, that's okay. I just had . . . an upset stomach. I'll be fine. Thanks."

The man's forehead furrowed, lines deepening. "Are you sure?" He raised his phone. "I have a phone right here."

"You know what . . . can I borrow that?"

"Sure." The man handed him the phone.

He dialed Michelle's number. Voice mail. He dialed Drako's number. Voice mail. He dialed Malek's number. Voice mail. Didn't anyone answer their fucking phone? Shaking his head, he handed it back to the man. "No answer. Thanks anyway."

"You're welcome." The man gave him a once-over. "Listen, I live right over the hill. Would you like a cup of coffee or something?"

"No, thanks. I should be going."

The man stepped back, and Talen hit the gas. The vehicle's tires dug into the soft earth for several seconds. Finally, they caught hold and the truck lurched forward, toward the road. He pressed on the accelerator to get it up the embankment. When it was finally on the road, he eased up. He had no idea where he was or which direction he should go.

Hoping there would be a town somewhere close by, he followed the winding road through the thick forest. He'd driven no more than a couple of miles when he heard his phone's ring-tone.

Heart thumping, he steered off the road, jumped out of the driver's seat, and opened the back door. It was on the floor. He scooped it up and checked the screen.

Michelle. She'd called. She was safe. Safe! But for how long?

He hit the button to call her back. It rang twice. Three times. Four. Just as he was about to give up, he heard a *click*.

"Talen."

"Michelle. I'm okay. Don't know where I am." Memories flooded his mind. "Are you still at your mother's place?"

"No. I'm not. I'm...I've been...they want to talk to you."

His blood turned to ice.

"You know why we've let you go," a voice said. It wasn't Angela's voice. It wasn't even a female.

He didn't respond. There was no need.

"We know about her *delicate condition*. Congratulations," the prick on the phone said.

Talen's heart stopped.

"Give us what we want, or they'll both die."

It took almost thirty minutes before Talen found any sign of life. He pulled into the somewhat dilapidated gas station-slash-coffee shop, killed the engine, and dialed his brother's number again.

This time Drako answered, "Talen. Tell me it hasn't gone bad."

"It's gone bad. The pricks found out I'd come back for her."

"Damn. Sorry."

"Yeah." Talen let his head fall forward. His forehead rested against the steering wheel.

"You know what we've been taught to do."

Talen closed his eyes. "I know." An image of Michelle's face flashed in his memory. His blood burned with rage.

"You can't do it, can you?" his brother asked.

"No. I can't. Could you?"

"No. Want some help?"

"No." Talen's heart thumped hard. He knew what he had to do. "I want you to go on without me, as if I were…dead. If I don't know where you are, and I can't reach you, they won't be able to torture or drug me into helping them find you."

" 'Kay. If that's what you want." Drako went silent.

Talen's hand shook as he pressed the phone tighter against his ear. Would this truly be the last time he spoke to his brothers? Would he never see them again alive? "I love you, bro. And Malek. And Rin and Lei. You'll tell them, won't you?"

"I will." Drako's voice wavered slightly.

"Thanks."

"You're sure about this?"

"I owe Michelle this much. She's carrying my child. I couldn't live with myself if I didn't go after her."

"We'll be thinking about you. Especially Lei."

Lei. His insides twisted. He would never see her again. It hurt, a lot, to realize she wouldn't be a part of his life anymore.

But it hurt even more imagining life without Michelle.

Yes, he was doing the right thing. He was sure of it.

"Love you," he said to his oldest brother. Drako would be okay without him. He would do just fine.

"Love you, too."

The call ended.

Talen took a moment to compose himself. It was hard to breathe, difficult to think. He needed a little time. Once he was sure he could concentrate, he dialed Michelle's number.

The bastard he'd talked to earlier answered on the first ring, "I knew you would make the right decision."

"We're not letting him do this alone," Drako announced as he slammed his phone down. "No fucking way." They were at a diner in some godforsaken town in the middle of nowhere. Exactly where they didn't need to be.

Malek leaned forward, looked left, right. "I didn't think you'd go for that," he whispered. "What's the plan?"

Drako glanced over his shoulder. The girls were in the bathroom, getting cleaned up. They would be back any minute. "I don't have a plan yet. We need to find out where they're holding Michelle. If Talen genuinely loves her, which I have no doubt, he'll discover his gift. Whatever it is, hopefully it, along with ours, will be enough to get us all out of danger."

Malek sighed. He shoved his fingers through his hair. "I'm so tired of this shit."

"Me too." That was no understatement. After what they'd been through this past year, he would do anything to live a normal life. And to give his wife a better life.

Their waitress came over to take their order. Drako ordered a burger and fries for himself, a salad for his wife. Malek ordered for himself and his wife.

When the waitress left to get their drinks, Malek said, "Too bad your plan to go on the offensive and knock them all out for good didn't work."

"There's too many of them." Drako checked for the girls again. Still no sign of them. Telling Rin what they were up to was going to be tough. He wanted to wait until they were alone. In private. "We're just going to have to be smarter. Move farther."

"Or..." Malek's eyes met his. "We could destroy it."

"No. We can't." Didn't he wish it could be that simple?

"Why not?" Malek challenged. "What the hell are we keeping the goddamn thing for anyway? If it'll cause the total destruction of our culture, our economy, our government, why not get rid of it? We won't be forced to live like this anymore."

Drako leaned closer and lowered his voice even more. "For one thing, they won't believe it's actually destroyed."

"What if we do it in front of them?" Malek suggested.

"They still would probably think it's a replica."

"There's got to be a way." Malek jammed his fingers through his hair again. "I'm so fucking tired of running, hiding, living in the shadows."

"Me too, Malek."

"And Lei..." Malek blinked several times. He was trying to hide his emotions. He wasn't succeeding. "I don't want to divorce her."

"You don't have to. No matter what."

"If we can't save Talen and Michelle, then that leaves you and Rin to have all three Gryffons. Who's to say she'll be able to have three boys?" He stopped short when Drako jumped to his feet. "What are you doing?"

Drako poked the buttons on his phone. "Getting ready to find Talen."

"You don't have a plan yet."

"No, I don't. I'm hoping something will come to me on the road. Go, tell your wife good-bye. We'll leave the girls here and take your car. I'm going to grab The Secret. We're taking it with us."

29

How long had it been? How long had she sat in this sterile effing room? Hours. Days. Weeks?

It had been tedious. But it could have been worse. When Michelle had first been abducted, she had been terrified. She'd feared being raped, beaten up, killed. None of those things had happened. Although she was relieved, every time her door's lock disengaged, her heart would start racing again.

Most of the time it had been someone delivering a meal.

Not this time.

"You must be relieved," Angela said as she sauntered into the room. "Talen has decided your life is worth something."

"I never doubted him." Standing by the window, Michelle sent her captor some serious squinty-eyes. Michelle had never despised anyone like she did this woman. Since bringing Michelle here, she'd proven to be inhumanely cruel. Sadistic.

"No, you wouldn't doubt him." Scowling, Angela brushed some nonexistent dirt off Michelle's bed and sat, crossing her knee. "You believe in the good in people. Me, I learned a long time ago that people always think about themselves first." She picked at her manicured fingernail. "As it turns out, Talen needs you. There's no other reason why he's coming for you. If he didn't need you, he wouldn't bother. He'd find another willing woman to carry his offspring." Snarling, she spat, "Breeder. That's what you are. His breed mare."

Michelle didn't bother responding to that insult. There was no point. She'd learned that by now. Angela was just being cruel for cruelty's sake. Giving her the benefit of a reaction only encouraged her.

Michelle just hoped she could continue to stay strong. Angela's words did sting, some more than others.

"Anyway, your breakfast will be here in a few minutes. Wouldn't want that little monster inside of you to die from lack of nutrition."

Monster. She'd called her baby a monster.

Michelle placed her hand on her stomach.

Angela leaned forward, one elbow on her knee. Her gaze jumped from Michelle's stomach to her face. "You don't know, do you?"

Whatever it was, Michelle didn't want to hear it.

A tray slid through the small opening at the bottom of the door. Breakfast. Ignoring Angela's taunt, Michelle picked up her tray and went to the tiny table bolted to the opposite wall.

Angela followed her. The bitch. "Did you hear me, Michelle?"

Michelle locked her gaze on her tray. If only she could swing it at that bitch's face. If only. But what good would that do? She would still be locked in this room. Still be at the bitch's mercy. Still be forced to sit around and wait for Talen to show up and be captured and killed.

Her insides revolted. She wasn't so hungry anymore.

"You win. I've had enough," Michelle muttered as she jerked around and scurried toward the window again. The view outside was blocked by a board. But a sliver of light cut between the outside wall and the ugly piece of wood. It was the only way she could tell what time of day it was. The light disappeared for hours when the sun went down and then it would reappear. As time crept by, the shaft's angle would change. "Just leave me alone."

Angela sat at the table and sniffed at Michelle's food, something that resembled eggs, along with some cold, stale toast and soggy fruit. "God, this slop is awful. You poor thing. Forced to eat something my dog wouldn't touch. And having that... *thing*... inside you. It's all those years of exposure. It's messed up their DNA. I know you hear me." Angela stood, swayed over to her. "You don't want to ignore what I'm telling you."

"Why should I believe a word you say? All you've done is lie and terrorize me."

"Oh, I suppose you're right. I have been a bit of a bitch. So sorry." She made something of an attempt at appearing apologetic. "It's working with all the assholes in this place. A girl has to be tough around here or she's walked all over. If I hadn't learned to be a bitch, I would still be sitting in that little fucking office, working that useless, meaningless, worthless job, collecting a measly paycheck and wondering when my life would turn around."

Michelle couldn't help it. She snapped, "Is it worth it, Angela? Where's the glory?"

"Of course it's going to be worth it. I didn't lie to you when I said I crave stability. With this job, I'll never need for anything."

"Then I'm glad for you."

"You're so fucking sweet. Rather, that's what you want me to think, don't you?" Smiling, Angela shook her head and plucked up a strand of Michelle's hair. Studying it, Angela ran her thumb over it. "The sweet-girl act doesn't work with me, beautiful. But that's beside the point. When we're done with this whole thing, you should get to a doctor pronto. That *thing* you're carrying isn't normal." Her gaze dropped to Michelle's stomach again. "You will probably want to get an abortion."

An abortion. No. Never.

"Thanks for the advice," Michelle said, pushing past Angela. Trapped. She was so fucking trapped. Rage was pounding through her now. But she couldn't let it out. Screaming, yelling, threatening, all encouraged Angela, made things worse. She had to remain silent. Quiet and calm.

"You're welcome. See? I'm not always a bitch," Angela said to her back.

Right.

"Well, I suppose I should get back to work." Hips swaying, Angela strolled to the door. She didn't leave without adding, "You're skeptical. I get it. But you won't be for long. Wait until he gets here, your…whatever you want to call him. Fiancé. Baby's father. Lover. You'll see what I mean. Then nobody will have to drag you to the doctor. You'll be so scared, you won't be able to get that thing out of you soon enough." She knocked, and the lock rattled. The door swung open. She stepped out and it closed with a resounding echo.

And as that reverberating sound vibrated through Michelle's body, she shuddered and silently prayed that the monster story was another lie.

Nicky's Family Diner. Quaint little place.

The perfect place to meet the enemy.

Talen pushed through the front door, and the bell over his head tinkled. A long counter stretched in front of him. Customers sat on every stool, consuming plates of burgers and fries and sandwiches. He checked all the patrons at the counter. No Angela. But probably several Chimera.

Inhaling the scents of grilled beef and deep fried chicken, he looked left, at the booths spaced evenly along the front wall.

No Angela in sight. A ponytailed waitress wearing a T-shirt that said "Eat at Nicky's," a pair of shorts, and a black apron scurried past him, scribbling on her order pad. Chimera? Probably not.

He looked right.

There. She was seated at the farthest table, her back to him.

His senses alert, he loped down the narrow passageway to the booth and sat across from her.

"Good afternoon." Angela beamed. "It's been too long. You look great. How have you been?"

Humoring her, he said, "I've been better."

She pushed a basket of fries toward him. "Care for a French fry?"

This fake friendly act was making him nauseous. "No thanks."

She poked a fry into her mouth, chewed. "Do you have it?"

"Yes."

Her eyes narrowed. "This is almost too easy."

"Not to me." He leaned closer and lowered his voice. "You have no idea how hard it was to get it away from my brothers. But I love Michelle. I don't want to risk her life. She doesn't deserve any of this."

Angela mirrored him, leaning closer. "Where is it? Do you have it with you?"

"I hid it nearby, in a safe place," he lied. "I want to see Michelle first."

Angela's faux smile broadened. "Don't trust me?"

"No."

She ate another fry. "That's unfortunate. Because you won't see her until I have what I want."

Of course she wasn't going to make this easy. He hadn't expected her to, though he'd hoped she might be so blinded by greed that she'd make a mistake or two. He was going to have to think his way through this and move very carefully.

She dug in her bag, sitting beside her on the bench, pulled her cell phone out, and placed it on the table, next to her basket of fries. "With just one phone call, Talen, I could either end Michelle's life or set her free."

He pulled his phone out of his pocket and set his in front of him. "And with one call, I could have The Secret destroyed."

Something flickered in Angela's eyes. "You wouldn't. Not after all of these years of protecting it. Decades. Generations."

Wouldn't he like to?

"I know all about the Black Gryffons," Angela said, plucking another fry from the basket. "You fools. It's all about honor and duty. But look what honor and duty has gotten you."

She wasn't entirely wrong. In fact, he somewhat agreed with her. There were aspects of his life that sucked. Having to move all the time, always aware that they could be discovered at any moment, being pressured to marry and produce children who would end up shouldering the same burden.

If he'd been the eldest, he probably would have destroyed that damn thing. At the first opportunity. He would have set his brothers free of this shitty obligation. But that call hadn't been his to make. And he respected Drako enough to trust his judgment.

Her brow slanted. "You don't have it, do you?" She was calling his bluff.

Dammit.

The truth was, he didn't have it, his brothers did. Not only didn't he want to give it to her, he couldn't. Once he'd severed ties with Drako, he'd lost all ability to contact him. He'd hoped he would be able to convince her to let him see Michelle on the promise of delivery.

"I do. I have it," he lied.

"Then you'll bring it to me." She made a shooing motion. "I don't know why you bothered to show up empty-handed. I should hold it against you. But I won't." She stood, circled the end of the table, and sat next to him. "There's some real chemistry between us. That makes it a little challenging to be too tough on you." She dragged an index finger up the center of his chest. It stopped just below the hollow of his throat and she moved closer, closer. "Don't underestimate me, Talen. I wouldn't think twice about killing that pathetic woman. She's nothing to me. Absolutely nothing." Laughing softly, she shifted back to study him. "Ah, don't like my threat, do you? Do something about it. Bring me what I want."

Fuck, it was hard keeping his head straight. All he wanted to do was snap this bitch's neck in two. "How do I know you have her?"

"Really?" She laughed. The sound was hollow, her expression humorless. "You doubt me? Come. I'll prove it to you." She poked at her phone, then lifted it toward him. "Look familiar?"

On the screen was a video of Michelle. She was lying on some kind of bed in a room with white-tiled walls. She was so still. Was she sleeping? Drugged?

"Aw, isn't that sweet. You look so worried," Angela cooed. "Your little breeder is fine...for now. We've taken good care of her for you. Fed her well. Provided medical care. But my hospitality won't be so convivial if you don't cooperate."

His blood was ice. Pure hatred lanced through him like a dagger. This was the third time he'd had to deal with the Chimera. The first couple of times he'd realized they were evil. To the core. But Angela was by far the worst. "She could be anywhere, in another state, another country. How do I know you have her under your direct care nearby? The Chimera is a large organization."

"She's nearby. You'll just have to trust me on that. As far as whether I have her in my custody"—she made a call on speakerphone—"wake the woman. Have her face the camera."

Seconds later, he watched a man enter the white room and

shake Michelle awake. He pointed at the camera, and she lifted her face to it.

Angela made a second call. "Now tell her to speak, to plead with Talen to cooperate."

He watched as Michelle gritted her teeth and glared at the screen. She had some fight in her. He adored that. "I won't beg. Screw that," she snapped.

Oh, how he adored her. His heart twisted.

"How do I know you'll release her if I give you The Secret?" he asked.

Angela considered his question for a handful of seconds as she munched on another fry. "I suppose you don't know that. But you can be assured that she will die if you don't bring me what I want."

That he was willing to believe.

He was in one hell of a spot. He didn't know where Michelle was being kept. He didn't have access to her. Nor did he have access to The Secret.

His only hope lay in the fact that hardly anyone knew what The Secret actually looked like. He would need to find something that could pass for a very old relic. Where the hell would he find that?

Angela stood, grabbed her purse. "Call me. I'll give you two hours."

Two hours.

One hundred twenty minutes.

He had only two hours to find something that would pass for a five-thousand-year-old relic. No pressure there.

30

Twenty seconds.

Fifteen.

Ten. Nine. Eight. Seven. Six. Five. Four. Three. Two.

Time was up.

Talen hoped this would work.

Carrying the small wooden case he'd bought from a local antique mart, he stood at the prearranged meeting place, an empty, abandoned parking lot on the fringe of a small town. Inside the box was some little piece of rusty metal he'd gotten for a buck. The dealer had told him it was a part from an old steam-powered engine. He didn't care, as long as Angela didn't know what it was.

All he needed was for it to fool her long enough to get to Michelle. That was all.

As the dark car pulled up, he said a little prayer.

The vehicle stopped. The door opened. Angela stepped out. Her gaze locked on the wood box in his hands. So far, so good.

"What do you have there?" she asked, standing back slightly.

"It's the item you asked for."

"Set the box down."

He followed her direction.

"Open it."

He unfastened the old latch and slowly lifted the lid.

Still standing far back, by the car, she commanded, "Take it out."

He scooped out the old piece of junk and lifted it, as if it was the priceless relic his brothers and his father and uncles before them and countless generations before them, had committed a lifetime to protecting.

Her brows furrowed. Her lips curled. "That's it? That piece of rusty trash?" Without waiting for his response, she raised her phone and snapped a picture.

"What did you expect?" he asked as he gingerly set it back in its box. "It's a few millennia old."

"It looks like it's steel. Was steel in use so long ago?" she asked as she poked at her phone.

"Yes, of course it was. Maybe not worldwide, but the people who created it were advanced. That's kind of the point. They created it. They knew how to use it safely. But humanity did not."

"Hmm." She took a step closer, and another. Just as she was taking a third step, her phone chimed. She turned her attention back to the screen.

"This is The Secret, the item my brothers and I have been protecting since our father died. Whether it's steel or something else, I couldn't say. We didn't have it analyzed. For obvious reasons."

She laughed. Hard.

He didn't take that as a good sign.

"A crankshaft," Angela said as she strolled over to him.

Oh shit.

She took the fake relic in her hands and inspected it. "How fitting. It isn't even that old." Her expression condemning, she shook her head. "Really, did you take me for such a fool?" She let the piece of junk fall to the ground at their feet. It landed with a heavy thud.

"No. I would never take you for a fool. It was a matter of necessity." What the hell was he going to do now? What the hell? "The truth is, I can't get what you want. My brothers have left town and have taken it with them, as they have been trained to do."

Her jaw clenched. "Of course they have. Contact them."

"It won't do any good. They've already changed their phone numbers."

Her jaw clenched tighter. "Try it. Now."

"Sure." Putting his phone on speaker, he dialed the number he'd called only a few hours ago. An irritating tone played, followed by a familiar recording: "The phone number you have dialed is no longer in service—" He hit the button, ending the call.

Her eyes narrowed to slits. "You intentionally misdialed."

"No, I didn't. You can try it yourself." Knowing there was nothing on his phone that could put his brothers at risk anymore, he handed it to her. He'd planned ahead, deleted everything but his brothers' initials.

Her squinty eyes narrowed even more. "Your brothers would not abandon you. They wouldn't."

"They will if it maintains the safety of their families."

"I don't believe you."

He shrugged.

After studying him for several moments, she poked the phone's screen. "You've deleted their real phone numbers."

"No."

Her eyes were as cool and lifeless as steel. "Then I guess you've got a problem. Because if you don't get The Secret here in the next twelve hours, your precious little Michelle will be dead. And so will that beast she's carrying in her stomach."

Beast. Who was that woman calling a beast? Who was less than human? Who?

Dammit, what the hell was he going to do now? He'd failed to protect Michelle and his child. Both Michelle and the child were innocent. Neither deserved this.

I should have let her be. It's because of my weakness that she's going to die. My failing.

He was left with only one option. But was there even a shred of humanity in that woman?

Lifting his arms in surrender, he said, "There's nothing I can do. Not in twelve hours. Not in twelve thousand. You have nothing to gain by killing her."

"That's what you think." Turning, she started back toward her car.

His blood turned to ice. He had to do something. Anything. "Take me instead," he yelled to Angela's back. "Maybe if you take me into custody, my brothers will find out and come to my aid. It's the only hope you have of luring them here."

Seeming skeptical, she considered his suggestion for a handful of heartbeats. "Well, fuck it." Swinging her arm up, she struck him in the shoulder. Sharp pain shot through his body. His gaze snapped to the shoulder she'd hit, and he spied the needle, thrust deep into his flesh.

Black blotches obscured his vision.

He heard her speaking as he went completely blind. Felt air brushing against his skin. Something hard slamming into his body.

"Shit, that was one hell of a fall," Drako whispered. He was staring into the binoculars, his body wedged between two trees. Malek was in the truck, listening to him via a wireless headset.

"I saw it. What a bitch," Malek said.

"Okay, they're dragging him into the car. Ready?"

"Yep. The engine's running."

"I'm coming." As Drako sprinted toward the waiting vehicle, he unzipped his pocket and slid his hand inside. It was still in there. Smooth. Hard. His finger traced one of the edges. He wasn't sure yet what he would do with it, or how it all was going to work, but this was it. He had sensed it for some time. The moment was coming, quickly. Two enemies would face off for one final time, and nothing would be the same afterward.

When he reached the car, Malek slammed the driver's side door.

They were off. To save their brother.

To change the future.

"Wake up, sleepyhead."

A voice. Female. Did he recognize it?

Maybe.

"Wake up."

No, he didn't know that voice.

"Damn, why is it taking so long?"

Wait, he did know that voice.

Memories started trickling through Talen's mind. Slowwwwwly. They moved like thick molasses. Images. A face. A woman's face.

Her. Angela.

A parking lot.

Had they met? Oh yes. They had.

Michelle. Where was she?

Angela wanted The Secret. And he'd tried to pass off a piece of old junk as it. It hadn't worked. He remembered everything now.

"Wake up, dammit."

Oh hell, his head hurt. Where was he?

His eyelids felt like they were glued shut. With huge effort he managed to slit them open.

"There you are. What a lightweight," his captor sneered. "Wake up. You're no use to me napping like a kindergartner."

He opened his mouth to speak but his throat was dry. All that came out was a painful cracking sound. He coughed.

"At least I know you can be easily subdued now."

"Where's Michelle?" he croaked.

"Get the hell up. We have work to do." Angela gave him a shake. "We need to find a way to communicate with your brothers."

"There isn't any. I told you, they disconnected their phones. Just let Michelle go. She's no use to you now."

"Wake your ass up and find a way to get your brothers here, and then I'll think about it," Angela snapped.

It wasn't easy, but he opened his eyes fully, avoiding direct light. Every beat of his heart pounded in his skull. It felt like the bones might shatter.

Get his brothers here? Wasn't going to happen. He was going to have to think of another way to get Michelle to safety. But how? His mind was still too foggy to think.

Sitting upright, he dropped his face into his hands and curled his fingers into his hair. At the moment, he was feeling defeated, powerless, lost. What the fuck was he going to do?

"You really don't know how to reach them?"

Face still covered, he shook his head. "I told you that. More than once."

"Fuck!" Angela left, slamming the door hard. His head felt the vibration in the air. Every fucking wave. His stomach twisted, and he almost heaved. When the nausea passed, he opened his eyes to stare down at the tile floor.

White.

His gaze slowly crept across the floor, then up a wall.

White tile.

Michelle was here somewhere. Close by. But he couldn't get to her, couldn't reassure her or protect her. They could do anything to her. Absolutely anything. And he was powerless to stop them.

This was hell. Pure and simple.

Someone was coming in her room. Again. Was it lunchtime? Dinnertime? Without anything to entertain her, distract her, hours dragged. Days dragged. Minutes dragged. Time had no meaning anymore.

Sleep. That was what Michelle did. As often as she could. In her dreams, she could go anywhere, with anyone. With Talen. Her mother.

Her stomach wasn't burning yet. She wasn't hungry. It seemed as if she'd just eaten lunch.

"Good afternoon," Angela said as she flounced into the room. The door slammed shut behind her. "How's your day going?"

Michelle didn't bother answering. Angela couldn't care less how her day was going. She pushed herself upright and hung her legs over the side of the bed.

Angela sat next to her. The thin mattress sank under her weight. "Well, I have a little good news for you."

Good news? Right. Sure.

"I'm going to let you speak with Talen," Angela announced. Talen?

Michelle's heart jerked. What did this mean? Was he here? Would she get to see him? Or would she talk to him on the phone? Most importantly, why did Angela want her to talk to him? This woman, as evil as she was, wouldn't let her do anything unless there was some ulterior motive. "You're going to let me call him?"

"Better than that. I'm going to let you *see* him. Face-to-face."

See him! "Is he here?"

"He is. Not far." Angela *click-clicked* toward the door in her little pointy-toed shoes. "Not far at all. You can go right now. This minute."

What the hell was this woman up to? "Why are you doing this?" Michelle asked.

Angela shrugged but didn't say a word. Instead, she knocked. The lock clicked. The door swung open, and she stepped one foot through the doorway. Pivoting, she asked over her shoulder, "Are you coming?"

Michelle hesitated for a moment. Was this a trick? Would she be lured to a room and killed? That didn't make a whole lot of sense.

Nervous, but hopeful that somehow this was a sign that Angela had given up trying to use her to get what she wanted, Michelle walked through the door.

This was the first time she'd been out of her room, at least, while she was conscious. She checked out every little detail, in case she needed to describe where she was.

The corridor was narrow. White-walled. Institutional. There were no windows, no signs, and no way to see where the building was located or what kind of structure it was. She followed Angela through a series of turns. Right. Left. Another left. A right. Several more. Right, left, right. She was soon completely confused and sure she could never get herself back to her room.

The place had to be huge, with so many hallways. A hospital. It reminded her of a hospital. The old kind, where everything was tiled white.

Old. Yes, the building was old. The linoleum floors showed signs of wear. Gray grunge had collected in the corners. Occasionally, a locked metal door would interrupt their progress, and Angela would have to unlock it with a key card to pass through.

Maybe it was a jail or prison.

Finally, Angela stopped at the end of yet another corridor that looked exactly like the last ten they'd walked down. "Here you are. You have thirty minutes." She slid her key card in the locking mechanism on the door and turned the knob. Smiling, she jerked her head. "Go ahead."

Michelle peered into the room.

There he was. It was him. Sitting on the bed, his head tipped down, elbows on knees. He didn't look up.

Something made her approach him slowly, cautiously. Was he sick? Angry?

Finally, he raised his eyes. Then he jerked his head upright. "Michelle."

She felt herself smiling for the first time since she'd been brought to this awful place. "Talen." Acting on pure instinct, she dashed to him. She leapt, catching her arms around his neck when she finally made contact. His arms wrapped around her, and their bodies melded. Oh, it was magical. He was here. Really here. Holding her.

"Tell me this isn't a dream," she whispered as she tipped her head back to look him in the eye.

"It's real." He lowered his head, lips hovering over hers. "This isn't the time or place, but now that I have you in my arms..." His mouth claimed hers. Hard. His lips smashed over hers. One of his hands cupped the back of her head, holding it in place. The fingers of the other dug into the flesh of her side as her back arched over his arm.

When his tongue pushed into her mouth, she couldn't help moaning. Her bones were softening, turning to mush. Her blood was simmering, blasting through her body in huge hot waves.

As need rushed through her, she clung to him and kissed him back. All the emotions she had pent up over the last few days surged to the surface. She released them all, the anger, confusion, fear, sadness, and now joy, in the kiss. With her tongue, lips, and body she told him how much she had missed him, how she had longed for his touch, and how terrified she'd been without him.

And with his tongue, lips, and body he told her how scared he'd been for her safety, how much he'd longed for her touch, and how much he wanted to cherish and protect her.

The kiss lasted a long time. It was as if neither of them could bear to let it end. Their mouths were connected, their breaths mingled, their bodies pressed so tightly together nothing could get between them. That was how it was meant to be. For always.

"Isn't this a pretty picture?" someone said.

Michelle knew that cold, cloying voice. The bitch. Of course there had been a reason why she'd let her come to see Talen. It couldn't be because she was trying to be nice. Michelle figured she was about to find out what that reason was.

It was Talen who broke the kiss. Gently but firmly, he turned her in his arms and held her with his arms crossed over her chest. "What now? What? You said we would have a half hour. It hasn't been a half hour."

"No, it hasn't. Unfortunately, I have to break up the party early." Angela made a fake pouty face. "But it's good news. At least for me. And maybe you." She pointed at Talen. "There's someone here to see you."

Michelle twisted to glance over her shoulder, at Talen. His brows were furrowed, confusion twisting his handsome features.

"Who?" he asked.

Angela shook her head. "You'll find out soon enough. In the

meantime, I need to escort your little friend here back to her room. We wouldn't want her to get hurt if things get a little... rough."

Dread settled into her stomach. It was heavy and hard, like a rock. Twisting as Angela pulled on her arm, she stole one last glance of Talen.

What was happening?

Would it be the last time she saw him alive?

"I love you," she whispered to him.

"I love you, too," he replied.

31

As he watched Angela escort Michelle away, his heart shattered. His eyes focused on her, only her. The slope of her neck, the curve of her cheek. If he didn't live to hold her again, he would remember that sweet moment when she'd molded her body to his and kissed him so fiercely. God, that moment had been like nothing before. Inside, he'd felt something, a spark ignite. It wasn't just lust or carnal need, it was more. A fire in his soul. And now, even though she was out of his sight, it still burned brightly, making him feel so strong and light that he wondered if he might take flight.

His senses seemed more acute, too. Especially his vision. Turning, he focused on the wall. There were slight imperfections between each tile. Had those been there before?

Sounds outside, beyond the locked door, caught his attention. Voices.

His brothers. They had come for him.

How had they known where he was?

Never mind that. Now that all three of them were together, here, in the clutches of the Chimera once again, the safety of

The Secret was in jeopardy. They had escaped twice before. Narrowly. And not without suffering serious injuries. Would they be so lucky this time? Or would one of them, or more, lose their lives?

His body energized as a surge of adrenaline coursed through it. His muscles tensed. His senses heightened even more. He still heard the voices, but he hadn't seen them yet. How long would he have to wait?

Restless, he paced. What would the enemy do this time? In the past, the individuals who had captured them hadn't known about or anticipated the supernatural gifts two of the three brothers had somehow acquired. Still, they weren't sure where those powers had come from. Drako had his own theory, and it related to the thing they'd been charged with protecting. Still, as far as he could tell, they were the first of the Gryffons to have possessed such powers. All Gryffons before them hadn't. If those powers had come from The Secret, wouldn't they have all received them?

Footsteps. He heard them tapping lightly on the floor. Little, light *click-clacks*. They were coming toward his room. Quickly. He guessed, based upon the pace and weight, they belonged to Angela.

She entered his room smiling. "This day will go down in history as the day when all humanity received the greatest gift of all. No longer will we rely upon expensive, dirty fossil fuels to power our cities. It will all come from us, from the Chimera. We will hold all nations in our grasp."

"You have it?" he asked.

"Not yet. But I will. Just as soon as I prove to your doubting brothers that you are here and still alive."

What was going to happen once Drako and Malek did see him? They couldn't hand over The Secret. Not a chance. Still, he told her, "If you are able to get The Secret from them, you need to think about the risks—"

"Risks? There are none." She sat in the one and only chair in the tiny room and crossed one leg over the other, revealing a lot of toned thigh. His stomach turned as memories of touching that thigh flashed through his head. "It's a never-ending, cost-free source of clean power. Strong enough to provide electricity to every nation in the world. Just think about all the good it will do. It'll not only shift the balance of world economic power but also improve living conditions in every part of the world. You and your Gryffons have been greedy, holding it to yourself all this time. Look at your wealth. Where does it come from? Who is paying you to keep it away from us?" Angela demanded.

"No one is paying us."

"You can't possibly tell me that you and your brothers earned all your wealth. You're a computer programmer. Your brother is a jewelry maker. Hardly the kinds of careers that produce the lifestyle that you seem to be living."

"Our father left us a large estate, worth quite a bit. We've merely built upon it," he reasoned, not that he owed this woman any explanation. But he wasn't ashamed of what he and his brothers had accomplished. They worked smart. They invested smart. And they spent smart.

"You built your wealth without the benefit of traceable incomes?" she asked.

"What does it matter whether we have been paid or not?"

"Maybe I would like to talk to whomever has been paying you. Perhaps I might agree to keep your secret safe if the price were right."

Ah, so that was what she was getting at. Interesting. He hadn't considered that angle. Was there any advantage to gain by making her think there was someone paying them? It might buy him a little time. But not enough to do any good. "There is nobody."

"Well, then. We meet your brothers." She stood and smoothed her skirt with her hands. "If you won't tell me who your benefactor is, I'll stick with Plan A. Making all the nations of the world completely dependent upon me for their electricity isn't a bad way to go."

Not a bad way, if she didn't blow herself, and tens of thousands of people around her, to smithereens. "You don't understand how it works. The power is beyond any human's capacity to control. The last time it was used, it caused a whole nation to collapse. Literally. Into the sea. And that was before the power had reached its fullest potential."

She scoffed. "That's a silly superstition. I've heard it so many times. Atlantis. The famous lost continent. Sunken into the sea."

"Doubting the truth is one sure way to destruction."

"I'm so scared." She rolled her eyes. "Obviously I have a team of scientists at my disposal, to make sure nothing like that happens. We've been preparing for this day for a long time, Talen. For centuries, since the first Chimera discovered the legend of The Secret and started their search for it. It's taken us a long time to finally get to this point. But we are prepared."

"If you were so prepared, how was it that you didn't know what it would look like?"

She tapped her chin. "Good question. While there was a lot of detail in the ancient documents those founding members of the Chimera found, a physical description wasn't in them. Enough chitchat. Let's go. I'm anxious to get on with this. Your brothers are waiting." She made a circle in the air with her index finger. She pulled a pair of handcuffs out of her pocket with the other hand. "Turn."

He turned his back to her and permitted her to clip on the handcuffs.

After she checked them to make sure they were secure, she rapped on the door. It opened.

"You will kill us once you have it," he said, allowing her to steer him down the hall by the arm.

"Of course. Can't have you trying to steal it back. You and your brothers would pose too big a risk to us."

"What about Michelle?"

"Ah, sweet little Michelle. You know, I might consider setting her free. Might. I kind of grew fond of her over the past few weeks. Especially when she was helping me plan my wedding. It'll be a game-day decision." Her smile broadened. "If things go smoothly, I might be inspired to be nice."

If there was any way he could make that happen, he had to. The farther away Michelle was from all of this, the better. Especially if Angela somehow really did get her hands on The Secret. If that happened, nobody within at least two hundred miles would be safe.

"Michelle served her purpose. Why won't you let her go now?" he demanded. Somehow he had to convince Angela to release Michelle. He had to protect her.

"But she might come in handy."

"You have me. You have my brothers. Why would you need her?"

"True. But I may need to motivate you at some point. No, I think I'll keep her around for a little while yet."

"Okay, so you know the plan," Talen heard Drako say. He could barely understand him, but it was loud enough that he worried Angela might hear him, too. "We'll destroy it just before we hand it over. We'll all die. But it's the best way. At least Rin and Lei, our children, they'll all be safe."

Shit.

Talen's heart sank.

They had brought it. They were going to destroy it, killing everyone within miles.

Somehow he had to get Michelle a safe distance away. Soon, this building would be vaporized.

"Can we destroy it somehow without risking the lives of everyone around us?" Malek asked.

"We are underground. That should help a little," Drako answered. "And if we made sure the power hadn't reached a high level yet, that'll be even better. But it's still going to blow. Big."

"Damn," Talen and Malek both said.

"But in the long run, we'll still be saving millions of lives," Drako said.

Malek said, "I wish there were another way."

Talen turned to Angela. Wasn't she hearing that conversation? If she was, she wasn't responding to anything his brothers were saying. No, she was jabbering on and on about how she would use Michelle to make him do everything she asked.

Wasn't she concerned? Or had she already anticipated their plan?

"Let's go. I'm getting bored." She pounded on the door and it swung open.

As Talen followed her through the maze of identical corridors, his muscles tensed, his senses heightened. His eyesight seemed extremely acute, every tiny detail of everything he looked at sharp and in focus. His brothers' voices were getting stronger. Even his sense of smell seemed stronger. When he turned his head, he could smell the sweet scent of coconut oil on Angela's skin. And jasmine. In her hair.

His brothers were still discussing their plan. They hadn't mentioned Michelle. He wondered if they knew she was here.

He knew, without Angela telling him, the minute he was outside of the room she was holding Drako and Malek in. Their voices were crystal-clear. Not once, throughout the journey from his room to theirs, did she seem to react or respond to anything they said. Not even when they talked about killing her.

She unlocked the door, then stepped aside. "Gentlemen first."

His gaze found Drako first, sitting on the floor, leaning against the wall directly opposite the door, his arms behind his back.

"We have made sure they aren't able to use those freakish powers," Angela stated as she closed the door shut, locking them all in. "Drako there is wearing some specially designed flameproof gloves. And Malek," she said, pointing to the right, "is secured with bindings made out of the strongest material known to mankind. Neither of them will be any help to you, outside of one thing." She turned to Drako. "You see him. Now, where is it?"

Talen pleaded, "Don't give it to her. We're going to be—"

Angela whirled around and kicked a foot into Talen's groin. The pain took about two seconds to reach his brain. Then he fell to the ground, breathless.

"Where's Michelle?" Drako demanded.

"What does she matter?" Angela snapped.

Pain. Blinding. Fire. Blazing.

Voice calm, Drako said, "I said I wanted to see Talen *and Michelle*. I'm not turning over anything until I see them both."

Agony. Couldn't breathe.

"I could take it from you," Angela said. "With those gloves on, you can't do your little fire thing."

"Maybe. Maybe not," Drako said calmly.

His insides were blistering hot. Acid burned up Talen's throat. He vomited. Dammit, he should have seen that coming.

A door slammed.

Had she left?

"Talen. Are you okay?" Drako.

Talen managed to groan. He wanted to say more. But the pain. Dammit, the fucking pain.

"Listen, we're going to destroy it. We have to. I'm going to get them to let you and Michelle go."

"No!" he shouted.

"Yes. Malek, too, if I can. Then I'll destroy it. Get as far away from here as you can. I'll put her off as long as possible to give you a chance."

"No," Talen repeated. He had to talk. Dammit. "You. Go."

"I'm the oldest. It's my duty," Drako said.

Talen gritted his teeth and slowly lifted his head to glare at his brothers. "Fuck that."

"Take care of Michelle. I had my chance to love and be loved. It's your time now."

This was not an option. "No."

"Do it, goddamnit!" Drako yelled. His face turned a deep crimson. The cloying scent of burning sulfur filled the room. "I'm the only one who can destroy it. Come here."

Come here? Oh hell. Drako was at least ten feet away.

Gagging and heaving, Talen staggered to his feet and shuffled over to Drako.

"Pocket."

Talen yanked off both gloves first, uncovering his brother's hands. Then he reached into Drako's pocket.

Smooth. Cool to the touch.

"You really did bring it?" Talen asked.

"Yes. Now, hand that to me. You take everything else."

Talen pulled the tiny cylinder out first and transferred that to his left hand. Then he reached back down and gathered what felt like a pen.

It was a hypodermic.

Ah, the irony.

"How the hell did you manage to get this in here?" Talen asked. "Didn't they search you?"

"They did." Drako grinned. "I didn't bring it in. I stole it. From one of them. It'll buy us some time," Drako explained. "Hit her with it the minute she comes back with Michelle. Then get yourself and Michelle out of here. Malek, too, if you can."

"I'm staying with you," Malek growled.

"No, you're not."

"Like hell."

"Lei needs you," Drako said slowly, carefully. "Think of her. Rin will be okay."

Talen had his own idea of how this whole thing should go down. It was all clear now. He knew exactly what he would do. And because he knew Drako wasn't going to like his plan, he kept it to himself.

There was no way he was going to leave either of his brothers in this building. Somehow he would make sure of that. Even if it meant he would pay with his own life.

Michelle. Their child. And his brothers. They would live. No matter what it took.

32

They were taking her somewhere. What was happening now? Michelle's heart was racing. Her hands were trembling. Something in the air told her this was it. Whatever she was about to face, it would be final.

Two men held her by the arms, one on each side. Her wrists were bound with cuffs. Angela was *click-clacking* in front of them on her stiletto heels. Michelle hoped someday she'd fall off those damn heels and land on her ass. That was what she deserved.

Angela barked into her phone, "This is it. Everyone in place."

Yes, whatever was about to happen, Michelle knew it would change her life. Her stomach twisted. Dread crept through her body like icy tentacles, winding around her heart and squeezing it. She couldn't breathe.

They stopped outside a room. Several more men came from the opposite direction. Two flanked Angela in the hallway. A third unlocked the door. A fourth hurried into the room with his gun drawn.

"Clear," the man inside called.

Angela and her escorts stepped inside. Michelle was pulled into the room after her.

Talen. She saw him first.

His eyes. Oh God, what was going on? He looked tortured. He didn't speak. Didn't take his gaze away from Michelle for several seconds.

"I've brought her as you asked. Now, it's time to hand it over," Angela demanded. Catching Michelle off guard, she grabbed Michelle's arm and yanked her forward, then shoved her toward Talen. "You can see for yourself, she's perfectly fine. Now I want The Secret. Enough fucking games."

Talen gave Michelle one last look. "I don't have it. Drako does." He went to Drako.

Drako's eyes widened. "What are you doing?"

"It's the only way we can all get out of this alive." Talen jammed his hand in Drako's pocket and pulled something out. Then he turned, and facing Angela, unfurled his fingers.

In his palm lay a small cylinder, roughly the diameter of a pencil.

It didn't look like a weapon of mass destruction.

"That's it? That little piece of scrap?" Angela's gaze jerked back and forth between Talen and Drako. Drako was glaring at his brother. Talen looked calm, resolved. She reached for it, but Talen yanked his hand away. "Set them free first. All of them."

"No, not until I know it's genuine."

"Set them free," Talen repeated. "I'll stay. I'll prove it's genuine."

Angela's eyes narrowed. "You're lying."

Talen raised his fist above his head, as if he would throw the cylinder. "I could destroy it. Right here. Right now. And then you'll have nothing. You're either going to have to believe I'm telling the truth or walk away with nothing. Your choice."

Michelle fought to inhale. What the hell was he doing? How

would he make it out of this alive? Did she trust him to have a plan?

His gaze found hers again. She searched his eyes.

Peace. She saw a deep sense of peace in them. And love.

The fear that had wound around her heart melted away.

She trusted him.

"He's telling the truth," she said.

Angela spun around and glared at her. "How do you know?"

"I know him. He's telling the truth."

"Release them," Angela ordered, motioning to Drako and Malek.

"Before you do that," Talen told her as he lowered his hand, "Drako's gloves have been removed."

"Dammit, Talen." A plume of smoke wafted from behind Drako's back.

"Secure him." Angela jerked her head to Drako.

"I'll do it." Talen circled behind Drako's back and bent down. After a few seconds, he straightened up. "It's safe now. Get them all out of here." He turned to Malek. "Take care of Michelle, please."

Malek said nothing. But Michelle could tell, by the clenched muscle along his jaw, that Malek didn't like Talen's plan, either.

Talen walked to her, cupped her face. "Michelle, no matter what happens today, know that I loved you. I would do anything for you and our child. Anything." His thumb caressed her cheek. He kissed her forehead, then nodded to Angela. "Now, get them out of here."

Loved.

He'd said it, past tense.

"Talen," she whispered.

Angela turned to the guards. "Do it."

Knowing that she had just felt Talen's touch for the last time, Michelle let the men lead her toward the door. Before she left, she said loudly, "Talen Gryffon, you are the most loving man I have ever known. I will make sure our son knows the sacrifice you made for him. I love you."

Ten minutes later, Michelle was standing in ankle-deep snow, shivering. "Where the heck are we? Snow? It's May."

"Minnesota. Freak storm brought in several inches," Drako said as he stared back at the building from which they'd just been expelled. "That bastard. Talen fucked up our plan."

"Now what?" Malek asked him.

"Take Michelle and get her as far from here as you can. I'm going back in there."

Malek shook his head. "Drako, if you're going back—"

"No, dammit," Drako shouted. "Get her out of here. Now. You're the only one who can make sure she's safe. Go back to the girls. Take care of them all."

"Drako—"

"Go! If we make it out of there alive, I know where to find you."

Malek glared at his brother for what felt like a lifetime. Michelle watched as at least a dozen different emotions played over his face. Then he turned to her, scooped her off her feet, and started running. Before she realized what was happening, the world around them became a blur.

He was running. Running! Faster than a car. How could a human being go so fast?

"Malek?" she screamed. Something flashed in her peripheral vision. Brilliant. An instant later, she felt as if they was sailing through the air. A blur of colors flew past her face.

And then silence.

Stillness.

She was lying down in a field, cradled in Malek's arms. He was beneath her, on his back in the snow.

Not moving.

"Malek?" she whispered.

Another flash blinded her. A wave of searing heat followed. One second there was snow everywhere, all around them. The next, it was gone. The earth was wet, muddy.

Malek groaned, shifted. "Fuck," he muttered.

Michelle scooted off him. Sweating. So hot. The air burned her lungs.

"Need to get you out of here." Malek pushed to his feet. He staggered. "Dammit." He shook his head and looked back over his shoulder. A tall column of smoke and fire blazed up to the sky. A huge mushroom cloud rolled high above, fed from the enormous inferno. "Dammit." He grabbed Michelle again and started running. They weren't going as fast as before. The heat. Her skin was stinging, itching. "Can't go fast enough."

Clinging to him, Michelle looked up, up, up. Past the gnarled and leafless trees to the rolling, thick gray cloud drifting toward them. Was it a nuclear explosion? Would they live?

He ran, but the cloud grew too fast, the heat spread too swiftly. When they reached a forest, he stumbled and slowed. He staggered and swayed. Finally, he stopped.

"Dammit, Drako, Talen! Damn you!" he screamed into the hellish darkness.

This was it. He couldn't outrun it.

The heat. It was getting worse. Now it burned her lungs, her nose, her face. Her eyes were tearing up. It was hard to see, to breathe.

Dragging a hand over her eyes to clear them, Michelle said, "It's okay. You tried."

"I failed," Malek said, shoving his fingers through his hair. "They're gone. They're both gone." He clapped a hand over his mouth, muffling a sob. "And I can't even get you out of this hell. That was all he'd asked."

"You did your best."

"I failed." He leaned back, a tree supporting him.

Sleepy.

She was getting tired, weak. Sit. She needed to rest. For just a minute.

Hot. So hot.

"If I hadn't hesitated, we might have made it far enough," Malek mumbled as he slowly sank to the ground. "If I had only done what he'd asked."

Michelle set her hand on her stomach. The baby was tiny yet, too small to feel pain, she hoped. A tear seeped from her eye. Sleepy. So hot.

Darkness. Drifting.

Heat. Burning her lungs.

Her senses were dulling. Sight, gone. Sounds muted.

She heard Malek's hard, heaving gasps. The rhythmic beat of something in the distance. *Thump, thump, thump.* No, not a beat, something else. Like the sound of a bird's wings as it took flight.

A helicopter?

Air stirring, caressing her skin.

Louder, it was getting louder.

She slitted open her eyes. Burned. Smoke. She couldn't see. Her lungs spasmed, and she coughed until she gagged.

Someone hauled her up, off the ground, cradling her in strong arms.

Malek?

She looked up.

"Talen?"

Was she dead? Dreaming? Hallucinating?

"Sssshh," he whispered. "Close your eyes. Rest. I'm here now. I have you."

The air swirled around them like a whirlwind.

She shut her eyes against the sting of dirt and soot and smoke. The wind was howling now in her ears. It felt as if the world was swooping and dipping and spinning around her, as if she were riding in an elevator that was falling, then surging skyward, then falling again.

"You trusted me, little one. Your trust, your love, has saved my life."

"What happened?" she wheezed.

"It's over. No more secrets. No more running."

"Malek? Drako?"

"I'll get them as soon as I know you're safe."

The air was cooling. She could breathe easier. Was it her imagination? She inhaled. Her nose didn't sting. She coughed, and his hold on her tightened.

She blinked open her eyes and looked up into the brilliant blue sky. The big cloud was gone. She glanced over her shoulder.

Her heart stopped.

Trees. Beneath her. Zooming past. No floor underneath. No walls or seats or windows.

She was flying. Soaring above the earth. Over houses and farms and trees and fields. How? She looked up again.

"Trust," he said, smiling.

Then she saw them, the wings, dark gray and white and ink-black feathers. They were stretched out, at least eight feet long, feathers at the tip spread out to catch the air currents.

Wings? Talen had wings?

"It makes sense now," he said. "I don't know how it happened, but... Gryphon. Dragon. Lion. Eagle. That's what we are, my brothers and I. The gryphon.

"But it was love that gave us our power. And, in the end, our humanity. Before we loved, we were... no better than monsters."

Michelle closed her eyes and relaxed in his strong embrace. How far she had come. How far Talen's love for her had taken her. She'd once been afraid to walk in a dark parking garage, imagining villains around every corner. Danger in every shadow. A coward who didn't trust anyone, anything, but herself.

Now, her life was completely changed. Not only had she faced a real honest-to-God villain, and not let her beat her down, but she'd learned to trust, to love, to let go of all the what-ifs and live life.

Her child, he or she would be taught to embrace life and everything it brought. Love. Joy. Peace. Danger. Sadness. And she would teach her child those lessons with the most loving, sexy, wonderful man in the world.

Her eagle.

Her hero.

Her master.

Turn the page for a sizzling preview of Tawny Taylor's

SURRENDER

An Aphrodisia trade paperback on sale now!

1

I closed my eyes. I pulled in a long, deep breath. I exhaled. My mind was racing, images flashing behind my eyelids.

Those eyes.

The sharp blade of a nose.

The chiseled jaw.

Those lips.

Those lips.

My heart was pounding. Hard. I felt a little dizzy.

I hadn't even talked to him yet. How would I ever convince him not to throw my baby brother in jail?

Pull it together, girl.

Twenty-three. Twenty. Three. That was how many times I'd heard Joss say, "Abby, I'm in trouble. Big trouble," since our father died. Twenty-freaking-three times too many.

I knew Joss could pull through his crap and get himself together, so I shouldn't have bothered stepping in to drag him out of one scrape after another. But I did. Because, despite his long, difficult struggle with addiction, Joss was a good person. He didn't go out of his way looking for trouble. Trouble seemed to always come looking for him.

And this time there might not be anything I could do about it.

Breathe.

If Kameron Maldonado, owner of MalTech Corporation, decided to report my brother's alleged crime to the police, he could end up in jail. For years.

My brother. A felon.

Breathe.

My brother. In prison.

Breathe.

The only family I had left, gone.

Breathe.

My sweating palms were sticking to the leather couch. I dragged them down my thighs. My scratchy polyester skirt wasn't going to dry them. But I wiped my hands on it anyway. When I heard the door to my right rattle a little, my heart skipped a beat. I jerked my head, glancing at it, then at the young woman sitting behind the reception desk directly in front of me. She was staring at a computer screen.

I glanced at my watch. Twelve twenty-five. I'd been sitting here for almost a half hour. My appointment had been at twelve.

God, this was torture.

The doorknob rattled again, and once more panic charged through my body. My head spun. The door swung open, and my breath caught in my throat.

Kameron Maldonado stepped out, moving out of the doorway. He was smiling over his shoulder at the man behind him. "We'll get together later this week to talk about the details. Thanks." Kameron extended a hand, and the man shook it.

The visitor returned Kameron's thank you and then, as he passed me, gave me a fleeting look before waving good-bye to the receptionist.

I turned my attention back to Kameron. He was standing next to the door, looking at me.

"Abigail Barnes?" he asked.

I nodded, stood on wobbly legs that felt boneless and heavy. Not expecting a handshake, but preparing for one anyway, I dragged my palms down my legs again as I shuffled toward his office.

After a quick, formal introduction and a brief handshake, Kameron closed his door behind me, circled his desk, and stood, waiting for me to sit in the chair facing him.

My stomach twisted.

Of all the situations Joss had put himself in, this was by far the worst. He had put not only his job in jeopardy, but mine too. Somehow I had to convince this man not to fire us both.

I sat, back straight, body stiff, heart thumping so hard I could hear it.

"How can I help you, Mrs. Barnes?"

"Miss," I corrected. My mouth was dry. I licked my lips, but that did nothing to help. My tongue was as dry as the Sahara.

He nodded. "Miss Barnes."

"I'm here on the behalf of Joss Barnes. My brother." A huge lump of something coagulated in my throat. I tried to swallow it. It didn't budge. I tried again.

Kameron's brows lifted. "Are you all right, Miss Barnes?"

Swallowing a third time, I nodded.

He stood, strolled to the cabinet recessed into the wall behind me, and opened a door. Within a second, he was standing over me, a cold bottle of water in his hand.

I accepted with a weak "Thank you," unscrewed the cap, and sipped.

"Better?" he asked as he leaned back against his desk.

I nodded.

Looming over me, he crossed his thick arms. God, he was big. Intimidating. Extremely intimidating.

"Your brother is in serious trouble, Miss Barnes. If what I heard is true, he not only violated more than one clause of his employment contract, but also broke the law. I was told he stole company property and sold it. I can't let that go with a warning."

We were so screwed.

Feeling utterly defeated, I nodded. "I understand." My nose was starting to burn. Dammit. This was just too much. It was all too much. Our father's death. Mom's disappearance. And my brother's rebellion and addiction. I was a fighter. I was a survivor. If I hadn't been, my brother and I wouldn't be where we were today. But I was too young to deal with this much crap. Every time things started to turn around, something new would come up and drag me right back down into the gutter.

When would life stop kicking me around? When?

My hands were shaking as I lifted them to drag my thumbs under my eyelashes. My eyes were burning now too. A sob was sitting in the pit of my stomach, but I was holding it in. Holding my breath.

I needed to get out of there. I couldn't cry in front of this man. No. *No-no-no.* I stood too fast and felt myself stumble. He caught me, hands clamped around my upper arms. Our gazes locked.

Something really strange happened. A crazy, unexpected bolt of electricity charged through my body. I heard myself gasp.

His eyes widened slightly. "Don't go." He gently forced me back into the chair. "I haven't finished yet."

What was there left to say? Was there any chance he was going to help me?

Afraid to hope anything decent could come out of this mess, I nodded and waited.

He released me, stared down, arms crossed over his chest once again. "Your brother has put me in a hell of a position."

"Is there anything I can do?" I asked, my voice cracking.

His eyes narrowed slightly. He tipped his head to the right. "Why? Why are you so willing to put your neck on the line for him?"

What kind of silly question was that? "He's my brother."

"But he just about got you thrown out of here. You understand that, don't you?"

Just about?

Just about!

I wasn't fired yet.

"Yes, sir. I do," I said, screwing and unscrewing the cap on the water bottle I clasped in my hand. "If my brother was a complete lost cause, I wouldn't have bothered trying to help him. I would've let you fire him. Hell, I would have stood by and watched him be arrested, too. But I can't. Because I know there's more to this situation than you and I know. He's not a bad guy. Sure, he's hit a bump or two lately. He'll get it figured out."

"Maybe you're right. Maybe there is more to this situation than we know. But, say he is guilty. What do I do with him until I figure out what really happened?"

"Good question."

"If he did do it, how could I risk keeping him on, knowing he might steal something else?"

"Another good question."

Leaning closer, he placed one hand on each arm of my chair, trapping me. I felt myself pushing back into the chair. I could smell his cologne, could see the flecks of silver-blue in dark, dark gray-brown eyes—the color of my favorite chocolates. I could feel the warm caress of his breath on my face.

My heart jerked again. But this time it wasn't because I was afraid. No, I was...warm. I was breathless. I was staring at his lips and wondering what they might taste like.

What was going on?

"How long have you been working for us, Miss Barnes?"

"T-two years," I stuttered, my gaze locked on his mouth. What was he getting at? What was he thinking?

"Hmmm."

My gaze inched up, following the line of his aristocratic nose to those dark eyes again. I saw something there, the flicker of something obscure, something wicked. My heart rate tripled, quadrupled, maybe. "Sir? Please don't fire me. My job is our primary source of income. Our father died. It's been really hard on us both, but especially Joss. He was only thirteen and a boy with no father—"

He leaned closer. "I'm sorry about your father." I was trapped, his body like a big wall hovering over me. Why was he standing so close? Why was he looking at me like *that?*

"Sir?" I murmured when he inched even closer. I'd never had a boss act this way with me before. If I didn't know better, I would swear he was...he was...

His head dipped down. Now, his mouth was hovering over mine. Not inches. No. It was a tiny fraction of an inch from mine. His breath softly caressed my lips. Warm. Sweet.

Was he going to kiss me?

Was he expecting some kind of bribe? A payment in return for my job?

I was frozen. Shocked. Unable to move. Unwilling to move. It was wrong for him to use his position to try something like this. Wrong. Illegal. Unethical. Immoral.

But, wow, was he a beautiful man. Sexy. Intelligent. Mysterious. I wanted him to kiss me. My lips were tingling already, and he hadn't even touched them yet. My blood was pounding hard through my body, too. My heart was slamming against my breastbone. I let my eyelids fall shut, enclosing myself in darkness and swirls of red.

"Miss Barnes?"

"Sir?" Something soft brushed against my lips. And again. Little sparks of electricity sizzled and zapped under my skin.

Heat whooshed through my body, up to my face, down between my legs.

The intensity of my body's reaction took my breath away. And still I couldn't move. A crazy impulse popped into my head. I wanted to throw my arms around his neck, tangle my fingers in his silky hair, and pull him to me.

I can't do that. I can't.

"I'm not going to fire you," he whispered. As he spoke, his lips grazed mine. The touches were minute, almost imperceptible. And yet the effect was mind-blowing. I wanted more. I needed more. A real kiss. Lips. Tongue. Teeth. Full body contact.

"Thank you." I shuddered. My fingers wrapped around the seat of the chair.

"Before you thank me, you need to know one thing."

"Yes?"

His mouth claimed mine. At last. And ohmygod, what a kiss it was. It started out smooth and gentle, a slow, patient seduction. But within seconds, his tongue traced the seam of my mouth. And once I opened to him, I was swept up into a wild, thrashing world of carnal need. His tongue stroked and stabbed, possessed. His hands cupped my face, holding me captive. I couldn't escape. I didn't want to escape. I craved more.

A moan swept up my throat, echoing in our joined mouths. Finally able to move, I lifted my hands, sliding them up his arms. I could feel the bulge of thick muscles under his crisp, starched dress shirt. They moved over his wide shoulders. My fingertips brushed silky curls at his nape.

Ohmygod, what was I doing? Kameron Maldonado was kissing me. The owner of the company! His tongue was stroking mine. One of his hands gliding down the column of my neck. The other slid to the back of my head. My scalp stung as he fisted a handful of my hair and pulled, forcing my head to one side.

He growled.

I groaned and licked my lips. They tasted like him. Sweet. Delicious. The swirls behind my eyelids were spinning now, and my heart was doing leaps in my chest.

His tongue flicked along the pounding pulse beating beneath my skin, down my neck to the ticklish spot at the crook. There he nipped me, and a shock wave of heat blazed down my body. Goose bumps coated my right arm. My nipples hardened.

Inside my head, I just kept saying, *Ohmygod, ohmygod, ohmygod.* I was lost in sensation, overcome with need. Eager to feel his weight and heat pressing against me, I pulled. But he didn't budge. The hand that had been at my neck inched lower, the palm sliding down to cover my breast. I whimpered, arched my back, pushing into his touch.

"Miss Barnes, you don't have to do this to keep your job," he murmured against my neck.

"I...I know." I didn't really know anything. I had no clue what this meant. I had no idea what would happen after it ended. But I did know I wanted what was happening and wished it would never end.

He kneaded my breast through my clothes, and I bit my lip, stifling a cry. "I want you," he said.

"I...I want you, too."

"No." He palmed my face. "Open your eyes."

I did as he asked, and my breath left my lungs in a soft huff. Wow, was he sexy. His hair was slightly messy, the curls a little unruly and wild. I'd never spoken to this man before. I'd only seen pictures of him down in the company cafeteria. In the pictures he looked good, but not anywhere as amazing as he did right now.

"I want you to be my assistant."

Was he offering me a promotion? And if he was, what kinds of strings were attached? There had to be strings.

"I...don't understand," I admitted.

"I'm offering you a job. You'll be my assistant. You'll be paid a salary that should meet your needs, and you'll have access to a company car, expense account, and business phone. But there is one condition, a fairly significant one."

I could imagine what that condition would be, considering where his hand was.

I felt the heat draining from my body as my brain started functioning. Reality was like a cold, hard slap to my face. It stung.

I would have to sleep with Kameron Maldonado. Not because I found him incredibly sexy. Not because I wanted to. But because I had to. I would be one of *those* women, the kind that fucked their bosses to get a job.

Me. Pretty-but-not-beautiful me.

I'd never, ever thought I would even consider such a proposition. For one thing, I'd never expected to have something like this come up. I wasn't a perfect ten. With a chest that was a little too small and hips a little too wide, eyes a little too big and wide-set and a jaw a little too narrow, I wasn't exactly Playboy Playmate material.

But it seemed Kameron Maldonado didn't care....

"What about my brother?" I asked.

"He's going to be let go. But I won't report what he did to the police or to my associates. It'll be kept between you and me. This is why I need you working as my assistant. Depending upon the fallout, I may need your help."

"I'll do anything I can to help."

"Good. I expected you to say that. And, as far as that condition I mentioned..." His hand inched down my stomach, stopping just above my pubic bone. "I'm accustomed to getting exactly what I want, when I want."

Despite the fact that I was so aroused—my panties were sodden—I whispered, somewhat coolly, "In other words, to keep my job, I have to sleep with you?"

"No, you'll sleep with me because you want to. I won't ask you to do that. I'll only ask you to allow me the liberty to touch you whenever, however, and wherever I want."

That was some "condition." But it wasn't exactly what I'd expected. By having pulled the actual act of intercourse off the table, Kameron had made it a little more palatable to me. I wouldn't be forced to have sex with him. Though I could almost believe he was telling the truth when he said I would want to. The way he touched me made me melt. What girl could resist?

After a few moments I nodded. "You have yourself a new assistant."